THE ILLUMINATED ORDER

THE ILLUMINATED ORDER

THE ILLUMINATED ORDER

SECRETS OF POWER IN AMERICA

T.M JEFFERSON

Copyright © 2024 T. Jefferson/TMJ Books

All rights reserved.

No part of this book may be reproduced in any form or by any electronic or mechanical means, including information storage and retrieval systems, without written permission from the author, except for the use of brief quotations in a book review.

This novel's story and characters are fictitious. Certain long-standing institutions, agencies, and public offices are mentioned, but the characters involved are wholly imaginary.

The information in this book can potentially get me into some trouble. But something inside of me is urging to enlighten. I wouldn't be doing my job if I didn't expose this information. This message is a warning. The content in this book will have you questioning everything and everyone around you. But let me tell you this... there is no greater power than God, and once you have belief in a higher power, your fear will subside. It is not my intention to scare you, I wrote this book to teach you.

"The world is governed by very different personages from what is imagined by those who are not behind the scenes."

- *BENJAMIN DISRAELI*

PROLOGUE

London, 1888

Lord Alexander Hawthorne presided over the ornate mahogany table like a king holding court, his fingers caressing the intricate carvings as if they held secrets of the universe within their grooves. The soft shimmer of the gaslight cast an ethereal glow on the grand library, the flames forming silhouettes that whispered secrets of their own. He carried the burden of centuries, the legacy of the Illuminated Order streaming through his veins like an ancient river.

"My esteemed colleagues," he began, his voice a rich baritone that commanded attention, "for centuries, we have worked tirelessly to guide the course of human history." The words tasted like honey on his tongue, sweet with the promise of power and control. He savored each syllable, letting them linger in the air like a fine wine.

"Let us reflect upon the foundations of our Order, the principles that have guided us through the centuries and shaped our destiny."

He paused, his eyes sweeping the room. "It was in the year 1534 that a great man, Ignatius of Loyola, founded the Society of Jesus, the Jesuit Order. His vision, his commitment to the cause, and his mastery of the arts of influence and persuasion laid the groundwork for what would one day become the Illuminated Order."

He leaned forward, his eyes intense with fervor. "It was through the study and application of Jesuit practices that the founders of the Illuminated Order first conceived of our great work. They saw in the Jesuits a path to power, a means to shape the world to their will, and they seized upon it with a fierce determination that continues to drive us to this very day."

Lord Hawthorne continued, "Like the Jesuits, we must be willing to adapt to changing circumstances, to use whatever means necessary to achieve our goals. We must be patient, methodical, and above all, ruthless in our pursuance of power."

Around the table, the faces of his fellow members shone with the same fierce determination that burned within his own heart. Lady Amelia Sinclair, her emerald eyes sparkling with a keen intelligence that rivaled his own. Sir Edward Blackwell, his weathered face a map of the battles he'd fought and won in service to the Order. These were the titans of their age, the true masters of the world, and he was proud to stand among them.

As he spoke, his mind drifted to their most recent triumph, the selection of a president who would dance to their tune like a marionette on a string. The memory brought a smile to his lips, a rush that set his heart racing. It was confirmation of their influence, their ability to shape the fabric of reality to their will.

The future stretched out before them, a canvas of infinite possibility waiting to be painted in the colors of their design. With each passing moment, he could feel the Order's power snaking out across the globe, infiltrating every corner of society like an invisible web. It was a heady sensation, a rush of adrenaline that left him feeling invincible.

He turned to the window, the fog-shrouded streets of London beckoning him like a siren's call. The world beyond these walls was a chessboard, and he the grandmaster moving the pieces with an invisible hand. The masses were pawns, ignorant of the true power that guided their lives, but he and his brethren knew the truth.

As he lost himself in visions of the future, the weight of destiny settled upon his shoulders like a mantle of power. The Illuminated Order had shaped the course of human history for centuries, and he would be damned if he let that legacy falter on his watch. The world would kneel before them, a grateful and obedient servant to the true masters of mankind's destiny.

The soft clearing of a throat jolted him back to the present, and he turned to see Lady Amelia watching him with a knowing smile. "The future is ours, Lord Hawthorne," she said, her voice a silken purr that sent shivers down his spine. "The world will tremble before the might of the Illuminated Order."

Lord Alexander nodded, a fierce grin spreading across his face. "And tremble it shall, my dear Lady Sinclair. Tremble it shall."

As the meeting adjourned and the members of the Order dispersed into the night, Lord Alexander Hawthorne was standing on the precipice of something momentous. The world was changing, the old order crumbling away like dust in the wind, and the Illuminated Order would be there to pick up the pieces and reshape them in their image.

He smiled, a cold and ruthless expression that would've made even the bravest of men quail in terror. The future was theirs, and he would stop at nothing to ensure that it was a future forged in the fires of their ambition. The Illuminated Order would reign supreme, and all who dared to stand in their way would be crushed beneath the wheels of their irrevocable march towards destiny.

1

Washington, D.C 2023

Jade sat in the living room of her cramped studio apartment, the only sound, the faint hum of the ceiling fan overhead. The blue glow of the computer monitor cast a pallid light across her intense expression, reflecting in the lenses of her black-rimmed glasses. She leaned forward, elbows resting on the cluttered desk as her eyes scanned the message on the screen.

Her fingers trembled over the keyboard, nails bitten to the quick in restless anticipation. The message contained references to a secret society known as the Illuminated Order operating unseen in Washington D.C. It was an invitation to pierce the veil and expose their hidden influence.

Her pulse quickened as she re-read the words. The stuffy apartment air seemed to stand still in the suspense of the moment. Outside, the sounds of traffic whirred as the city continued on, oblivious to the tempting proposition weighing on Jade's shoulders.

She reached for her mug, the dregs of coffee long cold, and took a sip to steady her nerves. She leaned back in the creaking desk chair, eyes still fixed on the screen as she contemplated her next move. This was the break she'd been waiting for, a chance to blow the doors off a story that could shake the foundations of power in Washington. The thrill of the hunt coursed through her veins, even as the hint of danger whispered caution.

The cursor blinked as if counting down the seconds until her decision. Jade's silhouette reflected back from the screen's surface, merging with the message that represented a threshold she couldn't return from. With a deep breath, she leaned forward again, fingers suspended over the keys before beginning to type out a response that would launch her into the unknown.

* * *

JADE STEPPED INTO DR. SOROS' *penthouse office, her eyes drawn to the floor-to-ceiling windows that offered a breathtaking view of the city skyline. The room itself was a testament to the woman's brilliance and eclectic tastes. Bookshelves lined the walls, filled with an array of scientific journals and philosophical texts. A wooden desk stood at the center, its surface adorned with a carefully curated selection of artifacts from various historical periods.*

As Jade settled into the plush armchair opposite Dr. Soros, she was overcome by a sense of awe. The older woman's presence filled the room, her intellect, visible in every carefully chosen detail of her surroundings. From the intricate tapestries depicting the great thinkers of history to the gleaming chess set resting on a side table, every element spoke to a mind that reveled in the complexities of the world.

Dr. Soros was an imposing woman, her silver hair perfectly coiffed and her tailored suit exuding an air of power and authority. As she began to speak, Jade found herself drawn into a world of arcane knowledge and philosophical musings.

"Life, my dear," Dr. Soros began, her eyes shining with a mixture of wisdom and mischief, "is a game. A grand, cosmic chess match played out across the eons ..." She rose from her chair, moving to stand before the crackling fireplace. "From the moment we're born, we're thrust into this

game, our moves dictated by forces beyond our control. Our families, our circumstances, the very blood that flows through our veins– all of these things shape the board on which we play."

Jade frowned. "But what about free will? The ability to choose our own paths, to make our own decisions?"

Dr. Soros smiled. "What do you believe about free will, Jade?"

Jade hesitated, caught off guard by the question. "I guess I've always thought that we have the power to make our own choices, to shape our own destinies."

"Ah, but what if I told you that free will is nothing more than an illusion? A comforting lie we tell ourselves to make sense of the chaos around us?"

Jade frowned. "What do you mean?"

Dr. Soros's stare intensified, her voice getting lower. "The truth, my dear, is that we're all slaves to the game. The game of power, of influence, of control. It's been played since the dawn of civilization, and it will continue long after we're gone."

"But that sounds so bleak, so hopeless," Jade said. "Are you saying that we have no control over our own lives?"

"On the contrary," Dr. Soros said, her eyes sparkling with an intensity that made Jade feel exhilarated and terrified. "There are some who have learned to rise above the game, to seize control and bend the world to their will. But it takes knowledge, cunning, and the willingness to do what others cannot."

Jade sat back, her mind reeling. "Just how deep does this rabbit hole go, Dr. Soros?"

The older woman smiled, her expression equal parts inviting and unsettling. "Deeper than you can possibly imagine, Jade. And if you're brave enough, I can show you just how far it goes."

Dr. Soros was a legend in the medical community, a brilliant researcher and philanthropist who dedicated her life to improving the lives of others. She was a mentor to Jade's mother for years, guiding her through the challenges of dental school and helping her establish her thriving practice.

8 T.M JEFFERSON

"Your mother is one of the most talented dentists I've ever known,"Dr. Soros said, her voice warm with affection. "She has a gift for healing, for making people feel safe and cared for. And that's something that can't be taught."

A swell of pride filled Jade's chest, a deep, abiding love for the woman who raised her and shaped her into the person she was today. Her mother had always been her hero, a shining example of compassion and dedication in a world that often seemed cold and indifferent.

"I remember when your mother first came to me," Dr. Soros continued, her eyes distant with memory. "She was just a young student then, full of passion and idealism. She wanted to change the world, to make a difference in people's lives."

Jade hung on every word. She heard this story before, but it never failed to inspire her, to fill her with a sense of awe and reverence for the two women who shaped her life in such profound ways.

"I knew from the moment I met her she was special," Dr. Soros said, a smile playing at the corners of her mouth. "She had a fire in her, a drive to succeed that I had never seen before. And so, I took her under my wing, showed her the ropes and helped her navigate the challenges of the medical world."

A lump formed in Jade's throat, a deep, overwhelming sense of gratitude for the woman who was such an important part of her family's life. She knew her mother's success, her ability to touch so many lives and make a real difference in the world, was due in no small part to the guidance and support of Dr. Evelyn Soros.

"I've learned so much from both of you," Jade said. "You've shown me what it means to be strong, to be compassionate, to fight for what you believe in. And I hope that someday, I can make you both proud, can carry on the work you've started."

Dr. Soros reached out, taking Jade's hand in her own. Her skin was soft and warm, her grip strong and reassuring.

"You already have, my dear," she said. "You have a bright future ahead of you. And I know whatever path you choose, whatever chal-

THE ILLUMINATED ORDER 9

lenges you face, you'll meet them with the same strength and determination that your mother has always shown."

A tear slipped down Jade's cheek, a sense of love and gratitude washing over her. She'd always known she was lucky, that she was blessed with two incredible women to guide and support her through life's obstacles.

But now, sitting in Dr. Soros' penthouse, surrounded by the love and wisdom, Jade felt a sense of purpose, a conviction that she was meant for something great.

She would make them proud, would carry on the legacy of compassion and dedication they instilled in her from the beginning.

And she would do it with the same strength, the same commitment to justice and truth, that had always been the hallmark of Dr. Evelyn Soros and her beloved mother.

* * *

THE RAIN-STREAKED HALLWAYS *of Harvard's Merrill Academic Building carried the ripple of Jade's purposeful strides. Though she tried to temper her excitement, she couldn't resist the swell of pride as her fingers traced the inscription carved into the plaque:*

"Jade Rose - Valedictorian, Class of 2012."

In that moment, the years of countless all-nighters, the relentless drive to outwork and outthink her privileged peers, all led to this crowning achievement. The sacrifices made sense as she reflected on her arduous journey from the quiet-surburban streets of New Rochelle, New York to these hallowed halls.

Jade's mind flashed back to her first day as a wide-eyed freshman, awestruck by the legacy surrounding her. The intimidation of ivy-covered buildings and students clad in tidy prep school blazers lingered, until she found her calling in Professor Woodson's Investigative Journalism seminar.

His lectures on seeking truth, remaining objective but impassioned in pursuit of justice, activated a ferocious passion within the scholarship

10 T.M JEFFERSON

student. Woodson's war stories of confronting corruption through intrepid reporting field research inspired Jade. She'd found her life's purpose.

From that point, she pursued every extracurricular avenue to hone her craft - pushing herself to be editor-in-chief of the Harvard Crimson by her junior year, finagling opportunities for one-on-one workshops with guest speakers like famed journalists Bob Woodward and Carl Bernstein, and even convincing the Dean to approve an independent study embedded with the AP in the Middle East conflict zones one summer.

Each experience galvanized her obsessive hunger for uncovering vital stories that held the powerful accountable. While her classmates partied at debutante balls and shmoozed for corporate jobs, Jade spent her nights devouring microfiche archives and shadowing local beat reporters.

Her tenacity carved a solitary path, but it soon paid off with a prestigious Soros Fellowship to launch her career after graduating as class valedictorian. With her diploma in hand, a profound sense of responsibility weighed on her shoulders. Having received an elite education, Jade now carried a moral obligation to use her work as a platform to advocate for the voiceless, propelling her forward with renewed determination.

Over the years since graduating from Harvard, Jade carved out a reputation by exposing scandal after scandal that the powerful tried to keep hidden.

There was her Pulitzer-nominated bombshell about defense contractors exploiting a legal loophole to import cheap metals tainted with carcinogens for military gear. Despite intense pressure from lobbyists, her months-long investigation forced several CEOs to resign in disgrace.

Her pursuit of the Panamaian money laundering operation that toppled three senators and crippled an international banking syndicate read like a John le Carré thriller. Jade spent weeks holed up in a dingy Panama City hostel, intercepting encrypted communications to unravel the sordid web.

Then there was the Washington, D.C. punk rock club that doubled as a front for underground Russian cybercrime forums she infiltrated. Going undercover as a South American heiress slumming as a groupie, she

THE ILLUMINATED ORDER   11

documented vast networks of identity theft, until narrowly escaping a biker gang intent on silencing her.

Each situation more hazardous than the last, but Jade remained dedicated in her mission to peel back every layer of deception, no matter how deeply embedded in the power structures.

Her apartment was a ramshackled chronicle of her crusades - FOIA requests and lawsuits stacked haphazardly, covered in scrawled notes like "DON'T TRUST ANYONE" and "They're watching ..."Burner phones filled shoeboxes, fake IDs and wigs stuffed in the air vents, all tools of her escalating tradecraft.

On the wall remained the solitary memorial to what set her on this uncompromising path– a ripped photograph in a frame of her six year old baby cousin smiling beside a tricycle, before his life was tragically taken in a hit-and-run incident. Jade was still enraged that the cover-up implicated city officials taking bribes to protect the culprit, a wealthy elite's son.

That defining moment crystallized her life's purpose– to give a voice to those systemically wronged or silenced by abuses of authority. It was the reason Yale's Poynter Fellowship and Peabody Award sat collecting dust in her closet. Abstract accolades meant little compared to the impact of her work dismantling injustice.

2

As the mysterious summons lit her laptop screen, Jade's heart raced, pounding against her ribs like a caged bird desperate for release. Her palms grew slick with sweat, and she wiped them nervously on her jeans, her mind spinning with the implications of what she was seeing.

This was big, bigger than anything she ever encountered before. A potential puppetmaster, pulling the strings of power on a global scale. The Illuminated Order, the very name making the hairs on the back of her neck stand on end.

Jade's breath came faster, her chest rising and falling with each rapid inhale and exhale. Her eyes flashed across the screen, taking in every word, every clue, every hint of the corruption and immorality waiting to be unraveled.

In her mind's eye, she could already see it: the cadaverous eyes of the powerful, the ones who thought themselves untouchable, withering under the blinding spotlight of truth. The thrill of the hunt, the exhilaration of the chase, it flowed through her veins like an electric current, setting every nerve ending alight with anticipation.

Her fingers trembled as she reached for her journal, flipping it open to a blank page. This was it, the next great challenge, the ultimate test of her skills and her resolve. She could feel it in her bones, in the beating of her heart and the buzzing of her mind.

The Illuminated Order was hiding in the shadows, pulling the strings of the world like a puppet master. But she would bring them into the light, expose their darkest secrets and their most heinous crimes. No matter the cost, no matter the danger, she would not rest until the truth was revealed.

Jade steadied her breath and glanced around her apartment. The countless awards and honors served as a counterpoint to the maxim that defined her existence: "Comfort is the enemy of truth."

This latest message heralding the existence of the Illuminated Order was simply the next challenge for her to confront. For Jade, her Harvard pedigree represented the high-minded ideals she'd been forged by– wielding the sanctity of facts to pull back the veil on those illicitly accumulating power.

As she stared at her laptop screen, she welcomed the thought that this could be her life's greatest investigation. One transcending Woodward and Bernstein, and cementing her as this generation's most fearless journalistic icon, even if it consumed her in the process.

No matter how dark or dangerous the path ahead turned, she was prepared to expose the forces controlling the world order. With her moleskin journal open, Jade wrote down her first impressions and leads to pursue, the fire now stoked for her next lonely crusade.

As the cursor blinked on the screen, she found herself in a bind, a choice between the ordinary and the extraordinary. *What truths lay hidden behind those cryptic words?* The allure of an exposé that could shake the foundations of power battled with the cautionary whispers of the dangers that awaited her.

Harvard was a training ground, but it hadn't prepared her for what was unfolding before her. The decision was a difficult one, a

THE ILLUMINATED ORDER   15

choice that could propel her further into the depths of corruption. The pursuit of justice was her guiding force, but this, this was something different.

Jade's eyes moved from the screen to the city outside her window, the heart of Washington, where power brokers and secrets entwined. The walls started closing in as she struggled with the decision that lay in her hands. With a determined breath, she closed her eyes and made the choice that would alter the course of her life forever.

She shifted from contemplation to action. The clatter of keys pinging through the room as she began her research, diving into the obscure history of the Illuminated Order. The secrets that eluded others were now hers to uncover.

Her journalistic instincts kicked in, and the messy desk became a command center. Red strings connected bits of information on a corkboard– a tangible map of the hidden world she was about to enter. As she sifted through government archives, conspiracy theories, and whistleblower accounts, a web of intrigue spun out before her. She continued to scour the internet for more information, and a single word caught her eye: 'grove.' It was mentioned in passing, almost as an afterthought, but something about it nagged at her. She made a mental note to investigate further, wondering if this term held any significance in the larger puzzle of the Illuminated Order.

The hours melded into the night. The white glow of her computer screen reflected in her eyes, now alight with the anticipation of unveiling the truth.

Jade's finger hovered over the 'send' button, the email address staring back at her. She took a deep breath and clicked, watching the message disappear into the digital ether.

Less than an hour later, her phone buzzed with a reply. A time and place. No signature, but she knew it was him.

3

The bar on the outskirts of D.C. was nearly empty when Jade arrived. She spotted him as soon as she walked in, hunched over a whiskey in the back booth. His once clean-cut appearance now obscured by a beard and tired eyes.

"David."

He looked up, surprised. "Jade. You look good."

Jade slid into the booth, her eyes locked on his. "I'm not here to catch up," she said, her tone clipped.

David leaned back, his jaw clenching as he studied her. "The Illuminated Order," he said, his voice low and rough. "Your message said you needed my help."

Jade nodded, her fingers tapping nervously on the table. "What do you know about them?"

David scanned the bar, checking for eavesdroppers. He took a long swig of his drink before answering, his voice just above a whisper. "More than I ever wanted to. They're not just some conspiracy theory, Jade. They're real, and they're ..." He paused, his eyes haunted. "They're fucking dangerous."

A chill crept down her spine. She leaned in closer, her voice urgent. "I've been piecing things together, but I keep hitting dead ends. I need someone with insider knowledge, someone who—"

"And you thought of me?" David interrupted, a humorless laugh escaping his lips. "I'm flattered."

"Don't be," Jade snapped. "You're the only person I know with connections to that world."

David studied her, his eyes searching hers. "What makes you think I'll help you?" he asked. "We didn't exactly part on the best of terms, Jade."

Jade held his stare, her heart drumming in her chest. "You owe me," she said quietly, her voice trembling. "And because I think, deep down, there's still a part of you that wants to do the right thing."

David was silent for a moment as he reached into his jacket. Jade watched him. She thought back to their time together at Harvard, the long nights spent researching and chasing leads.

It was the electricity between them, the way his touch sent a surge through her body. But she remembered the pain of his sudden disappearance, the unanswered questions that haunted her for years.

As David pulled out the flash drive and slid it across the table, Jade felt a rush of emotions. This was the break she'd been waiting for, the key to unlocking the secrets of the Illuminated Order. But it also meant delving back into a past she tried to leave behind.

Memories flashed through her mind unbidden. Late nights in the Harvard Crimson office, the strong smell of coffee and the hum of computers. Stolen kisses in the stacks of the library, the thrill of uncovering secrets together. And then the emptiness followed, the hole in her life that David's absence left.

Jade's fingers brushed against his as she took the flash drive, and for a moment, it was as if no time passed at all. She could feel the old connection between them, the pull that had always been there.

But they were no longer young students chasing the truth. They were two broken people, scarred by the battles they fought and the secrets they uncovered.

"Thank you," Jade said. She met David's eyes, seeing the obsessed look that mirrored her own.

"Don't thank me yet. You have no idea what you're getting yourself into."

Jade stood to leave, but David reached out, grabbing her wrist.

"Wait. There's something else you should know."

She looked down at his hand, then back at his face. "What?"

David's eyes were intense, pleading. "The Order ... They're everywhere. In the government, in corporations, in the media. And they'll stop at nothing to protect their secrets."

Jade pulled her arm away, her heart pounding. "I'm not afraid of them."

"You should be," David said, his voice low. "You need to be careful. Trust no one."

Jade stared at him before turning to leave. As she pushed through the door, the cold night air hit her like a blast, chilling her to the bone. The street was empty, save for a few shadows on the pavement from the streetlights.

She pulled her coat tighter around herself, David's words replaying in her mind. The Order was everywhere, their influence far-reaching and insidious. The task was daunting, almost insurmountable.

But beneath the fear and uncertainty, there was something else, something that pushed her to continue: determination. Jade dedicated her life to uncovering the truth, to exposing the corruption that lurked in the shadows of power. And now, with David's help, she finally had a chance to do just that.

With a deep breath, she squared her shoulders and continued walking, her steps filled with purpose. She would unravel the secrets of the Illuminated Order, no matter the cost. And maybe, just maybe, she and David could find a way to trust each other again, to heal the wounds of the past and forge a new partnership in the face of this daunting challenge.

* * *

INSIDE HIS TOWNHOUSE, David Montgomery sat at his kitchen table, a glass of whiskey in one hand and a tattered photograph in the other.

The face staring back at him was barely recognizable– a younger, cleaner-cut version of himself in a crisp military uniform. David's fingers traced the edge of the picture, his mind drifting to a time when he believed in the idea of serving a greater good.

But that was before. Before the CIA, before he crossed the lines between right and wrong, before the Illuminated Order.

* * *

IN THE SCORCHING *heat of Kandahar, Afghanistan, David Montgomery moved through the dusty streets, his mind a fractured maze of memories and half-formed thoughts. The effects of the MK Ultra program had taken hold, stripping away his sense of self and replacing it with a singular, all-consuming purpose: to track down and eliminate the high priest of the ancient cult that threatened the fragile balance of power in the region.*

The city was filled with narrow alleys and crowded bazaars, the air suffused with the scent of spices and the clamor of daily life. The sun beat down from a cloudless sky, emitting shadows across the crumbling mudbrick buildings and the faces of the people who called this place home.

David's routine was a cycle of surveillance and preparation, his every waking moment consumed by the task at hand. He rose before dawn each morning, his body conditioned by years of rigorous training and the chemical enhancements that flowed through his veins. He moved through the streets like a wraith, his eyes scanning for any sign of his target or the threat of danger.

THE ILLUMINATED ORDER 21

He spent long hours sitting on rooftops and crouched in alleyways, his eyes trained on the high priest's compound. He studied the comings and goings of the guards, memorized the patterns of their patrols and the layout of the buildings.

In the afternoons, when the heat was at its most oppressive, David retreated to the dingy room he rented on the outskirts of the city. The space was spartan and cramped, with little more than a cot and a few basic amenities to serve his needs. But it was here that he planned and prepared.

He pored over maps and satellite images. He cleaned and maintained his weapons, the tools of his trade that had become an extension of his body.

In the midst of his focus, the edges of his mind began to fray, the cracks in his psyche widening with each passing hour. The drugs that had been pumped into his system, the mental conditioning and the brutal training, had taken a toll on his sanity, his grasp on reality becoming more tenuous with every breath.

At night, when the city was draped in darkness and the sounds of gunfire resounded through the streets, David lay on his cot, his eyes staring blankly at the ceiling as he fought to hold onto the last shreds of his humanity. He saw faces in the shadows, heard whispers in the silence, the ghosts of his past and the demons of his present bleeding together in horror and despair.

Dressed in tactical gear, David moved through the rugged landscapes of Kandahar. He was a pawn in the CIA's twisted game. Under the influence of psychoactive drugs and subjected to brutal psychological tactics, David transformed into a programmed assassin, a killing machine stripped of moral constraints.

As he neared the decrepit temple, the air became stuffy. The high priest, a man of influence among the desperate and dispossessed, had become a thorn in the Order's side. His sermons contradicted their crafted lies.

Slipping through the darkness, David saw the glow of candles lighting the makeshift altar inside the temple. The high priest's voice could be heard through the night, resonating with the weary souls seeking guidance within the walls.

A surge of emotions shot through David's veins. Once a man of conviction, he now operated as a programmed instrument of death. MK Ultra stripped away his autonomy, turning him into a merciless executor of the Order's will.

Closing in on his target, David moved with precision. His silenced pistol felt cold against his gloved hand as he approached the temple's entrance. The candlelight revealed the silhouette of the high priest, deep in prayer.

Without hesitation, David breached the threshold, his movements a seamless blend of instinct and conditioning. The high priest, sensing an intruder, turned to face the person encroaching on his sacred space.

Their eyes locked, a moment pregnant with the weight of warring destinies. The high priest's eyes showed fear, while David's, once mirrors to a soul, now reflected the abyss that MK Ultra carved inside of him.

"Oh, great and mighty Gods, hear my prayer in this dark hour," he said. "For centuries, we have served as your faithful stewards, guiding the course of human history according to your divine will. But now, I fear that we have strayed from the path, that we have allowed our own hubris and ambition to cloud our judgment."

He paused, as if struggling to find the right words. "In our quest for power and control, we have forgotten the sacred trust that you have placed in us. We have sought to shape the world in our own image, to bend reality to our will. We have played God, and in doing so, we have brought darkness and suffering on the innocent."

The high priest's voice grew louder, as he continued. "Forgive us, oh Gods, for our arrogance and our folly. Forgive us for the lives we have taken, the souls we have corrupted, the chaos we have sown in your name. We are but mortal men, flawed and fallible, and we have let our own desires blind us to the true path."

He opened his eyes, his gaze falling on David, who stood before him like an avenging angel, his face hard and his eyes filled with a righteous fury. "And now, the reckoning is upon us," the high priest whispered. "The *forces of light have sent their champion to strike us down, to put an end to our misguided crusade. And though it pains me to admit it, I know that we deserve nothing less."*

He bowed his head, his shoulders slumping as if under a great weight. "So I beseech you, oh Gods, to have mercy on our souls. Judge us not for our actions, but for the purity of our intentions. And grant us the strength to face our fate with courage and dignity, knowing that we have served your will to the best of our ability."

As the high priest finished his prayer, David stepped forward, clutching the weapon at his side. The high priest looked up at him, his eyes filled with sadness and a deep, abiding faith.

"Do what you must," he said. "I am ready to face the judgment of the Gods, and to accept whatever fate they have ordained for me."

In that moment, David's training took over. The silenced pistol spat its deadly payload, extinguishing the life that dared challenge the Order's narrative. The high priest crumpled to the floor, his prayers silenced by the cold efficiency of the assassin.

* * *

DAVID TOOK a long swig of whiskey, relishing the burn in his throat. He tried to leave that world behind, but the past had a way of catching up with him.

He thought back to his and Jade's time together at Harvard– the heated debates, the stolen moments, the shared passion for finding the truth. Jade was a force of nature, and David was drawn to her like a bird to its nest.

But he had his own secrets, his own darkness that he couldn't share with her. When the CIA came calling, David saw it as a chance to make a real difference, to serve his country. He left without saying goodbye, knowing Jade would never understand.

Now, years later, he was a man haunted by his choices. The things he'd seen, the things he'd done in the name of national security– they clung to his back like a physical burden.

24 T.M JEFFERSON

David's eyes drifted to the stack of files on the table, the ones he managed to smuggle out of Langley before going off the grid. They were the key to unlocking the secrets of the Illuminated Order, the devilish cabal that had been pulling the strings behind the scenes for longer than anyone realized.

Helping Jade would put him back on their radar, paint a target on both their backs. But he couldn't keep running from the truth.

With a sigh, he drained the last of his whiskey and stood up, gathering the files and his few belongings. It was time to face his past and join Jade in her fight for justice.

As he stepped into the night, David felt something he hadn't felt in years– belief. Belief that maybe he could find a way to atone for his sins and make things right.

Even if it meant putting his life on the line in the process.

4

Senator Jonathan Bishop slithered through the corridors of the Capitol, his presence commanding attention and respect. His tailored suit, a perfect blend of elegance and authority, mirrored the persona he presented to the world. As he entered his office, the epitome of power and prestige, he prepared to face the inquisitive journalist who managed to secure an interview.

Jade Rose, a determined force in her own right, was prepared to unravel the enigma that was Senator Bishop. As she stepped into his office, the opulence of the surroundings struck her– the rich wooden desk, the plush leather chairs, the intricate artwork on the walls. Yet, beneath the veneer of sophistication, Jade sensed an undercurrent of something more sinister.

"Miss Rose, welcome," Senator Bishop greeted her, his smile polished and practiced. "I must say, I'm intrigued by your persistence in securing this meeting."

Jade's eyes met his, her smile masking the determination that burned inside of her. "Thank you for taking the time, Senator. I believe our conversation will be enlightening."

As they settled into their seats, Jade wasted no time diving into her questions. Each inquiry a calculated probe, designed to pierce through the senator's false image and uncover the truth behind his alleged ties to the Illuminated Order.

Senator Bishop, however, was a master of deflection. His responses were smooth and refined, his words chosen with meticulous care. "Miss Rose, while I admire your tenacity, I must say that these rumors of secret societies and hidden agendas are nothing more than sensationalism. My sole focus is serving the people who elected me."

But Jade was not so easily dissuaded. She pressed on, her questions growing more pointed, more specific. And for a moment, she saw something in the senator's eyes– a speckle of unease, a crack in his impeccable composure.

"Senator Bishop, with all due respect, the evidence suggests there may be more to your story than meets the eye. The connections, the coincidences ... they paint a picture that cannot be ignored."

The senator's smile tightened, his eyes hardening. "Miss Rose, I understand the allure of a good story, but I assure you, there is no grand conspiracy at play here. I am a public servant, nothing more, nothing less."

But, as Jade left the senator's office, a sense of unease lingered. The meeting only served to fuel her suspicions, to deepen the mystery surrounding Senator Bishop and his potential involvement with the Illuminated Order.

As she stepped out into the corridors of the Capitol, Jade understood this was just the beginning. The senator's persona was a mask, concealing secrets she was determined to uncover. And she would stop at nothing to bring the truth to the light.

* * *

SENATOR JONATHAN BISHOP stormed out of his office, his face twisted with rage and his eyes blazing with fury. He slammed the door behind him with such force that the walls shook, causing his staff to jump in alarm.

"Who the hell was that journalist?" he asked. "How did she get past security? And why the fuck wasn't I briefed on her before the meeting?"

His chief of staff, a thin, nervous-looking man named Eric, stepped forward, his hands trembling as he tried to placate his boss. "Sir, we had no idea she would be here. She must've used a fake identity to get through the screening process."

Bishop whirled on him, his eyes narrowing to slits. "I don't want excuses, Eric. I want answers. Who is this Jade Rose, and why is she sniffing around my business?"

Eric unfastened the top button of his shirt and swallowed hard. "I'm not sure, sir. We're still trying to gather information on her background and connections."

Bishop slammed his fist on his desk. "Well, you better find out fast. Because if that little bitch keeps digging, she's going to uncover things that could bring us all down."

He began to pace back and forth, thinking back on Jade's questions. She was well-informed, too sharp in her inquiries. It was clear she knew something, or at least suspected something, about his dealings with the Illuminated Order.

"I want a full dossier on her by the end of the day," he said, his voice cutting through the tense silence of the room. "I want to know everything about her– her family, her friends, her fucking kindergarten teacher. And I want to know who she's been talking to and what she knows."

His staff nodded, their faces pale with fear and apprehension. When the Senator was in this mood, there was no room for error or delay.

Bishop turned to face the window, his hands clasped behind his back and his jaw clenched tight. He worked too hard, sacrificed too much, to let some upstart journalist bring him down. He clawed his

28   T.M JEFFERSON

way to the top of the political heap, made the deals and compromises necessary to secure his place in the halls of power.

And he'd done it all with the backing of the Illuminated Order. They funded his campaigns, pulled the strings to ensure his victory, and in return, he was their loyal servant, their man on the inside.

But now, with Jade Rose sniffing around and asking dangerous questions, everything he built was at risk. If she kept digging, kept pulling at the threads of the web that bound him to the Order, it could all come crashing down around him.

He couldn't let that happen. He wouldn't let that happen. He was Senator Jonathan Bishop, and he would crush anyone who dared to stand in his way.

"Find out everything you can about this Jade Rose," he said. "And then we'll figure out how to deal with her. Permanently."

Jade and David entered the archive, a sanctuary of secrets tucked away in the heart of Washington. It was a stately edifice that exuded an air of history and knowledge. The building's exterior was crafted from smooth limestone, adorned with intricate carvings and columns that harkened back to the neoclassical architecture of the city's founding. The familiar scent of aged paper filled the air, transporting them back to their history of uncovering hidden truths. Shelves lined with dusty volumes reached toward the ceiling, each one a testament to the depth of knowledge waiting to be unraveled.

As they searched the cataloged records, David's fingers traced the spines with a practiced ease. Jade admired his focus, remembering the countless late nights they'd spent together, poring over documents in pursuit of a story.

She glanced at him, an inkling of their past sparking in her chest. "Just like old times, huh?"

David's eyes met hers, a hint of a smile tugging at his lips. "Some things never change."

They fell into a rhythm, their movements synchronized by the connection that never faded. Jade's heart skipped a beat as she read

30   T.M JEFFERSON

the headline of an old newspaper: "Illuminated Order Linked to Secret Society Gathering at Bohemian Grove." The article was dated back to the 1920s, but the implications were clear.

"David, look at this."

As he read the words, his brow furrowed. "That's where they meet."

"It's not the first time the Order's been connected to Bohemian Grove," she said. "This goes back decades, maybe even longer."

"This could be the key to exposing their secrets."

David's hand brushed against hers as he took the newspaper. His fingers lingered for a moment, the warmth of his skin seeping into hers, before he pulled away, his eyes scanning the pages with a practiced intensity.

"We're treading on thin ice here. One misstep, and the entire operation could collapse, taking us down with it."

Jade met David's eyes, seeing the determination that drew her to him. In that moment, the past and present collided, their mission reigniting the bond they once shared.

They gathered the pertinent documents, and as they stepped into the sunlight, Jade felt a renewed sense of purpose, fueled by the knowledge that she and David were once again fighting side by side. The ghosts of their past led them to this moment, and together, they were ready to face whatever lay ahead.

* * *

THE AUTUMN BREEZE *whispered through the ancient trees that adorned Harvard Yard, carrying with it the fragrance of knowledge and the promise of intellectual pursuits. Jade Rose, a tenacious journalist with a thirst for truth, navigated the maze of books and students with a focused determination. Her eyes, sharp and discerning, scanned the crowd for any hint of the mysteries she sought to unveil.*

Meanwhile, David Montgomery, a man with an air of quiet intensity, stood near the steps of Widener Library. His eyes swept over the academic landscape. The world seemed to fade into the background as he delved into his own thoughts, an island of introspection amidst the sea of academia.

Their first encounter was as unexpected as it was inevitable. In the shadow of John Harvard's statue, a symbolic guardian of knowledge, Jade and David's worlds collided. A collision of books and papers orchestrated by the hand of destiny.

"Oh, I'm so sorry," Jade said.

"No harm done," he replied.

Jade, with her insatiable curiosity, couldn't resist the opportunity. "Are you lost in thought, or is this just the usual Harvard contemplation pose?"

David laughed. "Perhaps a bit of both," he admitted. The ice broke, their dialogue flowed, weaving through topics ranging from literature to the complexities of life. Each word exchanged revealed layers of their personalities, creating an invisible bond that transcended the ordinary.

Little did they know that this chance meeting, bathed in the golden hues of a Harvard evening, would mark the beginning of an odyssey into the shadows of mystery and intrigue.

6

Councilman Michael Thornton's entanglement with the Illuminated Order began early in his political career. As a young, ambitious politician, Thornton caught the eye of the Order's recruiters, who saw in him a malleable and willing pawn to further their interests in the halls of power.

Thornton's rise through the ranks of D.C. politics was swift and explosive, fueled by the Order's influence and the considerable financial backing they provided. Behind the scenes, the Order pulled strings and called in favors, ensuring that Thornton's opponents were neutralized and his path to victory was all but assured.

In return for their support, Thornton became a loyal servant of the Order, using his position on the City Council to advance their agenda and protect their interests. He worked tirelessly to steer lucrative contracts and development deals to companies with ties to the Order, lining his own pockets in the process with kickbacks and bribes.

As Thornton's power and influence grew, so too did his corruption. He became involved in illicit activities, from money laundering and embezzlement to drug trafficking and prostitution. The

Order provided cover for his misdeeds, shielding him from investigation and ensuring that any potential whistleblowers were silenced.

Thornton's role as a corrupted councilman served the Order well, allowing them to maintain a stranglehold on the city's politics and economy. He was their eyes and ears in the corridors of power, reporting back on any potential threats or opportunities that might impact their operations.

However, as Thornton's behavior grew more reckless and his vices began to spiral out of control, he became a liability to the Order. His frequent dalliances with drugs and prostitutes made him vulnerable to blackmail, and his sloppy financial dealings threatened to expose the Order's own involvement in his corruption.

Despite the Order's best efforts to keep him in line, Thornton's self-destructive behavior finally caught up with him

His hand shook as he raised the glass of bourbon to his lips, the amber liquid sloshing against the sides. He could still taste the bitterness of the cocaine on his tongue, feel the rush of the high shooting through his veins.

On the bed beside him, the prostitute stirred, her naked body tangled in the sheets. Thornton's stomach twisted with a mixture of desire and disgust, the same conflicting emotions that drove him to this shady motel room in the first place.

He closed his eyes, memories flashing through his mind like a twisted highlight reel. The late nights at the office, the endless parties and fundraisers, the women who threw themselves at him with reckless abandon. He'd always been a man who craved more, who could never quite satisfy the gnawing hunger inside of him.

Power, influence, sex and drugs– they were all just different flavors of the same addictive cocktail, the one he couldn't seem to quit no matter how hard he tried. Each time he told himself it would be the last, that he would finally get his act together and be the man his constituents believed him to be.

THE ILLUMINATED ORDER   35

But then the temptation would come calling again, and he would find himself right back where he started, caught in a cycle of weakness and desperation that he couldn't seem to break.

Thornton's eyes snapped open as he heard the sound of sirens in the distance, growing louder with each passing second. His heart thudding in his chest. He glanced down at his trembling hands, realizing what he'd gotten himself into.

He'd gone too far this time, let his appetites get the best of him in a moment of reckless abandon. And now, as the consequences of his actions bore down on him like a freight train, he knew his luck had finally run out.

The door burst open, and a team of police officers swarmed the room, their weapons drawn. Thornton raised his hands in surrender, his eyes wide with fear and panic.

"Councilman Michael Thornton, you're under arrest," one of the officers said. "You have the right to remain silent. Anything you say can and will be used against you in a court of law."

As they led him out of one room and into another, a sense of numbness came over him, a dull acceptance of the fate that awaited him. He always knew his secrets would catch up with him one day, that the dark forces he aligned himself with would turn on him in the end.

In the other room, the detectives grilled him, their voices sharp and accusing as they laid out the evidence against him. The prostitute, the drugs, the corruption and deceit that stretched back years—it was all there, laid bare for the world to see.

But even in his desperation, Thornton clung to one last shred of hope, one final bargaining chip that could save him from the worst of the fallout. "I have information," he said. "About the Order, about the people behind all of this. I can give you names, dates, places. I can help you bring them down."

The detectives exchanged a look, their eyes narrowing with suspicion and interest. They heard whispers of the Illuminated Order before, caught glimpses of the secret cabal that pulled the strings of power from behind the scenes. But they never had someone so close to the inner circle, someone with the knowledge and the access to bring the whole house of cards tumbling down.

What Thornton didn't know, however, was that one of the detectives in the room, a man named Jack Caster, was himself a member of the Order. Caster rose through the ranks of law enforcement with the backing of his benefactors, and used his position to protect and serve their interests at every turn.

As he listened to Thornton's desperate pleas, Caster felt a cold fury growing in his gut, a sense of betrayal and disgust at the councilman's weakness and disloyalty. He had to act fast, had to contain the damage before Thornton could spill his secrets to the wrong people.

With a nod to his partner, Caster stepped out of the room. He pulled out his phone and dialed a number that he committed to memory long ago, the direct line to one of the Order's highest-ranking members.

"We have a problem," he said. "Thornton is talking, offering to spill everything he knows about the Order. We need to contain this, fast."

There was a moment of silence on the other end of the line, a pause that seemed to stretch out for an eternity. And then, with a voice that was as cold and unforgiving as the grave, the person on the other end spoke.

"Understood. Do what needs to be done. Thornton is now a liability. And we don't abide liabilities."

The call ended with a click. Caster knew what those words meant, knew the terrible price that Thornton would pay for his betrayal.

But he also knew he had no choice, his own survival depended on his loyalty to the Order. With a heavy heart, he stepped back into the room, ready to play his part in the dark drama that was about to unfold.

Thornton looked up at him with desperate, pleading eyes. But Caster's expression was hard as stone, his eyes cold and pitiless.

"I'm sorry, Councilman," he said. "But I'm afraid your information won't be enough to save you. You've crossed the wrong people, and now it's time to pay the price."

7

In a secluded corner of the city, Jade and David pored over the new information. The loud sounds outside seemed distant, muffled by the gravity of the moment.

Their voices hushed and urgent, they began to plot their next move. The information they held could change everything, but they had to tread carefully. The wrong step could put them in danger, exposing their knowledge to those who would stop at nothing to keep it hidden.

"We have to get more information about Bohemian Grove," Jade said. "Whatever they're planning, we need to bring it to the light."

She scanned the area, ensuring they were alone. The temporary sanctuary provided them a moment to catch their breath and gather their thoughts. David considered their options, his mind working through the potential outcomes of each path they could take.

"We're about to step into the lion's den, Jade. And Bohemian Grove is the beating heart of their twisted empire."

The discovery of the secret meeting location left them both stunned. Huddled together in the confines of the office, Jade and

David scrutinized maps and satellite imagery. Jade's fingers ghosted over the boundaries of Bohemian Grove, her touch delicate yet purposeful, as if trying to divine the secrets hidden within its borders.

"This is where the most powerful figures in the Order convene," she said. "A place of secrets and influence."

David leaned back in his chair. "It's a fortress of privilege, masked in exclusivity."

Jade met his eyes, the intensity of their past fluctuating between them. "We've faced risks before, David. This time, the stakes are higher than ever."

He reached out, his hand covering hers. "We're in this together, Jade. No matter what happens."

She nodded, drawing strength from his touch. "I'm with you, but we need someone who understands the inner workings of the Order."

David thought for a second. "Dr. Sophia Ramirez. She's our best bet. Her expertise on secret societies could be invaluable."

Jade stood up, the determination in her eyes mirroring David's. "Then let's pay her a visit. We have a Grove to infiltrate and secrets to uncover."

As they gathered their materials, Jade and David knew they were about to embark on a dangerous journey, but the truth was worth the risk. With Dr. Ramirez's guidance and their own unbreakable bond, they were ready to face the heart of the Illuminated Order's darkness.

Dr. Sophia Ramirez, a woman of academic distinction and age old wisdom, held court within the halls of academia. Her office, decorated with shelves laden with ancient tomes and manuscripts, served as a sanctuary for the pursuit of knowledge and the unraveling of mysteries that danced at the periphery of societal awareness.

With a demeanor that blended scholarly precision and a quiet intensity, Dr. Ramirez possessed an aura of intellectual authority. Her silver hair framed a face that bore the lines of countless hours spent delving into the secrets of clandestine societies. Behind a pair of glasses that hinted at the depth of her insights, her eyes gleamed with a keen intelligence that seemed to pierce through the layers of hidden truths.

As an expert in political science with a specialization in the study of secret societies and covert operations, Dr. Ramirez's reputation extended beyond the confines of her academic realm. She was sought after not only for her wealth of knowledge but also for her ability to connect historical threads and shed light on the shadows cast by the powerful.

Her attire, a subtle blend of professionalism and a hint of

mystery, reflected a woman who moved seamlessly between the worlds of higher education and intrigue. A small, gold owl pendant, an ancient symbol with roots lost in time, hung around her neck, a talisman that hinted at the depths of her understanding.

In her interactions, Dr. Ramirez exuded a calm assurance that inspired confidence. Her words carried the weight of decades spent deciphering the cryptic languages of secret societies. But beneath the veneer of academic authority, there was passion– a commitment to discovering the truths obscured by the veils of power.

Colleagues respected her insights, students revered her as a mentor, and those who sought the unraveling of secrets coveted her guidance. Dr. Sophia Ramirez, with her encyclopedic knowledge and intellect was ready to guide Jade and David through the maze of the Illuminated Order's secrets.

* * *

JADE AND DAVID stepped into Dr. Ramirez's office, a sanctuary of knowledge amidst the university. Towering bookcases lined the walls, filled with ancient tomes and obscure texts. The air was enveloped in the scent of aged leather and fresh brewed coffee.

At the center of it all sat Dr. Ramirez, engrossed in a manuscript. She looked up as they entered, her stare piercing through the secrets they sought to unravel.

"Jade Rose," she said, a hint of a smile playing at her lips. "I've been following your work. Tenacious, fearless. And driven by a hunger for truth that rivals my own."

Jade blinked, taken aback by the perceptiveness of the woman before her. She glanced at David, who gave a subtle nod. They were in the right place.

"Dr. Ramirez," Jade began, stepping forward. "We need your help. We've uncovered evidence of a secret society operating at the highest levels of power."

The professor's eyes widened, recognition passing over her face. She gestured for them to sit. "Tell me everything."

Jade wasted no time, placing the evidence on Dr. Ramirez's desk. "Bohemian Grove. The Illuminated Order's sanctuary. What can you tell us about this place, and how does it connect to the Order's influence?"

Dr. Ramirez scanned the documents. "Bohemian Grove has a storied history, intertwined with the elites of society. It's more than just a gathering place; it's a nexus of power and influence. The Order's choice of such a location signifies a deliberate move to shape events beyond the public eye."

She sat back in her chair, her eyes distant as if recalling the secrets she unearthed. "The Grove is divided into camps, each representing a facet of the Order's power structure. The Owl's Nest, the Cave, the Hilltop Lodge. Each has its own hierarchy and its own rituals."

David's jaw tightened. "We need to know what we're dealing with. The layout, the security, the key players."

Dr. Ramirez nodded, reaching for a worn leather journal. "I've spent years piecing together fragments of the Order's history. Bohemian Grove is a puzzle, but there are patterns, clues to its inner workings."

As the meeting stretched into the night, the trio pored over maps and documents. Jade and David's resolve grew stronger with each revelation, their determination fueled by the knowledge that they were on the cusp of exposing the truth.

"The Order has always employed assassins to carry out its darkest deeds," she said. "From the days of the Hashashin in ancient Persia to the modern era, they've relied on these skilled killers to eliminate threats and maintain their grip on power."

She paused, her voice dropping to a whisper. "And now, they have Elias Vale, a man whose reputation for brutality and efficiency is unmatched. He's the Order's most valuable asset, and their most closely guarded secret."

44   T.M JEFFERSON

Dr. Ramirez fixed them with a piercing gaze. "Remember, the Order's power lies in secrecy. The truth is your weapon. Wield it wisely, and the walls of Bohemian Grove will crumble."

As Jade and David sat in Dr. Ramirez's office, the professor leaned back in her chair, a distant look in her eyes. "I've been fascinated by secret societies since I was a young girl," she said. "My grandfather used to tell me stories of the Freemasons and the Illuminati, whispered tales of power and intrigue that captured my imagination."

She smiled ruefully. "When I lost him to cancer, I threw myself into my studies, determined to uncover the truth behind the myths. I spent years traveling the world, tracking down ancient texts and forgotten archives, piecing together the hidden history of these organizations. It became my life's work, my obsession."

Dr. Ramirez's stare turned serious. "I'm not just helping you because of my academic curiosity," she said. "I have my own reasons for wanting to see the Illuminated Order exposed."

She took a deep breath. "Years ago, my mentor, a brilliant historian named Dr. James Smithfield, stumbled on evidence of the Order's existence. He became consumed by his research, determined to bring their secrets to light. But before he could go public with his findings, he disappeared without a trace."

Her eyes glistened. "I never found out what happened to him, but I've always suspected the Order had a hand in his disappearance. Helping you uncover the truth is my way of honoring his memory and finishing the work he started."

As Jade and David listened to the professor, every so often, she would pause to adjust the small, gold pendant that hung around her neck, her fingers tracing the intricate engravings with a tender reverence. Jade wondered about the story behind the necklace, sensing it held a deep personal significance for the professor.

When Dr. Ramirez caught Jade staring, she smiled. "This was a gift from my grandmother," she said. "She said it would bring me

THE ILLUMINATED ORDER   45

luck and protect me from harm. I've worn it every day since, a little piece of her always close to my heart."

* * *

HIDDEN in the ancient redwood forests of Monte Rio, California, Bohemian Grove emerged as a sanctuary veiled in the mists of secrecy and exclusivity. The sprawling 2,700-acre expanse, bearing the address 20601 Bohemian Avenue, stood as a testament to the enclave's storied existence. A hallowed ground belonging to the private gentlemen's club known as the Bohemian Club, Bohemian Grove exuded an air of mystique that transcended its tranquil surroundings.

Founded with a vision that reflected through the corridors of time, Bohemian Grove traced its origins to a group of influential men seeking a retreat where they could escape the trappings of the ordinary world. Artists, musicians, businessmen, government officials, and former U.S. presidents converged within this redwood cathedral, the Bohemian Club's all-male membership forging bonds beneath the towering trees.

Each year, in mid-July, Bohemian Grove transformed into a sphere shrouded in secrecy, hosting an encampment that spanned more than two weeks. A privileged few, along with their invited guests, explored a world detached from the mundane, where the Club's motto, "*Weaving Spiders Come Not Here*," resonate through the ancient groves.

Beyond the falsehood of camaraderie lay the shadows of power and the undercurrents of influence that could sway the course of nations. Notorious for its Manhattan Project planning meeting in September 1942, which laid the groundwork for the atomic bomb, Bohemian Grove became a nexus where power and secrecy converged.

As the years passed, the Grove evolved, its significance growing as it became a symbol of privilege, influence, and the unspoken

46   T.M JEFFERSON

agreements forged within its secluded groves. The encampment became a rite of passage for the elite, and after 40 years of membership, individuals earned the revered *"Old Guard"* status, solidifying their position within the hierarchy.

* * *

AS THE TRIO delved into the historical significance of Bohemian Grove and the potential implications of the Illuminated Order's presence, Dr. Ramirez provided insights that transcended mere academic knowledge.

"You two are treading on slippery ground," she warned. "Bohemian Grove is a melting pot of influence, and those who seek to expose its secrets face powerful adversaries. But knowledge is your weapon, and understanding their methods is the key to unraveling the Order's web of deceit."

As they stepped out into the cool night air, they thought hard about what Dr. Ramirez told them. They exchanged a glance, and set forth, their footsteps carrying them towards the heart of the Illuminated Order's darkest secrets.

9

Jade and David maneuvered the small rowboat through the river's murky waters, the light from the moon guiding their path. The gentle splashing of the oars and the chirping of crickets were the only sounds that broke the silence of the night.

Jade sat at the bow, scanning the shoreline for any sign of their destination. "We should be getting close. The intel said Bohemian Grove is just a few miles upstream."

David nodded, his strong arms propelling the boat forward with steady strokes. "Let's hope the rumors are true," he said. "If the Order really is holding their meeting here, it could be our best chance to infiltrate their ranks and uncover their plans."

Jade rested her hand on the small pouch hanging from her waist, the weight of the camera inside a comforting presence. It was their silent weapon, a tool that could expose the Order's secrets to the world.

As they rounded a bend in the river, a faint glow appeared in the distance. David turned to Jade. "There, up ahead. That must be it."

David slowed his strokes, the boat gliding quietly through the water. They exchanged a glance. Whatever awaited them, they would have to face it together, their bond stronger than any force the Order could muster.

They crept through the forest surrounding Bohemian Grove. The moonlight filtered through the canopy, tossing shadows across the ground. As they approached the perimeter of the exclusive retreat, the distant sound of voices and the fizzling of a large fire tickled their ears.

A beam of light cut through the darkness, and a gruff voice called out, "Halt! You're trespassing on private property. Keep your hands where I can see them," he said, gun in one hand, reaching for his walkie talkie with the other. "We have a perimeter breach, possible suspicious activity. Requesting backup. Requesting backup."

Jade and David froze, their blood running cold as they realized they'd been spotted. They raised their hands in surrender as several security guards emerged from the trees.

Despite their pleas and explanations, they found themselves handcuffed and escorted off the property. The local police station was a blur of questioning and paperwork before they were finally released with a stern warning.

As they wandered through the nearby town, they approached several locals, hoping to gain some information about Bohemian Grove and the strange rituals rumored to take place there.

The town nestled on the fringes of Bohemian Grove was a study in contrasts, a place where the ordinary and the extraordinary collided. The air was suffused with the scent of pine and redwood, mixed with the tang of smoke from the Grove's nightly bonfires. The atmosphere was charged with an undercurrent of tension, a clear sign that something momentous was unfolding just beyond the reach of curious eyes.

The streets were lined with shops and cafes. The locals moved about their daily lives with a practiced nonchalance, their smiles warm but guarded, as if they were privy to secrets they dared not share. They spoke in whispered tones, their eyes darting furtively towards the grove's perimeter, ever mindful of the powerful figures who gathered there.

There was an energy to the town that was at once electric and subdued, a thrumming undercurrent of anticipation that set nerves on edge and hearts racing. The people here were no strangers to the weird and the extraordinary, living in the shadow of an enigma that long since become a part of their daily reality. They navigated the blurred lines between the mundane and the mystical with practiced ease, their lives forever intertwined with the fate of the Grove and the secrets it held.

As Jade and David walked the streets, they felt the weight of the town's history, the countless secrets and lies whispering on the breeze. The people they passed regarded them with a mix of curiosity and caution, their eyes filled with unspoken questions and warnings. In this place, where the veil between worlds seemed to wear thin, anything was possible, and the truth was often stranger than fiction.

Most of the residents were tight-lipped, unwilling to discuss the secretive retreat. However, one elderly man beckoned them closer.

He sat on a bench outside a small cafe, sipping a cup of coffee and watching the world go by with a knowing glint in his eye.

Jade and David approached him with caution, not wanting to scare him off with too many direct questions. They struck up a casual conversation, asking about the town's history and the local attractions.

The old man smiled, his eyes crinkling at the corners. "Folks 'round here tend to mind their own business, 'specially when it comes to the Grove," he said, his voice low and conspiratorial.

"Why is that?" Jade asked, keeping her tone light and friendly.

"Them rich fellas, they got their own way of doin' things, if ya catch my drift."

"Is there something unusual about the Grove?"

The old man chuckled, shaking his head. "Unusual doesn't even begin to cover it," he said. "Strange things happen up there, or so

50   T.M JEFFERSON

they say. Rituals and such. But you didn't hear that from me, ya understand?"

David exchanged a glance with Jade, his interest clearly piqued as well. "What kind of rituals?" He asked, trying to keep his voice casual.

The old man shrugged, taking another sip of his coffee. "Who knows for sure? Some say they worship ancient gods, make sacrifices and whatnot. Others say it's just a bunch of rich folks playing dress-up and getting up to no good."

He paused, his eyes growing distant as if lost in thought. "But there is one thing I've heard, something that always stuck with me. They say on the last night of the gathering, they burn an effigy in a big old bonfire. Some kind of symbolic thing, supposed to represent casting off the cares of the world or some such nonsense."

Jade and David listened to the old man's words. They couldn't take everything he said at face value, but the mention of the effigy burning was too specific to ignore.

They thanked the old man for his time and bought him another cup of coffee before leaving, their heads buzzing with new questions and theories.

As they walked back, Jade turned to David. "The effigy burning ritual seems significant," she said. "That has to mean something. It's too specific to be just a random rumor."

David nodded, his own mind working overtime to piece together the clues. "Agreed. The old man's intel lines up with some of the documents I've seen. It's a lead worth pursuing. We should cross-reference it against the historical records and see if any patterns emerge. Even the smallest detail could crack this case wide open."

They climbed into a cab, their determination renewed by the glimpse of the truth the old man provided. They still had a long way to go, but every scrap of information, no matter how small or insignificant, brought them one step closer to unraveling the secrets of Bohemian Grove and the Illuminated Order's dark agenda.

10

In her office, where the secrets were about to be unveiled, Jade leaned forward, her eyes fixed on David Montgomery. The atmosphere was tinged with anticipation as David, the former government operative haunted by his past, prepared to unravel the guarded mysteries.

Seated in front of an array of computer screens and classified documents, David's eyes held a steely resolve. His voice, measured and laden with the weight of disclosure, cut through the silence. "The Illuminated Order," he began, "is not just a name. It's a secret force that weaves its influence through the corridors of power."

As he spoke, images flashed on the screens– symbols, encrypted messages, and glimpses of powerful figures obscured in the shadows. "Founded centuries ago," David continued, "by three individuals whose ambitions transcended the ordinary. Lord Alexander Hawthorne, a wealthy aristocrat with a vision; Lady Amelia Sinclair, a brilliant intellectual and socialite; and Sir Edward Blackwell, a seasoned military commander."

Jade absorbed every word, and David pressed on, delving into the inner workings of the Order. "Within the Order's hierarchy, there's the Inner Circle—Baroness Isabella Devereaux, a shrewd businesswoman managing the vast wealth; Dr. Marcus Bennett, a brilliant scientist developing advanced technology; and Madame Celeste Duval, a master of espionage and deception."

The images shifted, revealing faces and roles that painted a vivid picture of the Order's power structure. "And then there's the High Council," David continued. "Lord Sebastian Monroe, a charismatic politician; Lady Eleanor Worthington, a renowned philanthropist; and Sir William Hastings, a ruthless enforcer and tactician."

Jade's mind raced trying to connect the dots. "But there's more," David added, lowering his voice. "Junior Members like Miss Victoria Sterling, manipulating financial markets; Mr. Jameson Shaw, a brilliant hacker and cyber warfare expert; and Ms. Cassandra Blackwell, Sir Edward Blackwell's great, great granddaughter, a skilled diplomat forging global alliances."

The room seemed to close in as David's knowledge unraveled the intricate web of the Illuminated Order. "And then there's Senator Jonathan Bishop," he concluded, "charismatic in public, but a high-ranking member within the Order, using political influence to further its agenda."

David pointed to an image of an owl. "The owl. It keeps appearing in these texts, always in connection with the Order. At first, I thought it was just a coincidence, but the more I studied their history and symbolism, the more I realized it was a deliberate choice."

"But why an owl? What does it represent?"

"In many ancient cultures, the owl was seen as a symbol of wisdom, knowledge, and insight. It was believed to have the ability to see through the darkness, to perceive truths that were hidden from ordinary sight."

He stared at the owl on the screen.

"But there was also a darker side to the owl's symbolism. In some traditions, it was associated with death, with the underworld

THE ILLUMINATED ORDER 53

and the forces of darkness. It was seen as a vessel of doom, a messenger of the gods that brought tidings of sorrow and despair.

As the weight of the information settled, Jade and David exchanged a knowing look. The journey to expose the Illuminated Order's secrets had only just begun, and the road ahead promised treacherous twists and turns. The shadows of power cast by the Order loomed large, and Jade felt the gravity of the path she'd chosen– a path that would lead them into the heart of darkness.

11

London, 1888

The members of the Illuminated Order, dressed in velvet robes, stood in a circle around a raised marble altar, their faces concealed behind masks.

At the head of the circle, Lord Alexander Hawthorne, the Grand Master of the Order, raised his hands. "Brothers and sisters, we gather here tonight to reaffirm our sacred oaths and to celebrate the bonds that unite us in our noble cause."

The assembled members bowed their heads in reverence, their voices rising in unison. "Knowledge is our currency, secrecy our shield. In silence, we govern, in darkness, we yield ..."

Lord Hawthorne surveyed the room. "The six pillars of our Order are the foundation upon which we build our power and influence. Let us speak of them now, that we may never forget the principles that guide us."

He turned to his right, where Lady Amelia Sinclair stood, her auburn hair cascading down the back of her robe. "Lady Sinclair, speak to us of the first pillar: Secrecy."

Lady Sinclair stepped forward, her voice clear and commanding. "Secrecy is the cornerstone of our Order. It is the veil that shrouds us from the prying eyes of the world, allowing us to wield power and influence from the shadows. We are bound by a sacred oath, pledging never to reveal the existence of our Order or its activities to outsiders. In secrecy, we find our strength."

Lord Hawthorne nodded. "And what of loyalty, Sir Blackwell?" he asked, turning to the tall, imposing man on his left.

Sir Edward Blackwell, his chest filled with military medals, spoke with conviction. "Loyalty is the lifeblood of our Order. It is the unbreakable bond that unites us, the fire that fuels our determination. We must always put the needs of the Order before our own, supporting our fellow members and upholding our values in all that we do. Betrayal of loyalty is a grave offense, punishable by the severest of consequences."

As each member spoke, the air in the hall seemed to grow thicker with the weight of their words. The candles flickered, casting ghostly shadows on the faces of the assembled members.

"Manipulation is our tool, our means of shaping the world to our will," declared Baroness Isabella Devereaux. "We must use it wisely and judiciously, always in service of the greater good of our Order."

Dr. Marcus Bennett, his voice tinged with a hint of warning, spoke of the importance of hierarchy. "Structure and discipline are the pillars upon which our Order stands. We must defer to those above us, following orders without question and maintaining the chain of command. Disobedience will not be tolerated."

Madame Celeste Duval emphasized the protection of secrets. "Our secrets are our most valuable asset, the key to our power and influence. We must guard them with our lives, ensuring that they never fall into the hands of our enemies. Betrayal of our secrets is an act of treason, punishable by death."

Finally, Lord Sebastian Monroe spoke of the importance of unity. "In unity, we find our strength. We must set aside our differences and work together towards our common goals, supporting one another and prioritizing the success of our Order above all else. Division and discord will only weaken us, leaving us vulnerable to our adversaries."

As the last words faded into the flickering candlelight, Lord

Hawthorne raised his hands once more. "Let us reaffirm our oaths, brothers and sisters. Knowledge is our currency, secrecy our shield. In silence, we govern, in darkness, we yield ..."

The assembled members raised their voices in a resounding chorus, their words vibrating through the grand hall like a thunderous proclamation. "In the name of the Illuminated Order, we so swear."

As they began to disperse, slipping away into the shadows of the manor, they knew the true work of the Order lay ahead, in the whispered conversations of parlors and the backroom dealings of power. But for now, they basked in the glow of their shared purpose, secure in the knowledge that they were part of something greater than themselves.

The Illuminated Order continued its work, spinning its influence and power throughout society, always guided by the six pillars that formed the foundation of their secret brotherhood.

As Jade stepped onto the grounds of Harvard University, a wave of nostalgia and purpose washed over her. The crimson hues of the ivy-covered buildings whispered secrets of centuries past. The scent of old books and the feel of worn leather chairs in the libraries transported her back to her days as a student, but now she returned as an investigator, determined to unravel the mysteries that lurked beneath the surface.

Walking the corridors of her alma mater, Jade encountered familiar faces. Professors with whom she dissected the nuances of journalism greeted her with knowing smiles, while classmates who once shared her aspirations now pursued diverse paths. Yet, beneath the veneer of routine academic life, Jade sensed an under-current– a hidden tapestry woven with threads of power and influence.

Her questions led her to the depths of the archives, where she uncovered references to Lord Alexander Hawthorne, Lady Amelia Sinclair, and Sir Edward Blackwell– names that resonated through Harvard's past. The trio, founders of the Illuminated Order, left a mark on the institution, their influence seeping into the foundations of knowledge.

As Jade pored over the documents, a pattern began to emerge. The same names kept appearing in connection with the major financial institutions at the heart of the 2008 crisis. *Could it be the Order manipulated the markets, engineering the collapse that devastated so many lives? And if so, to what end?*

In the crowded libraries, Jade overheard conversations hinting at the Order's far-reaching influence. Professors spoke in veiled terms of secret meetings and power dynamics that shifted like shadows. A sense of unease prickled the back of her neck, as if hidden eyes were watching her every move.

As she dug deeper, Jade stumbled on an old photograph tucked away in the pages of an ancient manuscript. The image depicted a gathering of distinguished individuals, their faces obscured by the passage of time. But one figure stood out– a man bearing a striking resemblance to Senator Jonathan Bishop. The discovery sent a shivering chill through Jade's body, connecting the threads of the past to the present.

Her investigation had taken on a deep personal nature. The Illuminated Order's influence not only shaped the course of history but also cast a shade over her own educational journey. The secrets she uncovered threatened the validity of the institutions she once revered.

With a sense of urgency, Jade continued on, her footsteps ringing through the halls of Harvard. Each revelation propelled her further into the depths of the Order's influence, drawing her closer to the heart of the mystery. As she filtered through the maze of archives and secret meeting places, the path ahead was fraught with danger, but the truth was worth the risk.

As she moved through the university, an hidden observer tracked her every step. A woman emerged from the shadows and delivered a chilling warning: "Tread with caution, Miss Rose. Pursuing the truth may cost you dearly."

The message served as a reminder that powerful forces were determined to keep the Order's secrets concealed at any cost.

13

Senator Bishop paced behind his desk. The news he just received from his chief of staff sent him into a fit of anger.

"What do you mean, she got another interview?" he said. "I thought we had this under control."

He slammed his fist on the desk, sending papers and pens scattering across the polished wood. His staff stood around him, their faces pale and their eyes wide with fear.

"I want to know how this happened," Bishop said, his eyes sweeping the room like a predator searching for prey. "I want to know who dropped the ball, who let this little bitch slip through our fingers."

His chief of staff stepped forward. "Sir, we did everything we could. We put pressure on her editors, threatened to pull our advertising, but she just wouldn't back down."

Bishop's eyes narrowed. "Then you didn't do enough. You failed me, Eric, and you know how I feel about failure."

He turned to his press secretary, a young woman named Samantha who'd been watching the exchange. "Get me everything you can on this interview. I want to know what she knows, what she's planning to ask. And I want it done yesterday."

Samantha's fingers were already flying across the screen of her phone as she set to work. Bishop turned back to Eric. "And you, I want you to fix this. I don't care how you do it, but I want Jade Rose out of the picture. Permanently."

Eric swallowed hard, his Adam's apple bobbing in his throat. "Yes, sir. I understand."

With a final, dismissive wave of his hand, he sent his staff scurrying from the room. He had a meeting to prepare for, a battle to wage against the forces that sought to undermine his authority.

* * *

JADE ROSE STEPPED inside Senator Bishop's office, her heart pounding against her ribcage. The senator, a towering man, greeted her with a practiced smile that did little to mask the intensity of his stare.

"Miss Rose," Senator Bishop's voice resonated through the room, smooth and commanding, "I don't recall having you on my schedule today. To what do I owe this ... unexpected interruption?"

Jade squared her shoulders, her eyes locking with the senator's as she took a bold step forward. The plush carpet beneath her feet seemed to swallow her footsteps, but she stood firm, determined to confront the truth. "I'm here to discuss the Illuminated Order, Senator," she said.

A hint of surprise flashed across the senator's face before he regained his composure. "Ah, the Illuminated Order," he replied, leaning back in his leather chair. "A figment of conspiracy theorists' imaginations, I assure you."

Jade refused to be intimidated. She reached into her bag and pulled out a file, the evidence she gathered. "I have proof, Senator," she said, her voice steady despite the fear flowing through her veins. "Irrefutable evidence that ties you directly to the Order. Your involvement behind the scenes– it's all here."

Senator Bishop's mask slipped further, uncertainty crossing his

THE ILLUMINATED ORDER   63

expression before he schooled his features into a composed authority. "You have no proof, Miss Rose," he countered, his eyes narrowing. "And even if you did, it would be wise to be careful. The Order's reach extends far beyond what you can imagine."

The weight of his words hung between them, but Jade refused to back down. She thought of all the secrets she uncovered, the threads that tied the Illuminated Order to the highest echelons of power. "Senator Bishop, the secrets of the Illuminated Order are no longer hidden. We know of your involvement, the puppeteer pulling strings from within the heart of our government."

"Miss Rose, I'm afraid you've stumbled into matters beyond your understanding. The Illuminated Order is a force for stability, guiding the nation through turbulent times."

Jade shook her head. "Stability built on corruption and manipulation? Your Order thrives in the darkness, preying on the vulnerabilities of our democracy."

The senator's smile, a veneer of charm concealing deeper motives, remained intact. "You underestimate the complexities of governance, Miss Rose. The Order ensures the wheels of progress turn smoothly."

Jade kept at it, armed with the knowledge of Harvard's history and the Order's intricate web. "Harvard, Senator, the institution that shaped leaders, incubated a dark legacy. Lord Hawthorne, Lady Sinclair, Sir Blackwell—all founders of the Illuminated Order with ties to this prestigious university."

"Miss Rose, you're involving yourself in matters that surpass your role as a journalist. The Order safeguards the nation's interests; we ensure balance in the face of chaos."

"You call it balance, I call it deception," Jade countered. "The public deserves to know the truth, Senator. They deserve to know the depths of secrets, betrayal, and manipulation that the Order has sunk to in the name of power. And I won't rest until that truth is exposed, no matter the cost."

As the verbal duel escalated, the room pulsed with an energy of

64   T.M JEFFERSON

its own. Jade felt the weight of the moment, realizing her actions could have far-reaching consequences.

Senator Bishop leaned back in his chair, his eyes never leaving Jades'. "You have spirit, Miss Rose. I'll give you that," he said, his tone almost amused. "But spirit alone won't save you from the consequences of your actions. The Order has eyes and ears everywhere, in places you can't even begin to fathom. If you continue down this path, you'll find yourself in a world of trouble. Is that really a price you're willing to pay?"

Jade met his stare. "I'm prepared to face the consequences, Senator. The truth cannot be buried forever."

The senator sighed. "Very well, Miss Rose. But remember, you've been warned. The Order does not take kindly to those who threaten its existence."

With those parting words, Senator Bishop rose from his chair, signaling the end of their meeting, and Jade gathered her belongings. As she stepped out of the office and into the hallway, she couldn't shake the feeling she just crossed a threshold from which there was no turning back.

The battle lines were drawn, and Jade knew her investigation would now take on a new level of urgency. The Illuminated Order's influence ran deep, and exposing their secrets would require every ounce of her determination and skill. But she was ready to face whatever challenges lay ahead, armed with the truth and a commitment to justice.

As she walked out into the fading light of the evening, Jade's determination only grew stronger. The confrontation with Senator Bishop only fueled her to continue to unravel the yarn ball of the Illuminated Order and bring their dark deeds to the light.

* * *

SENATOR JONATHAN BISHOP seethed in his office. Jade's findings ignited a tempest of anger and frustration inside of him.

With a clenched jaw, he reached for his phone, fingers tapping with controlled fury as he dialed numbers that vibrated through the echelons of power.

"Get me Director Harris," he said.

The line clicked, and a voice on the other end responded.

"Senator Bishop, what can I do for you?" Director Harris asked, the sound of shuffling papers in the background.

"We have a situation," Senator Bishop replied. "Jade Rose, a journalist, is digging into matters that could jeopardize everything we've built. She's uncovered secrets that threaten the foundation of the Order."

"I see," Director Harris said, his voice growing serious. "What do you need from me, Senator?"

"I need you to mobilize our assets," Senator Bishop instructed. "Put surveillance on Rose and her accomplice, David Montgomery. He's ex-CIA and a former member. His involvement makes this even more delicate."

The senator's words set the wheels in motion. Director Harris assured him the necessary measures would be taken, and the call ended.

Under the shadows of power, unseen forces prepared to counteract the threat posed by Jade and David. Operatives were dispatched, their orders clear: monitor, disrupt, and contain. The Illuminated Order's network of influence began to churn, targeting the intrepid duo who dared to challenge their secrets.

Senator Bishop's fury, however, was not satisfied with only surveillance. His mind turned to David Montgomery, the former CIA operative who was once part of the Order. The betrayal stung, and the senator's desire for retribution grew.

In conversations with his inner circle, Senator Bishop concocted a sinister plot to silence David. Whispers of assassins and covert operations danced through the air as the senator, driven by a ruthless determination to protect the Order, set in motion a plan that would thrust Jade and David into a dance with the devil.

66   T.M JEFFERSON

"David Montgomery is a loose end that needs to be tied up," Senator Bishop said to his most trusted confidant. "His CIA training and knowledge of the Order make him a formidable threat. We need to send a message that no one can threaten the Order and walk away unscathed."

The confidant nodded, understanding the gravity of the situation. "I'll make the necessary arrangements, Senator. Montgomery will be dealt with swiftly and discreetly."

As the plot against David took shape, Jade remained unaware of the lurking danger. She continued her investigation, driven by the truth. But the senator's moves were already in motion.

14

In the heartbeat of Washington D.C., David Montgomery's residence occupied a quiet corner in the historic neighborhood of Georgetown. The cobblestone streets carried the weight of history beneath the soles of those who tread on them, and the air was redolent with the fragrance of cherry blossoms, a subtle reminder of the city's transient beauty.

David's townhouse stood proudly amidst its neighbors, its red-bricks adorned with ivy that clung to the walls like a living tapestry. Gas lanterns flanked the entrance, reflecting a warm glow that danced on the wrought-iron railings and illuminated the lush greenery at the doorstep, a testament to David's appreciation for the simple elegance of nature in the urban sprawl.

Inside, the townhouse unfolded into a sanctuary of colors and refined taste. Antique furniture, bearing the patina of time, while sunlight filtered through heavy curtains, creating shadows that played on the hardwood floors. The gentle creaking of the floorboards beneath David's feet and the soft ticking of an antique clock were the only sounds that disrupted the tranquil atmosphere.

In David's study, books lined the shelves with leather-bound spines, their musty scent filling the air. An old-fashioned globe marked with the scars of exploration, sat atop a carved wooden desk where David escaped into the mysteries that unfolded before him. His mind raced with thoughts of the investigation, the pieces of the puzzle slowly falling into place as he connected the dots between the Illuminated Order and the secrets that lay hidden within the corridors of power.

A sharp knock at the door shattered the tranquility, the sound reverberating through the townhouse like a gunshot. David rose from his seat. With cautious steps, he approached the door, the hairs on the back of his neck at attention. His heart pounded in his ears, a primal rhythm that seemed to magnify the growing tension.

As he reached for the doorknob, the door burst open with a crash of shattered wood, splinters flying through the air like shrapnel. In the doorway stood a trio of suited men, their faces hidden behind masks, their presence an intrusion into David's sanctuary. The bitter taste of adrenaline flooded David's mouth as he faced them, his body coiled like a spring, ready to fight.

"David Montgomery," one of the men said. "We've been sent to deliver a message."

"Who sent you?"

The man stepped forward, his footsteps heavy on the creaking floorboards. "Senator Bishop," he said. "He's not too pleased with your little investigation. You're poking your nose where it doesn't belong, Montgomery. The Senator sends his regards and a warning."

The pieces of the puzzle clicked into place. Senator Bishop's involvement in the Illuminated Order was deeper than he initially suspected, and this confrontation only served to reinforce the importance of his collaboration with Jade. They were getting closer to the truth, and the Order was clearly willing to go to great lengths to keep their secrets buried.

With a smirk, the man nodded to his companions, and they

THE ILLUMINATED ORDER 69

rushed David. The room erupted into mayhem as fists flew and furniture crashed to the ground. The sound of shattering glass and splintering wood filled the air.

David fought for his life, his training as a former CIA operative kicking in as he parried blows and delivered precise strikes. The coppery taste of blood filled his mouth as he took a punch to the jaw, but he pushed through the pain, his resolve unbreakable. He knew this was just the beginning, the Illuminated Order would stop at nothing to maintain their grip on power.

As the dust settled and the intruders vanished into the night, David stood battered and beaten but unbowed. His breath came in ragged gasps, and the throbbing pain of his injuries served as a reminder of the price he was willing to pay for the truth. In that moment of defiance, he vowed to continue his quest for justice, undeterred by the threats that lurked in the darkness.

He picked up the phone and dialed Jade's number. They had work to do, and the Illuminated Order's attempts to silence them only fueled their dedication to expose the secrets that threatened to tear the nation apart.

* * *

THE EVENING SKY draped Washington D.C. in a blanket of dusky hues as Jade Rose made her way to David Montgomery's residence in Georgetown. A thick sense of trepidation hung in the air as she climbed the worn steps to David's door, the events of the night unfolding in her mind like a haunting prelude.

Upon entering, Jade was greeted by the dim light of candles in the hallway. The scent of melted wax mingled with the musty aroma of aged wood, creating a heady mixture that whispered secrets of the past. The air was charged with tension, each step Jade took towards the study feeling like a weight on her shoulders.

As the door creaked open, Jade's eyes widened at the sight of

David, his face bearing the bruised remnants of the earlier altercation. The room felt heavy with the weight of his resilience, the struggle still lingering in the air like a tangible presence. Jade's heart ached at the sight of his battered face, a reminder of the sacrifices they were making in pursuit of the truth.

"David," Jade whispered, her voice trembling. "What happened? Who did this to you?"

David's eyes met hers. "They came," he replied, his voice rough with emotion. "The Order. They came to send a message. They're trying to scare me off."

Jade's heart sank at his words, a cold dread coiling in her chest like a serpent ready to strike. It dawned on her with chilling clarity —the forces they were up against were far more powerful and ruthless than she ever imagined.

"David, this is dangerous," Jade said. "Maybe we should reconsider. They mean business. We could get hurt, or worse."

As the words left her lips, Jade thought about the potential consequences of their actions. Images of dark figures lurking in the shadows, of powerful men with sinister agendas, flashed before her eyes. The fear of the unknown, of the dangers that lay ahead, threatened to consume her.

But as she looked into David's eyes, Jade saw determination, a resolve that burned brighter than the candles in the room. His eyes held a steadiness that anchored her, a silent reminder of the strength they possessed together.

David reached out, grasping her hand, the warmth of his touch a comforting presence amidst the chaos. "I know the risks, Jade. We can't let fear dictate our actions," he said, his voice firm yet gentle. "And we can't back down now. The truth is worth fighting for, no matter the cost."

His words settled on her shoulders like a mantle of determination, pushing aside her doubts and fears with a new sense of purpose. In that moment, Jade knew their journey had only just begun, a path fraught with danger and uncertainty, but illuminated by the light of truth.

With a deep breath, she nodded. "You're right. We can't give up. The Order may think they can silence us, but we'll show them the power of the truth."

David smiled. "Together. We'll face this together."

15

The flashing lights of police cars lit up the entrance to The Capitol Inn, where the body of Councilman Michael Thornton was found. Detective Marcus Reynolds stood in the middle of the chaos, his eyes on the gruesome scene before him. Thornton, once a respected figure in D.C. politics, now lay motionless, his blood pooling on the cold motel room floor.

As Detective Reynolds surveyed the crime scene, his eyes fell on a peculiar detail— a tattoo on Thornton's wrist, an owl with piercing eyes that seemed to stare directly into his soul. A sense of recognition washed over him, a distant memory of whispered rumors and shadowy conspiracies.

The owl hinted at a connection to a hidden world, where power and secrecy intertwined. He heard whispers of secret societies pulling the strings behind the scenes, but he always dismissed them as mere speculation. Until now.

As the crime scene technicians went about their work, Detective Reynolds knew this was more than a routine murder. The pieces of the puzzle began to fall into place, forming a picture that both thrilled and terrified him. The trail of breadcrumbs leading to

74 T.M JEFFERSON

the Illuminated Order lay before him, and he was ready to follow it, no matter where it led.

As he stepped away from the crime scene, the weight of the investigation settled on his shoulders. Detective Reynolds knew the path ahead would be treacherous, filled with secrets and dangers he could scarcely imagine.

* * *

IN THE HEART of the concrete jungle that is Washington D.C., Detective Marcus Reynolds emerged from the shadows of the Lincoln Memorial, a man of quiet determination. Tall and broad-shouldered, he moved with the fluid grace of someone who navigated the city's myriad alleyways and backstreets with a purpose. His salt-and-pepper hair, cropped close to his scalp, hinted at years of experience, each strand a testament to the weight of the investigations he carried on his shoulders.

Marcus's eyes reflected the city's complexities—a hint of skepticism, a residue of countless cases that tested his faith in the system. The lines on his face, like a map of his career, told stories of sleepless nights, of chasing leads through the corridors of power. His gait, steady and purposeful, embodied a blend of pragmatism and a commitment to justice.

Decked in the worn but impeccably maintained attire of a seasoned detective, Marcus bore the badges of his experiences. The crease between his eyebrows deepened as his mind drifted to a recent case, the images of bloodstained hands and shattered promises haunting his thoughts. But his fingers, calloused from countless hours sifting through evidence, now traced the outline of the owl tattoo on Councilman Thornton's wrist—an unexpected detail that would catapult him into a world far beyond the confines of routine police work.

The curiosity and apprehension that rose when he first saw the tattoo now burned brighter within him, a flame that refused to be extinguished. Outside of the crime scenes and investigations, Marcus was a man of few words, his thoughts often hidden behind a contemplative stare. Little did he know, the murder of Councilman Thornton would be the catalyst propelling him into a maelstrom of conspiracies, where the pursuit of justice would become a journey into the shadows of power, where secrets lurked and the truth waited to be unveiled.

16

The loud ring pierced through the silence of the night, waking Jade from a fitful slumber. She fumbled for her phone, a sense of dread washing over her. As she answered, the voice on the other end was laden with urgency.

"Jade, it's David," came the breathless voice. "You need to turn on the news. Something's happened."

With trembling hands, she reached for the remote, her fingers numb as she pressed the button. The television came to life, the glare of the breaking news alert glowing on the screen.

Good evening, and welcome to Global Network News. Our top story tonight is the shocking murder of Councilman Michael Thornton. Thornton's body was found early this morning in The Capitol Inn motel on the outskirts of town, surrounded by empty bottles of booze and a dusting of cocaine that would make Tony Montana blush.

Police were called to the scene at approximately 5:30 AM after a housekeeper, who wished to remain anonymous, found the councilman's body in one of the motel rooms. According to sources close to the investigation, the scene that greeted officers was one of unimaginable horror and brutality.

Thornton's body was found on the floor, his lifeless eyes staring up at

78 T.M JEFFERSON

the ceiling. He had been brutally stabbed multiple times in the chest and abdomen, the carpet beneath him soaked through with blood.

Investigators quickly cordoned off the area, and forensic teams worked to gather evidence and piece together the events that led to this tragic and senseless loss of life. As they combed through the room, they found signs of a struggle, with furniture overturned and broken glass littering the floor.

But perhaps most shocking of all were the revelations that began to emerge about Councilman Thornton's personal life. As detectives dug deeper, they uncovered evidence of the councilman's involvement with drugs and prostitution, a sordid underworld that few could've imagined him being a part of.

Witnesses reported seeing Thornton entering the motel with a young woman, believed to be a sex worker, just hours before his death. They described the councilman as appearing agitated and paranoid, constantly looking over his shoulder as if he feared he was being followed.

As the investigation into Thornton's murder continues, many are left wondering what could've driven someone to commit such a heinous act of violence. Some have speculated the councilman's illicit activities may have put him in contact with dangerous individuals, while others believe his death may be connected to his role in city politics.

Regardless of the motive, one thing is clear: the loss of Councilman Michael Thornton has left a deep wound in the heart of our community. He was a man who dedicated his life to public service, working tirelessly to make our city a better place for all its residents.

As we mourn his passing and struggle to come to terms with the shocking circumstances surrounding his death, we must also remember the legacy he leaves behind. Councilman Thornton was a champion for the underdog, a voice for those who often went unheard in the halls of power.

His commitment to justice and equality will not be forgotten, and his memory will live on in the hearts and minds of all those who knew him.

The investigation into Councilman Thornton's murder is still ongoing, and police have urged anyone with information about the crime to *come forward. In the meantime, the city has announced that flags will be flown at half-mast in honor of the fallen councilman, and a memorial service will be held in the coming days.*

We will continue to bring you updates on this developing story as they become available. For Global Network News, this is Lila Matsumoto, reporting live from the scene of the crime.

Jade's breath was caught in her throat as she listened to the details unfold. This was no ordinary crime. The owl tattoo on Thornton's wrist flashed across the screen.

"David, what's going on?" Jade's voice trembled. "Is this connected to ... them?"

There was a pause on the other end of the line, a heavy silence that seemed to stretch for an eternity.

"Yes, Jade," David's voice was grave. "I think it's time we delve deeper into this. We can't ignore the signs any longer. The Order is playing a dangerous game, and we're right in the middle of it. Meet me at the usual spot. We need to strategize."

Jade closed her eyes. The murder of Councilman Thornton shattered any illusions of safety, and any hope they could unravel the secrets of the Illuminated Order without consequences.

As she sat in darkness, the images of the crime scene burned into her mind, Jade knew the stakes had been raised. The truth they sought was now more elusive—and more dangerous—than ever before. With a heavy heart and a determination that burned like a flame, she prepared to meet David, ready to face the shadows that loomed ahead.

Dr. Ramirez sat behind her desk, surrounded by stacks of papers and ancient tomes that whispered secrets from another era. The glow of the desk lamp cast shadows on the walls as Jade and David entered, the creak of the door echoing in the hallowed space.

"Jade, David, please have a seat," Dr. Ramirez said, gesturing to the worn leather chairs opposite her desk.

Jade's voice was low and urgent. "Dr. Ramirez, we need your expertise. Councilman Thornton's murder is linked to the Illuminated Order, and we believe there's more at play here."

"What do you seek to uncover?"

David met her eyes. "We need to understand their motives, their hierarchy, and any historical patterns that might guide their actions. Councilman Thornton's death feels like a message, and we want to decipher it."

Dr. Ramirez nodded. "The Illuminated Order has roots that extend into the depths of history, tracing back to the founding of this nation. To comprehend their actions, we must dig into their origins and the symbolism that shapes their worldview."

As she spoke, Dr. Ramirez guided them through the world of secret societies, weaving a narrative that connected dots across centuries. She spoke of whispers in the halls of power, of clandestine meetings where the fate of nations was decided. From the Bohemian Grove's influence to the subtle threads linking political figures, she painted a vivid picture of a secret network manipulating the strings of power.

"The Owl," she emphasized, her voice taking on a reverent tone, "has been a symbol associated with the Order for centuries. Its wisdom signifies knowledge held only by the select few within the organization. The founding fathers themselves were said to have borne the mark of the Owl."

Jade and David exchanged a glance.

"How do we confront an organization so entrenched in secrecy?" Jade asked.

Dr. Ramirez leaned back in her chair, her eyes distant as if peering into the very heart of the mystery. "You must infiltrate their world, understand their rituals, and expose the truth. But beware, the Order guards its secrets fiercely. Trust no one, and follow the trail of the Owl. It will guide you to the answers you seek."

With those words, Dr. Ramirez handed them an old journal, its pages filled with symbols and ciphers. "This may prove useful in your quest. Remember, the truth often lies in the shadows."

As Jade and David left Dr. Ramirez's office, the weight of the task before them settled on their shoulders. The path ahead was fraught with danger, but armed with new knowledge and hope. They were ready to face the challenges that awaited them in the heart of the Illuminated Order's web of secrets.

Jade and David dug into the heart of Councilman Thornton's life. The energy of the streets, with its honking horns and hurried footsteps, mirrored the urgency of their investigation. They navigated the corridors of power, where shadows concealed more than they revealed.

They approached Thornton's former office, the glass exterior towering above them, concealing the secrets within. Jade, notepad in hand, jotted down questions, while David, ever observant, scanned their surroundings for any subtle cues that might help unravel the mystery they sought to decipher.

As they interviewed Thornton's colleagues, tension filled the air, their whispers bouncing through the polished hallways. They spoke of the councilman's charisma and his ability to sway opinions, but their words also hinted at a darker undercurrent beneath his public persona, suggesting the man they once knew danced on the edges of power, flirting with forces beyond his control.

"He was always well-connected," one colleague said, his eyes darting nervously. "Had friends in high places, you know? Some say his influence reached far beyond City Hall."

The duo continued on, chasing leads through upscale restaurants, cocktail parties, and exclusive clubs frequented by the city's elite. Each conversation uncovered a new layer, a puzzle piece that refused to fit neatly into the narrative they were constructing.

Jade never wavered. Her questions probed into the shadows of Councilman Thornton's life, seeking the truth that seemed to elude them. She sensed the fear lingering in the responses, the acknowledgment that some secrets were best left buried.

David listened. His instincts guided the investigation, weaving together threads of information that hinted at a secret network of influence.

The investigation took an unexpected turn when they stumbled on a connection to an exclusive gathering—at the Bohemian Grove. The mention of the Grove sent a chill down Jade's spine, a recognition of the elite circle it represented.

As they navigated the intricate dance of politics and secrecy, Jade and David found themselves drawn deeper into the tangled web of Councilman Thornton's alliances.

"Did you hear what they said about Thornton's connections?" Jade's voice was soft.

"Yeah, it seems like he had his fingers in more than a few pies. And the mention of the Grove? That's not your typical hangout spot for a councilman."

"Agreed. If Thornton's connections lead to the Grove, then we're onto something big."

"Exactly. We need to find out what he was involved in and why it led to his demise. But we can't afford to make any missteps. The truth is out there, but it won't come easy."

As they stepped back out into the streets, Jade and David knew their investigation had taken a pivotal turn. The Bohemian Grove connection was big, a thread that could unravel the entire mystery surrounding Councilman Thornton's death.

The city's noise faded into the background as they focused on the task at hand, determined to uncover the truth, no matter the cost.

19

In the newsroom of the Washington Post, the clatter of typewriters and journalistic chatter filled the air. The scent of coffee wafted through the room. Jade sat at her cubicle, her fingers tapping the keyboard as she pieced together the threads of Councilman Thornton's murder. The light from the screen brightening her expression.

As she worked, lost in thought, a familiar voice broke through her concentration.

"Jade, got a minute?" her boss, Mr. Anderson, asked.

Jade looked up, surprised by the interruption. "Sure, Mr. Anderson. What's up?"

Mr. Anderson pulled up a chair and sat down, his expression serious. "I've been hearing some rumblings about your investigation into Councilman Thornton's murder."

Jade nodded, pulling up her draft on the screen. "I'm making progress. It's a complex story, but I think I'm onto something big."

"Jade, I know you're a talented journalist, and I respect your dedication. But I need you to be careful with this one."

Jade frowned. "Careful? I'm just doing my job, following the facts."

"I know, and I appreciate that," Mr. Anderson said. "But this story, it's attracted some attention from higher up. There's pressure to handle it a certain way."

"Pressure? From who?"

Mr. Anderson sighed. "I can't give you names, but let's just say there are some powerful people who have an interest in how this story is told. Or if it's told at all."

"So, what are you saying? That I should back off, let it go?"

"I'm saying you need to be smart about this. I don't want to see you get in over your head. This story, it's bigger than just Councilman Thornton. There are forces at play that we don't fully understand."

Jade's mind raced with questions. "But isn't that all the more reason to pursue it? To uncover the truth, no matter where it leads?"

Mr. Anderson stood up, placing a hand on Jade's shoulder. "Just be careful, Jade. I know you're a hell of a reporter, but sometimes, the biggest stories are the ones that can do the most damage. To the subjects, and to the journalists who cover them."

With those final words, Mr. Anderson walked away, leaving Jade alone with her thoughts.

As she sat there, the sounds of the newsroom fading into the background, Jade's persistence grew stronger. She knew there were risks, that the story was bigger than she ever imagined. But she also knew she couldn't turn away, not when the truth was so close.

No matter the cost, she would follow this story to the end. And if there were forces trying to stop her, well, she'd just have to be smarter, more resilient. The truth, after all, had a way of coming to light, no matter how hard some tried to keep it hidden.

* * *

IN THE DARK PARKING GARAGE, Jade fumbled through her purse, searching for her car keys. The clatter of distant footsteps and the buzzing lights overhead added to the atmosphere. A lingering sense of unease settled over her, a weight that made her glance around.

Finally, keys in hand, Jade hurried to her car, the sharp click of her heels vibrating against the cold walls. As she entered the vehicle and started the engine, a chill traveled through her body. She couldn't shake the sensation of being watched. Her eyes went to the rearview mirror, looking for any signs of an unwelcome presence.

The engine roared to life, and Jade navigated the massive parking garage, her heart pounding in her chest. Every shadow seemed to conceal a potential threat, and the hair on the back of her neck stood on end.

Jade's breath grew more ragged. The Illuminated Order had a way of making their presence known, and the recent encounter with her boss fueled her paranoia. The notion they may have sent someone to intimidate him gnawed at her thoughts, sending a fresh wave of fear through her veins.

As she merged onto the highway, Jade noticed a black van with tinted windows trailing her. Panic set in as she realized she might be the target. Determined not to lead them to her house, she made a sudden decision and swerved into the exit lane without a second thought, her tires screeching against the asphalt.

The sign blurred overhead as she exited the unfamiliar off-ramp. She was sweating, gasping to control her breath. Fear pulsating through her body as she stole a glance back– the black van still in pursuit, its headlights glaring.

Her mind raced, and the highway lights blurred into streaks as she sped through the streets, trying to evade her pursuer. Jade's heart was beating so loud she could hear it over the roar of the engine.

With adrenaline surging through her veins, she weighed her options. Before she could make a move, the van surged forward, closing the gap between them with frightening speed. Panic seized her as the van's headlights filled her vision, blinding her to everything else.

Jade swerved, narrowly avoiding a collision with a light pole. The screech of her tires screaming through the night as her car drifted to the side, the van speeding past with reckless abandon.

Breathless and shaken, Jade pulled over to the side of the road, her hands trembling. The black van disappeared into the night, leaving behind a trail of uncertainty and fear. As the adrenaline subsided, Jade's entire body shook, and she struggled to steady her breathing.

She reached for her phone, her mind racing with the need to find safety and regroup. She scrolled through her contacts, her vision blurred with unshed tears, until she found the one person she knew she could trust.

"David," she whispered, her voice cracking with emotion. "I need your help. Something's happened, and I don't know who else to turn to."

As she waited for David's response, Jade leaned back in her seat, her heart still racing. The events of the night had unveiled a chilling reality– she was in far deeper waters than she ever imagined, and the Illuminated Order would stop at nothing to keep their secrets buried.

* * *

IN THE LIVING ROOM, David paced back and forth, his footsteps loud against the hardwood floor. Jade's words stuck in his mind. She recounted the warnings from her boss and the terrifying high-speed chase through the streets, her voice trembling with fear and determination.

As he listened, a knot of dread tightened in his chest.

Memories of his past involvement with the secretive organization flooded his brain, each one a painful reminder of the consequences of defiance. He recalled the night he tried to leave, the cold barrel of a gun pressed against his temple, the whispered threats that haunted his dreams ever since. David's hands clenched into fists, his nails digging into his palms as he struggled to suppress the rising tide of fear and uncertainty.

Jade was in over her head, he realized, feeling guilty. She had stumbled into a world of power and corruption, unaware of the threat that awaited her. David's heart raced as he imagined the dangers she faced, the thought of losing her sent a shiver down his spine. He felt a surge of protectiveness towards her, and a gnawing sense of responsibility for dragging her into this dangerous game.

But as he struggled with his own demons, David couldn't shake the doubts that overcame him. *Was it worth risking his life– and Jade's– to pursue the truth?* He wondered if he'd made a mistake by involving himself in this situation.

Despite the risks and the uncertainty, he wouldn't abandon Jade. He couldn't bear the thought of leaving her to face these monsters alone. With a heavy sigh, David made his decision– he would stand by her side, no matter what happened.

20

Jade sat on the plush sofa in Dr. Evelyn Soros penthouse, her hands wrapped around a steaming mug of tea, the delicate aroma of jasmine and honey filling her senses.

Across from her, Dr. Soros settled into a leather armchair, her movements graceful and poised. The years had been kind to her, the lines around her eyes and mouth a testament to a life filled with laughter and wisdom. She regarded Jade with a gentle smile, her eyes sparkling with the same warmth and compassion that drew so many to her side.

"Jade, my dear," she said, "it's so good to see you. But I can tell something is troubling you. Please, tell me what's on your mind."

Jade took a deep breath, the weight of the past few weeks pressing on her like a physical force. She came here seeking solace and guidance, a momentary respite from the chaos and danger that consumed her life.

"Dr. Soros," she said, "I feel like I'm drowning. My work, my life ... everything seems to be spiraling out of control. I'm pursuing a story, one that I believe in with all my heart, but the closer I get to the truth, the more I feel like I'm losing myself in the process."

Dr. Soros' eyes were filled with understanding and empathy.

"The pursuit of truth is never an easy path. It requires sacrifice and perseverance, a willingness to confront the darkness and uncertainty that lurks at the edges of our understanding."

Jade nodded, her eyes glistening. "I know. But sometimes, I can't help but wonder if it's all worth it. The secrets I'm uncovering, the people I'm going up against ... it feels like I'm in over my head, like I'm risking everything for a cause that might be hopeless."

Dr. Soros reached out, her hand resting on Jade's arm. The warmth of her touch was a balm to Jade's frayed nerves, a reminder of the love and support that existed in a world that often felt cold and merciless.

"Jade, listen to me," she said, her voice filled with quiet conviction. "You're one of the strongest, most resilient people I have ever known. Your passion for the truth, your commitment to justice ... those are the qualities that make you who you are."

Jade felt a tear slide down her cheek, the knot in her chest loosening at Dr. Soros' words. She always looked up to this woman, always seen her as a mentor and a friend, a guiding light in a world that often seemed shrouded in shadow.

"But what if I'm not strong enough?" she whispered, her voice raw with emotion. "What if I fail, or worse, what if I lose myself in the process?"

Dr. Soros smiled. "Failure is a part of life, Jade. It's the price we pay for daring to dream, for reaching beyond our grasp and striving for something greater than ourselves. But it is not the end, nor is it a reflection of our worth or our courage."

She leaned back, her eyes distant and thoughtful. "I've seen you overcome countless obstacles in your life. I've watched you rise from adversity time and time again. And I know, with every fiber of my being, that you'll emerge from this stronger and wiser than ever before."

A rush of emotions surged through Jade's chest; gratitude, love and fierce determination. Dr. Soros' words struck a chord, and rekindled the fire that was dampened by doubt and fear.

THE ILLUMINATED ORDER   93

"Thank you, Dr. Soros," she said, her voice thick with emotion. "I don't know what I would do without you, without your guidance and your wisdom."

Dr. Soros smiled, her eyes crinkling at the corners. "You're never alone, Jade. You have a network of people who love and support you, who believe in you and the work that you do. Draw strength from that love, from that faith, and let it be your light in the darkness."

She reached out, taking Jade's hand in her own. "And remember, my dear, that the path you've chosen is not an easy one. But it is a path that leads to truth, to justice, and to a better world for all of us. Never lose sight of that, even in your darkest moments."

Jade nodded, a watery smile spreading across her face. The road ahead would be long and treacherous, and the dangers and challenges she faced were far from over. But in that moment, sitting in the warm glow of Dr. Soros' living room, she felt a renewed sense of purpose and determination, a fierce conviction that she was exactly where she needed to be.

"I won't, Dr. Soros," she said. "I promise you that. I'll see this through to the end, no matter what it takes."

Dr. Soros smiled, pride and affection shining in her eyes. "I know you will, Jade. And I'll be here for you, every step of the way. Never forget that."

As Jade left the penthouse that afternoon, her heart felt lighter than it had in weeks. The burdens she carried were still there, the dangers and uncertainties lingering on the horizon no less daunting than before. But she wasn't alone, she had the love and support of those who believed in her, and the guidance of a woman who stood for hope and inspiration throughout her life.

21

In the quiet confines of a Georgetown coffee shop, Jade stirred her latte nervously, the clinking of the spoon against the ceramic mug creating an anxious rhythm. David, watchful as ever, scanned the surroundings before proposing the introduction to one of his long-time friends, Detective Marcus Reynolds.

As Marcus settled into his seat, his eyes narrowed, assessing the situation. David, with a nod, initiated the introductions. "Marcus, this is Jade Rose. Jade, meet Detective Marcus Reynolds."

Detective Marcus extended a hand, his grip firm and his eyes intense. "Pleasure to meet you, Jade. David's mentioned you've got some interesting insights into the recent councilman's murder."

"Yes, Detective. It's not just a murder; it's tied to something much deeper– the Illuminated Order."

"The who? You mean those conspiracy theorists' bogeymen? I've heard the rumors, but I deal with facts, not fantasy."

David sipped his coffee, his expression serious. "They're not a myth, Marcus. I've been there, and they're real. I've seen the lengths they'll go to protect their secrets."

"We believe they're involved in the councilman's death," Jade said. "We need your help to dig deeper, to expose them."

96 T.M JEFFERSON

The coffee shop provided some privacy for their conversations. The trio forged a bond, each sip of coffee marking a pact to unravel the secrets woven by the Illuminated Order. The exchange of information, ideas, and suspicions flowed like a river, carving a path through the fog of uncertainty.

As the hour wore on, Marcus' skepticism gave way to a cautious trust. He saw in Jade and David the fire of justice and a commitment to exposing the hidden truths. A shared glance between Jade and David, a silent acknowledgment of their partnership, didn't go unnoticed by the detective.

"Alright, let's get to work," Marcus said. "But I warn you– it's dangerous. I've seen good people get hurt chasing shadows. You sure you're ready for what you might uncover?"

Their expressions hardened in response to Marcus's words. Locking eyes, they exchanged a knowing glance, and in unison said, "Count us in."

As they prepared to leave the coffee shop, Jade approached the counter, ready to settle the bill. The aroma of brewed coffee lingered in the air, creating an illusion of normalcy. However, the illusion shattered when she attempted to use her debit card, and it declined.

Panic gripped her as she reached for her credit card, hoping for a different outcome. But the universe seemed determined to deny her. David, seeing her distress, stepped in, offering to cover the expenses. But his attempt to use his debit card mirrored Jade's.

In the silence that followed, a sense of vulnerability took over them. Jade's voice cut through the tension, "Well, this is embarrassing. I guess the Illuminati decided to put a hold on our coffee privilege."

David smirked and his jaw clenched. "It seems they're sending us a message. They know we're getting close."

"Are they this powerful? Can they really control our finances?"

Detective Marcus leaned in. "This is just the beginning. If they can do this, imagine what else they're capable of. We need to watch our backs at every turn."

* * *

AFTER THE COFFEE SHOP ORDEAL, Jade and David reached out to their respective banks, desperate for some clarity amid the distortion. They were hoping for a logical explanation. However, what they discovered only added fuel to the fire of their escalating fears– all their accounts, every hard-earned penny saved, had been frozen. The voice on the other end of the line, was cold and impersonal, and offered no explanation for the sudden travesty.

Jade ended the call, the phone nearly slipping from her grasp. David's jaw clenched, a vein throbbing in his temple as he processed the news. It was as if the ground had been yanked from beneath them, leaving them suspended in a state of helpless uncertainty.

The world around them felt surreal, the once-familiar surroundings now tinged with a sense of unease. It was a reminder of the power wielded by the Order, a chilling demonstration of their ability to dismantle lives with the snap of a finger. As the reality of their situation sank in, they realized– they were only pawns in a dangerous game, and the Order held all the pieces.

With a sinking feeling in their hearts, Jade and David understood their adversaries had the power to unravel their lives with ease. The image of puppet strings, invisible yet ever-present, danced in their minds, a haunting reminder of the forces that sought to control their fate.

Jade took a deep breath as she turned to face David. "We can't afford to let them maintain their grip on power. We need to double down on our efforts, leverage every resource at our disposal, and keep pushing forward, no matter the obstacles they place in our path."

"I agree. We'll need to be strategic in our approach, though.

They have eyes and ears everywhere, and they won't hesitate to use their network of influence to shut us down if we're not careful."

"What if we focus on building a coalition of allies? Reach out to other journalists, whistleblowers, and activists who share our goals? Together, we might be able to create enough pressure to force the Order's secrets out into the open."

"That's a start, but we'll need more than just numbers. We should look into leveraging technology to our advantage. Encrypted communication channels, secure data storage, maybe even some advanced surveillance equipment to gather evidence on the Order's activities."

"I like the way you think. We could also explore alternative media platforms to disseminate our findings, bypassing the mainstream channels that the Order likely has under their control."

"Exactly. We'll need to be adaptable, ready to pivot our strategy at a moment's notice. They'll try to anticipate our moves, so we'll have to stay one step ahead."

Jade's smile faded, replaced by a look of focus and determination. "It won't be easy, David. They've had centuries to perfect their methods, to entrench themselves in the halls of power."

David reached out, his hand touching hers in a gesture of solidarity. "We'll find a way, Jade. We'll pool our resources, leverage every tool and ally at our disposal, and keep chipping away until the whole world can see them for what they really are."

The Illuminated Order had shown their hand, and the stakes had never been higher. But they had each other, a bond forged in the fires of adversity. Together, they would move through the maze of secrets and lies, and bring the truth to light, no matter the cost.

22

For weeks, Jade put on a brave face, trying to downplay the mounting money issues closing in around her. But each unpaid bill, each past-due notice that arrived in her mailbox, chipped away at her already fragile sense of security.

She was skating on thin ice, living well beyond her means in a city that devoured dreams and aspirations with a cold, indifferent hunger. But she was too proud, too stubborn, to admit defeat– to herself or to anyone else.

That all changed the day the final eviction notice came. Holding that plain white envelope, the weight of her situation became inescapable. She was out of options, out of time, and out of hope of finding her way back.

For hours, Jade sat on her sofa, that simple piece of paper mocking her. She failed, completely. And now, she would be forced to do the one thing she swore she never would– ask her parents for help.

The thought made her recoil, shame and self-loathing rose up from the depths of her gut. Her relationship with her parents had always been strained, fraught with unrealistic expectations and suffocating obligations. To reach out to them now, admitting her

100   T.M JEFFERSON

inability to make it on her own, felt like an indictment of her own self-worth.

But as the hours ticked by, and the shadows grew long across her apartment, Jade was out of choices. Either she could break the cycle of her pride and ask for help, or she could lose everything– her home, her career, her dreams. And that was something she couldn't bear to let happen.

* * *

THE SOUND of the highway beneath the tires provided a soundtrack to the whirlwind of thoughts in Jade's mind. The decision to turn to her parents for help was not an easy one. As the miles stretched before her, she thought about how to shield them from the storm that became her life.

The landscape transformed from the towering structures of Washington D.C. to the serene suburbs of New Rochelle, New York. Rolling hills and manicured lawns replaced the concrete jungle, signaling Jade's arrival in her hometown. The streets lined with trees stood as sentinels of memories long past, their leaves rustling in the gentle breeze. The warmth of the sun on her skin was a fleeting comfort, a momentary reprieve from the chaos that awaited her.

The Rose family home was a grand structure in a field of greenery. A white picket fence framed the front yard, leading to a majestic entrance with blooming flowers. The scent of fresh-cut grass filled the air, mixed with the delicate aroma of roses from the nearby garden. The tranquility of the neighborhood stood in stark contrast to the turmoil in Jade's heart. It was a reminder of the life she left behind.

Pulling into the driveway, she marveled at the sight of her parents' home. It was a haven of comfort and elegance, the fruits of her mother's success as a renowned dentist and her father's achievements in the entertainment industry. The pristine exterior, with its cream-colored walls and large windows, hinted at a life of prosperity, but Jade knew that behind the polished facade, a loving family awaited her.

Entering the house, she was greeted by the warm embrace of familiarity. The tastefully decorated living room, with its plush sofas and curated artwork, and the subtle melody of soft jazz playing in the background. Pictures capturing moments of joy filled the walls, encapsulating a lifetime of shared experiences. Jade's eyes lingered on a family portrait, a reminder of simpler times when the weight of the world seemed far away.

Dr. Thalia Rose, Jade's mother, appeared from the kitchen, her face lighting up at the sight of her daughter. She was a poised and compassionate woman, her dark hair elegantly styled and her warm brown eyes behind sleek glasses. Concern lingered as she wrapped Jade in a comforting hug. "Jade, darling, it's been too long. How are you?" she asked, her voice soft and soothing.

Jade smiled, but it didn't quite reach her eyes. "I'm okay, Mom. Just needed a break from the city, you know?" The words were heavy on her tongue, a half-truth that only scratched the surface of her troubles.

Her father, a tall and charismatic man with salt-and-pepper hair and a winning smile, entered the room. "Jade, my girl, good to have you back. What brings you home?" His dark brown eyes seemed to search her face for answers she wasn't ready to give.

As they settled in, Jade struggled with the choice she faced– to burden her parents with the truth or to act as if nothing was amiss. The delicate dance between love and protection played out in the living room of the Rose family home.

A few hours later, the dining room held a warmth that emanated from the shared laughter and the strength of the family bond. As they savored the last bites of a delicious home-cooked meal, Jade seized the opportunity to broach a delicate subject with her mother, while her father was momentarily absent.

As they cleared the plates and moved to the living room, Jade's heart thumped. Her chest tightened, a physical manifestation of the guilt that gnawed at her conscience.

"Mom," Jade began, her voice trembling, "there's something I need to talk to you about. It's important."

Dr. Thalia Rose settled onto the sofa, her eyes reflecting concern. She reached out, placing a hand on Jade's knee. "Of course, sweetheart. You can always talk to me. What's on your mind?"

Jade hesitated, the words sticking in her throat. She swallowed hard, trying to find the right way to frame her predicament. "I ... I've been facing some financial troubles. The bank made a mistake, and they froze my accounts. I need some money to sort things out."

"Oh, Jade, I had no idea." Dr. Rose said. "Why didn't you tell us sooner? We can figure this out together."

Jade took a deep breath, her eyes moving to the doorway where her father reappeared. The knot in her stomach tightened as she prepared to extend her deception. "It's embarrassing, Mom. I didn't want to burden you. But I need a loan, about fifty thousand dollars."

Her father's eyebrows shot up. "What's going on, Jade? Why do you need such a significant amount of money?"

Caught off guard, Jade scrambled to concoct an explanation. "Dad, it's a mix-up. The bank made an error in their systems, and they're working to fix it. But in the meantime, I need to cover some expenses. It's all going to be sorted out soon."

Throughout her childhood, Jade's relationship with her father was marked by his absence, a void that grew with each passing year. As a successful figure in the music industry, he was constantly on the move, chasing the next big hit or touring with the latest sensation. While Jade understood the demands of his career on an intellectual level, the emotional toll of his absence was harder to rationalize.

Growing up, she couldn't help but resent the missed birthdays, the empty seats at school recitals, and the broken promises of quality time that never seemed to materialize. However, as she matured and pursued her own passions, she began to see her father in a new light. She recognized the sacrifices he made to provide for their family and the dedication he poured into his craft. Slowly but surely, they began to bridge the gap between them, learning to appreciate each other not just as father and daughter, but as individuals with their own dreams and challenges. Though their relationship would always bear the scars of those early years, Jade and her father were determined to forge a new path together, one built on mutual understanding, respect, and the unbreakable bond of family.

Her father stared at her, a silent plea for honesty hanging in the air between them. Jade felt the weight of her own deception, a fracture in the trust she always cherished with her parents. In that moment, in the tasteful decor of their family home, Jade told half-truths, desperate to shield her loved ones from the shadows closing in on her life.

Dr. Thalia and her husband exchanged a glance, a silent communication born of years of partnership. In the affluent New Rochelle neighborhood, financial concerns were a foreign concept to the Roses. Their elegant home rest among manicured lawns and stately trees, exuding an air of prosperity that belied any hint of hardship.

"We'll take care of this, Jade," her mother said. "Your father and I will sort out the paperwork and get you the money you need. You don't have to worry about a thing."

"Absolutely. Your mother's right. We're a family, and we'll tackle this together. Now, let's focus on finding a solution." Jade's father nodded, his expression a mix of concern and determination.

As they discussed the intricacies of resolving the financial hiccup, the shadows of suspicion remained dormant, concealed by the facade of family unity. The Rose family, accustomed to the rhythm of prosperity, extended their protective embrace, unaware their daughter's request was covered in a blanket of deceit.

104 T.M JEFFERSON

The comfortable cocoon of financial stability shielded them from the storm gathering on the horizon, its distant rumblings unheard within the sanctuary of their home. But as Jade sat there, the weight of her lies pressing on her shoulders, her deception would have consequences she couldn't begin to fathom. The image of a tangled web, each strand representing a truth untold, flashed in her mind, a haunting reminder of the dangerous game she was playing.

23

As Jade and David delved deeper into Councilman Thornton's death, a new lead emerged, one that threatened to unravel their entire investigation. In the confines of David's apartment, amidst a sea of scattered documents and computer screens, they stumbled on a connection.

Councilman Thornton's name appeared alongside a mysterious international corporation that stretched far beyond the borders of the United States. The company known only as Octavian Global, seemed to exist in the shadows, its true purpose covered in secrecy.

Jade's fingers flew across the keyboard, her eyes narrowing as she dug deeper into Octavian Global's history. "David, look at this," she said. "I think I found something."

"What is it?"

"Bank statements, going back several years. Looks like our dear departed Councilman was receiving some pretty hefty payments from a shell corporation based in the Cayman Islands. Says here that Octavian Global has ties to several high-level government officials, including ..." She paused, her eyes widening. "Including President Adrian Blackwell."

"A shell corporation? That screams money laundering." David

leaned in closer, his eyes intense as he scanned the document. "That can't be a coincidence," he said. "Thornton, Octavian Global, and now the President himself? There's something bigger going on here."

Jade leaned back in her chair, rubbing her eyes with a groan. "I feel like my brain is about to melt. How do you do this all day?"

David smirked. "It's called stamina. Something you reporters wouldn't know anything about, chasing after your next big scoop."

"Oh, really? This from the guy who probably spends his weekends binge-watching conspiracy theory videos on YouTube?"

David clutched his chest in mock offense. "You wound me, Jade. I'll have you know that my weekends are reserved for much more sophisticated pursuits, like building model airplanes and practicing my origami skills."

Jade snorted, shaking her head with a grin. "I never pegged you for an arts and crafts kind of guy."

"I'm full of surprises," David said, waggling his eyebrows. "Stick around long enough, and you might just learn a thing or two."

Jade felt a knot of dread tighten in her stomach. They had stumbled onto a conspiracy far more enormous and insidious than they ever imagined. The pieces of the puzzle were clicking into place with a chilling clarity.

"If the President is involved with Octavian Global," she said, "and Octavian Global is connected to the Illuminated Order ... then that means ..."

"It means the Order's influence goes to the highest levels of our government," David finished. "And if they're willing to silence someone like Thornton to keep their secrets hidden, then there's no telling what else they're capable of."

Jade shook her head, a feeling of helplessness washing over her. The enemy they were facing was no longer just a secret group of elites and power brokers– it was the system itself, the institutions and leaders that were supposed to protect and serve the people.

"We should be careful, David," she said, her eyes locking with his. "If the President's involved, then we're not just up against the Order anymore. We're taking on the full might of the U.S. government."

David's hand found Jade's, his fingers intertwining with hers in a gesture that spoke volumes about their bond. He caught her gaze, his eyes filled with a fierce intensity that seemed to burn straight through to her core. "I know the risks we're facing, the dangers that lurks around every corner. But we can't let that stop us, not when we're on the cusp of something so monumental."

He paused, his thumb tracing a gentle circle on the back of her hand. "Think about all we've uncovered, all the secrets we've dragged into the light. Their power is built on a foundation of lies and manipulation, and every truth we expose brings us one step closer to dismantling their empire."

Jade took a deep breath, drawing strength from his touch. He was right– they'd come too far, sacrificed too much to let the Illuminated Order win.

"Okay," she said. "But we need to be smart about this. We can't just go charging in blindly. We need a plan, and we need allies we can trust."

David smiled. "You can trust me."

Jade rolled her eyes, but she couldn't help the smile that tugged at the corners of her mouth. "Come on, Casanova. We've got a conspiracy to unravel."

In the days that followed, they pored over financial records and encrypted communications, piecing together a puzzle that grew more complex with each passing moment. The Illuminated Order's influence, it seemed, knew no bounds, and the stakes grew higher with every revelation.

President Adrian Blackwell stood at the window of the Oval Office, his eyes on the distant Washington Monument as it pierced the skyline. The weight of the nation rested on his shoulders, a mantle he wore with pride since the day he took the oath of office. His tall, lean frame exuded an air of quiet authority, the silver at his temples a testament to the decades he spent navigating the treacherous waters of American politics.

To the public, he was a man of integrity and vision, a leader who promised to bridge the divides that fractured the nation and guide the country into a new era of prosperity and unity. His charisma and eloquence won him legions of devoted followers, his face a fixture on every news channel and magazine cover.

But beneath the polished veneer, there were whispers of something darker, murmurs of secrets and alliances that stretched beyond the halls of power and into the realms of global influence. And at the center of those whispers was a name that few dared to speak aloud: Octavian Global.

The corporation rose to prominence in recent years, spreading across every sector of the economy and its influence felt in the highest stages of government. Some saw it as innovation and progress, a shining example of the boundless potential of free enterprise. Others viewed it with suspicion and fear, a faceless entity with an agenda that remained a mystery.

For President Blackwell, the truth lay somewhere in between. He first crossed paths with Octavian Global during his days as a senator, when a chance meeting with the company's founder opened his eyes to a world of possibilities he never before imagined. The man spoke of a future where the boundaries between politics and business, between nations and corporations, would be no more, giving rise to a new order that would reshape society.

At first, Blackwell was skeptical, his instincts honed by a lifetime in the cutthroat world of politics. But as he looked deeper into Octavian Global's operations, he began to see the truth behind the founder's words. The company's reach was broad and its resources limitless, its fingers in every pie from cutting-edge technology to global finance.

And so, a partnership forged, a secret alliance that helped propel Blackwell to the highest office in the land and cemented Octavian Global's place at the forefront of the new world order. It was a partnership that brought him power and influence beyond his wildest dreams, but one that also comes with a price.

As he stood at the window, staring out at the city before him, President Blackwell sensed he was no longer the master of his own destiny, the strings that guided his actions were being pulled by forces beyond his control. The weight of the secrets he carried seemed to grow heavier each day, and the lines between his public persona and his private allegiances were so mixed up he could no longer tell where one ended and the other began.

With whispers of investigations and exposes swirling, the fragile web of power and influence he wove was in danger of unraveling at any moment. The name of Councilman Thornton, a pawn in a game whose true scope remained hidden even to Blackwell, surfaced, and it threatened to bring the entire house of cards crashing down around him.

25

As Jade and David continued their pursuit of the truth, another lead came forth, it was a whisper of a secret gathering which promised to shed light on the Illuminated Order's global domination. Amidst the chaos of their investigation, they uncovered a fragment of information that set their pulses racing and their minds reeling.

It was a single line of code, buried deep in a file they managed to extract from Octavian Global's servers. At first glance, it appeared to be nothing more than a random string of characters, a digital ghost that danced across the screen. But as Jade and David dug deeper, the true significance of their discovery took shape.

"It's a date and a location," Jade said, as she deciphered the code. "London, two weeks from now. And look at this ..." She pointed to a series of symbols that followed the date.

David studied the symbols. "I've seen this before," he said. "It's the Order's cipher, used for their most sensitive communications."

The reality hit them like a thunderbolt, the pieces of the puzzle falling into place with a sickening clarity. The secret meeting in London, the presence of high-ranking members of the Order, the whispers of a global agenda ... it all pointed to a truth that was as terrifying as it was undeniable.

"They're planning something big," Jade said. "Something that could change the course of history."

"We have to be there. We have to find out what they're planning and stop them before it's too late."

The decision was made, a pact sealed. They would go to London, infiltrate the secret meeting, and uncover the truth behind the Illuminated Order's global agenda.

With the knowledge of the meeting in London burning in their minds, Jade and David set about planning their next move. Infiltrating the gathering of the Illuminated Order's high-ranking members would be no easy feat, but it was a chance they couldn't afford to pass up.

In David's apartment, they huddled over a map of London, their eyes tracing the winding streets and ancient buildings that held the key to unlocking the Order's global agenda. They studied the location of the meeting, the Royal Institute of International Affairs. The building, known as Chatham House, was a grand Edwardian manor. The institute was renowned as a hub of global policy and diplomacy, hosting conferences and events that brought together the world's most influential minds.

"We'll need aliases," Jade said. "Identities that can withstand the scrutiny of the Order's security."

"I have a contact in London, someone who can help us create backstories that will hold up under pressure." David said.

They spent long hours crafting their new identities, weaving together threads of truth and fiction until they created personas that felt as real as their own skin. Jade became Sophia Steele, a wealthy socialite with a penchant for brushing elbows with the powerful and influential. And David took on the role of Milton Ashton, a successful businessman with ties to the upper echelons of society.

With their aliases in place, they turned their attention to the

THE ILLUMINATED ORDER   113

logistics of their journey. They booked flights under their new names, careful to leave no trace of their true identities. They packed bags with the essentials, including the tools of their trade—cameras, recording devices, and the ever-present notebooks that held the secrets they had uncovered.

On the eve of their departure, they met one last time in David's apartment to go over the final details of their plan.

"You ready for this?" David asked, his voice low and earnest as he met Jade's eyes.

"I'm ready," she said. "We'll uncover the truth, no matter what it takes."

David reached out, his hand finding hers in the dim light of the room. "Together," he said, his fingers intertwining with hers.

"Together," Jade replied, the word a promise and a prayer.

As the night wore on and the city slept, Jade and David remained awake, consumed with thoughts of the journey ahead. The road would be treacherous, and the dangers they faced were real and deadly.

As Jade and David prepared to embark on their trip to London, Detective Marcus Reynolds struggled with a lead that threatened to shatter his investigation. In the depths of the Washington D.C. police department, amidst the chaos of ringing phones and scattering officers, he stumbled on a piece of evidence that raised the hairs on his arm.

It was a single sheet of paper, buried deep in the files of the Thornton murder case. At first glance, it appeared to be nothing more than a regular document, a record of a financial transaction that had no place in a homicide investigation. But as Reynolds studied the paper more closely, a pattern began to emerge, a trail of breadcrumbs that led him down a darker path than he ever imagined.

The transaction was linked to a shell company, a faceless entity that seemed to exist only on paper. But as Reynolds dug deeper, he discovered the company was connected to a web of secret organizations, each one more enigmatic than the last.

And at the center of that web, like a spider spinning a deadly trap, was a name he had become all too familiar with: The Illuminated Order.

116   T.M JEFFERSON

Reynolds heard the whispers, rumors of a secret society that pulled the strings of power from behind the scenes. He always dismissed such talk as the stuff of conspiracy theories and paranoid delusions. But now, as he stared at the evidence before him, he couldn't deny the truth any longer.

The Illuminated Order was real, and they had their fingers in every corner of the city's power structure. And if the evidence he uncovered was to be believed, they played a role in the murder of Councilman Michael Thornton.

Reynolds leaned back in his chair. *If the Order orchestrated Thornton's death, then the councilman's murder was more than just a simple homicide. It was a political assassination, a message sent by those who held the reins of power.*

He couldn't trust anyone with this information, not even his fellow officers. The Order's reach was too wide, their influence too deep. He would have to tread carefully, gathering evidence and building a case in secret, until he had enough to take them down.

As he sat in his office, Reynolds promised himself. He would not rest until he uncovered the truth behind Councilman Thornton's murder, no matter the cost. He would follow the trail to the very heart of their dark empire, and he would bring them to justice.

27

As the plane touched down on the rain-slicked tarmac of Heathrow Airport, Jade and David felt a rush of adrenaline. They arrived in London, the heart of an ancient empire, where the secrets of the Illuminated Order lay waiting to be uncovered.

The multiple languages, the whir of luggage carousels, and the distant roar of jet engines created a disorienting backdrop as they scanned the sea of faces around them. Each passing glance, each fleeting expression, was analyzed with a meticulous eye, searching for any hint of recognition or malicious intent.

Their first stop was a building located at 33 Cannon Street, in the heart of London's financial district. The building, known as Cannon Place, was a glass and steel structure that seemed to blend into the cityscape, belying the secrets that lay within its walls.

As Jade and David approached the entrance, they took a moment to compose themselves. The contact they were about to meet, known only as 'Rafael,' held the key to unlocking the Order's activities in London.

With a deep breath, they stepped through the revolving doors and into the lobby of Cannon Place. The space was a study in understated elegance, with polished marble floors, sleek metal

118   T.M JEFFERSON

accents, and a sweeping reception desk manned by a solitary guard. The air was filled with soft conversation and the distant ding of elevators, the everyday sounds of corporate life masking the true nature of their visit.

The elevator ride to the 14th floor seemed to stretch on forever, the confined space filled with a tense, electric silence. When the doors slid open, they found themselves in a hallway, the walls lined with anonymous doors and the air heavy with the weight of secrets untold.

As they approached the office of their contact, Jade and David exchanged a loaded glance. With a final, steadying breath, David raised his hand and knocked on the door.

Moments later, the door swung open. On the other side, Rafael, a man with a reputation for international espionage, stood before them, his face an inscrutable mask of professionalism.

Rafael's office was a study in opulence and strategic discretion. The space was modest in size, belying the true scope of his influence and reach. The walls, lined with dark, richly grained wood paneling, created an atmosphere of warmth and sophistication. A large, antique mahogany desk dominated the room, its polished surface adorned with high-tech gadgets and encrypted communication devices. Behind the desk, a floor-to-ceiling window offered a breathtaking view of the London skyline, a reminder of the city's vast and complex network of power and influence.

A vintage world map hung on one wall, marked with a series of symbols and notations only Rafael could decipher. On another wall, a set of ancient, leather-bound books sat on a shelf, their titles obscured by a thin layer of dust that suggested they hadn't been touched in years.

"Come in," he said. "We have much to discuss, and time is not on our side."

Rafael was a nervous-looking man with shifty eyes and a twitchy demeanor. He reached into his leather satchel and pulled out a thick, brown envelope, the edges frayed and the surface marred by coffee stains and creases. With a glance over his shoulder, as if checking for any signs of unwanted observers, he slid the envelope across the table to Jade and David.

"Everything I have on the Order's operations in the city," he said. "I've managed to gather intel on some of their key players, including a few high-ranking members. There's names, addresses, and even some photos of them attending secret meetings."

He paused, licking his dry lips before continuing, "I've also got a list of suspected front companies and shell corporations they use to funnel money and resources. It's not a complete picture, but it's a start. Also, addresses for a few of their safe houses and storage facilities scattered throughout the city."

Rafael's eyes darted back and forth, his voice dropping even lower, "I managed to intercept some of their financial records, too. Bank statements, transaction logs, and encrypted files that I haven't been able to crack yet. Not the full scope of their financial network, but it's enough to give you an idea of the scale of their operations."

His shoulders slumped as if a weight was lifted from them. "It's not much, I know. The Order is notoriously secretive, and getting any information on them is like trying to catch smoke with your bare hands. But it's a start, a foundation for you to build on as you dig deeper into their activities."

Jade and David pored over the file, scanning the pages with a fierce intensity. The information was in fragments and incomplete, but it was enough to give them a sense of the scope of the Order's influence.

There were shell companies and front organizations, dummy corporations and secret bank accounts. There were names of politicians and businessmen, socialites and celebrities, all connected by a web of money and power that stretched across the globe.

A picture began to emerge of a city within a city, a secret realm where the Illuminated Order held sway. They would have to encounter this dark underbelly if they hoped to uncover the truth behind the Order's global agenda.

120   T.M JEFFERSON

Over the next few days, Jade and David followed the leads in the file, chasing down whispers and rumors in hidden corners of the city. They posed as wealthy investors and influential power brokers, using their aliases to gain access to the inner circles of London's elite.

28

The ballroom of the Ritz London was a sea of elegance and opulence, a glittery tableau of wealth and power. Jade and David moved through the crowd like two predators, their eyes searching the faces of the assembled guests for any sign of their prey.

Jade was dressed in a black gown that clung to her curves like a second skin, her dark hair swept up in an elegant chignon that exposed the graceful curve of her neck. She carried herself with the easy confidence of a woman born to wealth and privilege, her smile dazzling as she greeted the other guests.

At her side, David projected an air of sophistication in a tailored tuxedo, his hair cut low and his eyes shined with a dangerous charm. He played the role of the successful businessman to perfection, his every gesture and word calculated to project an air of power and influence.

As they mingled with the cream of London's high society, Jade and David kept their ears open for any whisper of the Order's presence. They listened in on conversations about politics and finance, about art and culture and the latest gossip from the city's most exclusive circles.

122   T.M JEFFERSON

Somewhere in this throng of people, there were members of the Order, men and women who held the fate of nations in their hands.

As the evening wore on and the champagne flowed, Jade was drawn into a conversation with a woman named Amelia, the daughter of a prominent British politician. Amelia was charming and vivacious, with quick wit and a sharp intellect.

Jade sensed there was something more to Amelia than what she presented. She had a glow in her eye, secrets that lurked just beneath the surface.

"Tell me, Sophia," Amelia said, using Jade's alias with a smile. "What brings you to London? Business or pleasure?"

Jade laughed, the sound light and airy. "A little of both, I suppose. My husband and I are always on the lookout for new opportunities."

Amelia's smile widened, and she leaned in closer, her voice dropping to a whisper. "And have you found any interesting opportunities here in London?"

Excitement culminated in Jade's chest, she was on the verge of a breakthrough. "We're always open to new possibilities," she said. "Especially if they involve people of influence and power."

"Well, then, you've certainly come to the right place. London is full of people who know how to wield power, if you know where to look."

She reached into her clutch and pulled out a small, embossed business card, pressing it into Jade's hand with a meaningful look. "If you and your husband are interested in exploring some of those possibilities, come to this address tomorrow evening. I think you'll find it very enlightening."

With that, Amelia melted back into the crowd, leaving Jade standing alone with the card in her hand. She glanced down at it.

The address was in one of the oldest and most exclusive neighborhoods in London, a place where the wealthy and powerful held court for centuries. Jade slipped the card into her purse, she knew

THE ILLUMINATED ORDER   123

they were one step closer to uncovering the secrets of the Illuminated Order.

* * *

IT WAS at a private art gallery opening where they first encountered the man who would become one of their most valuable allies.

Jade analyzed the crowd, landing on a man across the room. At first glance he looked like any other well-dressed patron– expensive suit, easy smile, flute of champagne in hand. But there was something else about him, an air of alertness, of coiled potential energy that put Jade on edge.

As she watched, the man's eyes roamed the gallery almost imperceptibly, cataloging every exit, weighing every potential threat. His movements were self-assured yet economical, each gesture stripped of any wasted motion. This was no idle socialite killing time– this was a predator stalking his prey.

"David," Jade mumbled under her breath. "The man by the Warhol print, do you see him?"

"I see him. There's something off about the way he moves. Military training, possibly intelligence? If I had to venture a guess, I'd say he's MI6."

As if on cue, Ashford drained his flute and began weaving through the crowd towards them, a shark catching the faint copper scent of blood in the water. Up close, the man's aura of quiet, assured menace was even more evident.

"Sophia Steele and Milton Ashton, I presume?" His cut-glass Received Pronunciation accent caressed the syllables with a sort of casual arrogance. "Forgive me for being so dreadfully direct, but we have some matters of grave importance to discuss."

Jade and David exchanged a glance. They'd been careful to maintain their cover identities, and the fact that Ashford knew their aliases was a red flag.

124 T.M JEFFERSON

Jade refused to be cowed, fixing him with a level stare. "I'm afraid you have us at a disadvantage, Mr ...?"

"Ashford. James Ashford." He extended a hand calloused by decades of service. "But you already knew that, didn't you, Mr. Ashton?"

David's eyes narrowed. "I don't know what you're talking about."

Ashford's smile widened. "Come now, Mr. Ashton. We both know you and your lovely wife are not here for the art. You're investigating the Illuminated Order, and I can help you. We've been tracking your movements for months now," Ashford continued, "Ever since you first started poking that clever nose of yours into matters that should've remained undisturbed."

He leaned in, his voice thick with the promise of untold secrets. "The Illuminated Order has been a thorn in the side of His Majesty's government for longer than you can possibly imagine. We know they're planning something momentous here in London– the first domino in a larger campaign of manipulation and destabilization."

Ashford's eyes bored into Jade's with the intensity of a killing stare. "Make no mistake, Miss Steele– we want to stop them just as badly as you do. But we'll need to work together if we want any hope of succeeding where so many others before us have failed." He paused. "And time ... is rapidly running out."

Jade and David exchanged another glance. They couldn't trust him, not yet, but they also couldn't afford to turn down any potential leads.

"I suppose you're wondering how I knew who you were and how to find you," he said.

"The thought crossed our minds," Jade replied.

James laughed. "You have to understand, the Order isn't just a concern for the United States."

"So you've been watching us, gathering intelligence on our movements and our findings?"

"We have. And I must say, I've been impressed by your tenacity and your resourcefulness. You've managed to uncover secrets that have eluded us for years, to connect dots we never even knew existed."

"But why come to us now?" David said. "Why not reach out earlier, when we were still in the States?"

"Because the stakes have never been higher. The meeting you witnessed last night was just the tip of the iceberg. There are forces at work here that even I don't fully understand, players moving on a chessboard that span the globe."

He fixed them with a piercing stare. "But one thing is clear. If we don't act now, if we don't find a way to stop the Order's plans, the consequences could be catastrophic. And that's where you come in. With your skills, your knowledge, and your determination, you may be the only ones who can unlock the secrets of the Illuminated Order and bring them to light."

With those words, he pressed a small card into Jade's hand. "Meet me at this address tomorrow, and we'll talk further. I think you'll find that I can be a very valuable ally."

He melted back into the crowd, leaving Jade and David alone with their thoughts. They were taking a risk by trusting Ashford, but they needed all the help they could get.

As they made their way out of the gallery and into the cool London night, they were aware the Order had eyes and ears everywhere, and their every move was being monitored.

29

Jade sipped her coffee as she watched David pore over the thick dossier on their new ally– a dossier compiled by none other than MI6 itself.

"You know, for an intelligence agency that prides itself on discretion, they sure don't mind documenting their own history," she mused.

"Maybe it's their way of ensuring their legacy lives on," David said. You have to admit, it's a compelling one."

He turned a page, his expression growing more pensive. "Listen to this– 'The roots of MI6 trace back to the late 19th century, an informal Secret Service Bureau tasked with cultivating informants and stealing intelligence about the British Empire's rivals and threats abroad ...'"

As David recounted the twisting path that led to the modern Secret Intelligence Service's formation, Jade found herself transfixed. She learned of the crucial role MI6 played in both World War I and II, running deception operations and infiltrating enemy networks with legendary operatives like 'Lady Spy' Gertrude Bell.

"They were instrumental in finally bringing down the Nazi

regime,"David said. "Including securing a copy of Hitler's last will and testament that proved invaluable."

He shook his head in admiration. "After the war, it was a new front against the Soviets and the spread of communist influence worldwide. High-profile defectors, pioneering new techniques– MI6 was at the vanguard of realigning the entire global chessboard in those Cold War years."

Flipping ahead, David's voice took on a somber tone. "Of course, it hasn't all been triumph after triumph. There have been more than a few controversies and scandals that get glossed over in this official narrative...."

Jade held up a hand. "I'm sure there have been. No intelligence service's hands can be completely clean after decades of operating in the shadows." She exhaled slowly. "What matters now is how deep their present-day investment is in uncovering and stopping the Illuminated Order's schemes."

David nodded. "Well, according to these records, that obsession goes back over seventy years to the waning days of World War II. When Allied forces first uncovered hints of the Order's involvement with the worst excesses of Nazi cruelty and ambition ..."

As David recounted the agency's generational commitment to shining light onto the Order's darkest secrets, no matter how murky or far-flung the frontlines may be, Jade realized they may have finally found the ally they needed. An ally born from the same embers of conspiracy that gave rise to the diabolical force they were now battling.

She just hoped when the time came to confront the Illuminated Order's existence, MI6 would have the fortitude and perseverance to see the fight through to its bitter conclusion– no matter the cost.

30

In a room, deep in the heart of an centuries-old manor in the exclusive Belgravia district of London, a group of individuals stood around a mahogany table.

At the head of the table was Sir William Hastings, a distinguished gentleman with silver hair and striking blue eyes. He was the leader of the Illuminated Order's London chapter, a man whose influence reached the highest echelons of British society.

"My dear friends," he began, his voice a rich, sonorous baritone. "The time has come for us to set in motion the final phases of our grand plan. For too long, the world has been mired in chaos and uncertainty, lacking the guiding hand of enlightened leadership. But soon, the Illuminated Order will step out of the shadows and take its rightful place as the architects of a new global order."

To his right, Miss Victoria Sterling. She was the Order's master manipulator, a woman who could bend the wills of even the most powerful men with a mere whisper and a smile.

As Victoria took her seat at the table, her mind drifted to the past, to the moment that set her on this path. She was a young woman then, barely out of college, when she first learned of her family's long-standing ties to the Illuminated Order.

Her father, a powerful businessman with a ruthless streak, groomed her from a young age to take his place within the Order's ranks. He drilled into her the importance of power, of control, and of the sacrifices that must be made to maintain them.

But Victoria had her own reasons for embracing the Order's cause. She'd seen firsthand the corruption and weakness of those who claimed to lead, the politicians and bureaucrats who were too spineless to make the hard choices. The Order offered a different path, a way to shape the world to her will and create a future where the strong ruled over the weak.

"Our influence has never been stronger," she said. "The media, the entertainment industry, the halls of academia– all dance to our tune, shaping the hearts and minds of the masses to our purpose. The stage is set for a cultural revolution, one that will pave the way for our ascendancy."

Across from her, was Mr. Jameson Shaw. His youthful features belying the razor-sharp intellect that made him the Order's rising star. As the mastermind behind their cutting-edge technology initiatives, he held the key to unlocking the next frontier of human potential.

Jameson leaned back in his chair as he listened to his fellow members discuss their latest plans. He'd always been a loyal soldier of the Order, a tech prodigy who used his skills to further their cause without question.

But lately, he found himself plagued by doubts, by a nagging sense that the Order's methods were becoming ruthless and indiscriminate. He thought of the lives that were ruined, the innocent who'd become collateral damage in the Order's quest for power.

He joined the Order because he believed in their vision of a better world, a world where reason and enlightenment triumphed over chaos and ignorance. But now, as he sat in this room, surrounded by people who seemed all too eager to spill blood in the name of their cause, he wondered if they'd lost their way.

THE ILLUMINATED ORDER   131

"Our advances in artificial intelligence and biotechnology are poised to reshape society," he said, his eyes alight with a fervent intensity. "Imagine a world where the lines between man and machine are blurred, where the limits of the human mind and body are cast aside in pursuit of a higher purpose. That world is within our grasp, and it will be the Illuminated Order that ushers it in."

Finally, Ms. Cassandra Blackwell spoke. As the Order's spiritual guide and oracle, she held sway over the deepest mysteries and darkest secrets of the human soul.

"The ancient prophecies are aligning," she said, her eyes distant and unfocused. "The stars themselves bear witness to the dawning of a new age, one in which the true believers will rise from the ashes of the old world."

She paused, focusing on her fellow council members. "For too long, the Illuminated Order has been shackled by the constraints of secrecy and subterfuge. But the time has come for us to step out of the shadows and claim our rightful place as the architects of humanity's future."

Cassandra's voice took on a note of fervor, a hint of the zealotry that drove her every action. "The Children of the Light are the beating heart of the Order, the true guardians of the ancient wisdom and the sacred mysteries. We are the ones who will lead the Order into a new era of enlightenment and transcendence, shedding the chains of the past and embracing the glorious destiny that awaits us."

Her eyes flashed with intensity. "But there are those within the Order who would stand in our way, those who cling to the old ways and fear the power of true revelation. They are the rot that must be purged, the cancer that must be excised before it can spread and corrupt all that we have built."

Cassandra smiled; equal parts seductive and terrifying. "The Children of the Light will be the instrument of that purification, the cleansing flame that will burn away the impurities and leave only the shining core of truth. And those who oppose us, those who seek to thwart our sacred mission ... they will be consumed by the fire of our righteousness, reduced to ash and scattered on the winds of change."

Sir William Hastings smiled. "Indeed, my friends. The pieces are in place, the board is set. All that remains is for us to make our final moves, to strike at the heart of the old order and watch as it crumbles to dust."

He rose from his seat. "The Illuminated Order has guided the course of human history for centuries, working from the shadows to shape the destiny of nations. But now, the time has come for us to step into the light, to claim our birthright as the true masters of the world. Knowledge is our currency, secrecy our shield. In silence, we govern, in darkness, we yield ..."

As the meeting came to a close, Victoria noticed the subtle glances and gestures exchanged between Jameson and Cassandra. It was clear there was a history there, alliances and rivalries that extended beyond the walls of this room.

Cassandra always resented Victoria's influence within the Order, seeing her as a threat to her own ambitions. And Jameson, for all his brilliance, was still just a pawn in their games, a tool to be used and discarded as necessary.

But Victoria was no fool. She learned long ago to play the game of power, to navigate the treacherous currents of the Order's inner circle with a deft hand and a ruthless heart. She would not be outmaneuvered, not by Cassandra or anyone else. The future of the Order, and of the world itself, depended on her ability to stay one step ahead of her rivals.

The meeting adjourned and the four members of the Order went their separate ways. The endgame was upon them, the final battle between the forces of secrecy and revelation, tradition and progress, darkness and light.

And in the heart of London, the Illuminated Order prepared to unleash its most audacious plan yet, a scheme that would reshape human civilization and bring about a new era of enlightenment, one in which they alone would hold the reins of power and the keys to the future.

31

Jade and David continued to navigate the waters of London's secret societies and hidden agendas, they found themselves drawn ever deeper into a web of conspiracy and intrigue. With each passing day, they uncovered new pieces of the puzzle, their investigation leading them closer and closer to the heart of the Illuminated Order's dark designs.

It was a rainy afternoon when they finally discovered the truth that would change everything. They'd been following a lead from James Ashford, their MI6 contact, and it brought them to a building in the the city.

As they made their way inside, posing as potential clients for a front company, they found themselves in a small, cramped room, surrounded by stacks of papers and computer screens.

It was there, amidst the chaos of the office, that they found the file that would blow the lid off the Illuminated Order's plans. It was a innocuous-looking document, buried beneath a pile of financial reports and business proposals.

As Jade and David pored over its contents, their eyes widening with each passing moment, they realized they stumbled on a bombshell.

136   T.M JEFFERSON

The file detailed a plan, years in the making, for a global event that would reshape society. It was a scheme so audacious, so far-reaching, that it took their breath away.

The Illuminated Order, it seemed, was not content with just pulling the strings of power from behind the scenes. They wanted to fundamentally alter the course of human history, to create a new world order in their own image.

The plan involved a series of coordinated attacks, staged in cities around the world, that would sow chaos and confusion on a scale never before seen. Governments would fall, economies would collapse, and entire nations would be plunged into anarchy.

And in the midst of the mayhem, the Illuminated Order would emerge as the saviors of humanity, the only force capable of restoring order and stability to a world gone mad.

Jade and David sat in stunned silence. They'd always known the Order was powerful, but this ... this was beyond anything they ever imagined.

They had to act fast. They had to find a way to stop the Order's plan before it was too late. But they were against an enemy with resources and influence beyond their wildest dreams.

32

The room was suffocating as Detective Marcus Reynolds sat across from his long-time mentor and superior, Chief of Police John Thompson. The chief's office, usually a place of respect and admiration, felt like a cage, trapping Reynolds in a web of politics and deceit.

Chief Thompson stared at Reynolds, a mixture of disappointment and regret on his face. The fluorescent lights overhead accentuated the deep lines of stress and fatigue on his forehead.

"Detective Reynolds," he said. "I'm afraid I have no choice but to place you on administrative leave, effective immediately."

Reynold's heart sank. "But why, Chief? I've given everything to this case, to finding justice for Councilman Thornton. You can't just pull me off now, not when I'm so close to the truth."

Chief Thompson sighed. "It's not about your dedication, Marcus. It's about your methods, your obsession with this case. You've gotten too personal, too involved. It's clouding your judgment and putting the entire investigation at risk."

"With all due respect, sir, that's bullshit. I've followed every lead, every protocol. I've done everything by the book. This isn't about

138   T.M JEFFERSON

my judgment; it's about politics, isn't it? Someone higher up wants me gone, wants me to back off."

"Watch your tone, Detective. I won't have you making baseless accusations in my office. This decision comes from me and me alone. It's for your own good, and for the good of the department."

Reynolds shot up from his chair. "For my own good? I thought you had my back, Chief. I thought you believed in the work we were doing, in the truth we were fighting for."

The chief rose to meet him. "I do believe in the truth. But I also believe in the chain of command, in the integrity of this department. If you can't trust my decisions, then maybe you don't belong here after all."

Reynolds felt like he'd been slapped, the chief's words hit him like a blow to the gut. He took a step back, his eyes searching Thompson's face for any sign of the mentor he once knew, the man who taught him everything about being a good cop.

But all he saw was a stranger, a man he no longer recognized. In that moment, something dawned on him, a truth he'd been too blind to see before.

"You're one of them, aren't you?" Reynolds asked. "The Order. They got to you. That's what this is really about."

"I don't know what you're talking about. But I suggest you take some time off, clear your head. Don't make this any harder than it needs to be."

Reynolds shook his head, a bitter laugh escaping his lips. "I used to look up to you, Chief. I used to think you were the one man in this city who couldn't be bought, who couldn't be corrupted. But now I see the truth. You're just another pawn in their game, another puppet dancing on their strings."

He turned to leave, his hand on the doorknob, his back to the man he once called a friend. "I won't stop, Chief. I won't rest until I expose the truth, until I bring the Illuminated Order to justice. And if that means going through you to do it, then so be it."

THE ILLUMINATED ORDER 139

* * *

IN THE CONFINES of his office, Reynolds leaned back in his chair, his eyes fixed on the ceiling as he tried to make sense of it all. He always believed in the system, in the idea that justice would prevail no matter what. But now, he was beginning to understand just how naive he'd been.

The Order's reach extended far beyond anything he imagined. They were a hydra, a monster with a thousand heads, and he'd been foolish enough to think he could take them on alone.

As he sat there, lost in thought, a knock at the door jolted him back to reality. He looked up and a familiar face stood in the doorway, a man he'd come to know as a friend and a confidant.

It was Detective Sanchez; who'd been helping Reynolds on the Thornton case from the beginning. Sanchez had a grim expression on his face, his eyes filled with a mixture of sympathy and determination.

"I heard about the suspension," he said. "It's bullshit, and we both know it."

Reynolds nodded, a bitter smile tugging at the corners of his mouth. "Yeah, well, that's the way the game's played, I guess. The Order doesn't like it when people start poking around in their business."

"Listen, I know this is a tough blow, but you can't give up. You're onto something big here, something that could blow the lid off this whole damn thing."

Reynolds sighed, his shoulders slumping. "I don't know, Sanchez. Maybe I should just walk away, let someone else take up the fight."

"No way, man. You're the only one who can see this through. You've got the skills, the knowledge, and the guts to take these bastards down. And I'll be with you every step of the way."

Reynolds looked up at his friend. Sanchez was right. He couldn't turn his back on this fight, no matter how hard it got.

140   T.M JEFFERSON

* * *

CHIEF JOHN THOMPSON hung up the phone, his jaw clenched tight as he replayed the conversation in his mind. He was a man used to giving orders, not taking them.

A light rap on the door broke his trance. "Come in," his voice gruffer than intended.

His secretary poked her head in. "Sir, line two for you. They say it's urgent."

Thompson frowned. He knew who was on the other end of that line. With a curt nod, he waved her away and lifted the receiver.

"This is Thompson," he answered.

"John." The voice on the other end was clipped, precise– a voice used to deference. "I trust my instructions have been carried out regarding Detective Reynolds?"

Thompson's free hand clenched into a fist on the desktop. "Your boy's been put out to pasture, like you asked. Suspended indefinitely for 'crossing professional lines' on the Councilman Thornton case."

"Excellent. And I have your assurance he'll be ... dissuaded from continuing his extracurricular pursuits during this hiatus?"

A muscle ticked in Thompson's cheek. "Yeah, you have my assurance. Guy's a bloodhound, but even he knows to obey the leash when it's yanked tight enough."

"See that he does," the person on the other end replied. "Reynolds has already stumbled too close to certain ... sensitive operations for my comfort. The last thing we need is a testosterone– addled detective poking around where he shouldn't."

Thompson bristled at the insult, barely biting back a heated retort. He was the Chief of Police, not some errand boy to get sneered at by.

The voice cut through his thoughts like a scalpel. "I trusting I'm making myself unmistakably clear, Chief Thompson? Our friends have worked too hard, sacrificed too much, to let one man's misguided moral crusade threaten the grand design. Not when we are so. Damn. Close."

Thompson swallowed hard, anger replaced by a sliver of ice trailing down his spine. "Crystal clear," he said. "Reynolds is a dead end, I'll make sure of it. You got nothing to worry about on my end."

"For all our sakes," the person agreed, "I certainly hope that's the case. Good day, Chief."

The line went dead, leaving Thompson alone with the bitter taste of his compromised position. Somehow, after decades of unblemished service and adherence to the virtues he once held so dear, he'd become just another crooked cop on the take– a willing conscript in some grand scheme he couldn't begin to fathom.

As he reached for the glass paperweight, a gift from his wife on his first promotion, the words carved into the steel began to blur behind a sheen of unshed tears:

"Quis custodiet ipsos custodes?"

Who watches the watchmen, indeed?

33

The London night was cold and damp, a clinging mist covering the city's streets. Jade and David moved through the shadows, their footsteps echoing on the rain-slicked cobblestones.

They were ghosts in this ancient city, hunters stalking their prey through a realm where secrets lurked in every darkened alley and shadowed doorway. The weight of history pressed on them, the whispers of long-dead kings and poets in the stones beneath their feet.

But Jade and David pushed forward, driven by a desperate need to uncover the truth behind the Illuminated Order. They spent days preparing for this moment, pouring over maps and intelligence reports, gathering every scrap of information they could about their enemy's stronghold.

As they approached the building where the secret meeting was taking place, everything relied on their ability to blend in, to become one with the darkness that covered the city.

Jade underwent a stunning transformation for this mission. Gone was the hard-edged reporter who chased down leads and faced threats. In her place was a figure of aristocratic grace and poise, a woman who could move through the highest levels of society without raising an eyebrow.

Her gown was a masterpiece of midnight silk and lace, hugging her curves and trailing behind her like a shadow. Her hair was swept up in a braided bun, exposing the swan-like curve of her neck and the glittering diamonds at her throat.

But beneath the finery and the polish, Jade's heart raced with anticipation and fear. They were walking into the lion's den, the slightest misstep could expose them and bring the full wrath of the Order down on their heads.

Beside her, David was a man of coiled energy and quiet strength, his eyes surveyed the shadows for any hint of danger. He wore a tailored tuxedo like a second skin, the picture of refined wealth and power.

Together, they ascended the steps of the building, their hearts pounding in sync as they prepared to infiltrate the Order's inner sanctum. The fate of the world hung in the balance, and only they could prevent the unthinkable from coming to pass.

As they stepped over the threshold and into the light of the ballroom, they were no longer mortals, but players in a game of cosmic proportions. The secrets they uncovered tonight could change the course of history, but only if they could survive long enough to bring them to light.

At the front of the room, a stage was set up, a podium flanked by towering screens that pulsed with an otherworldly light.

Jade looked around the room, taking in every detail, every face, searching for any sign of the grand master or his inner circle. And then she saw it– a small, black laptop resting on the podium.

This was what they'd come for. It was the key to unlocking the Order's darkest secrets. The laptop would contain the files, the plans, and the evidence they needed to expose the conspiracy to the world.

With a subtle nod to David, Jade began to move through the crowd, her smile fixed firmly in place. She laughed at the right moments, clinked glasses with the right people, all the while edging closer and closer to the podium.

As she approached, a small group of guards stood nearby, their eyes watchful and alert. She would only have one chance, one moment to make her move.

A commotion broke out on the other side of the room– a drunk guest, stumbling and slurring, drawing the attention of the guards. Jade seized her opportunity, darting forward with lightning speed.

Her fingers closed around a small flash-drive sticking out the side of the laptop, yanking it in one smooth motion, she tucked it beneath her gown, her heart racing as she turned and made her escape.

As the mumbles of conversation died away and a quietness fell over the crowd, a man stepped out onto the stage, his face obscured by a glittery golden mask.

"Brothers and sisters," he said, his voice deep and resonant, vibrating off the vaulted ceilings of the hall. "We stand on the threshold of a new era, a time of great change and upheaval. And it is our duty, as the guardians of the ancient wisdom, to guide humanity through the darkness and into the light."

As he spoke, the screens behind him came to life, a dizzying array of images and symbols flashing across their surface. Jade and David watched in mounting horror as the Illuminated Order's plans for global domination unfolded before their eyes.

There were maps of the world, with swathes of territory marked in red, indicating the areas the Order sought to control. There were images of weapons and technology, of armies and mercenaries, all bearing the Order's distinctive emblem.

And at the center of it all, a single, chilling phrase: "The Great Reset."

Jade and David looked at each other. They were witnessing something monumental, a plan that threatened to reshape human society.

As the presentation continued, the speaker outlined the Order's vision for a new world order, a global government that would unite all of humanity under a single banner. There would be no more nations, no more borders, no more wars or conflicts.

But there would also be no more freedom, no more individual liberty or self-determination. The Illuminated Order would rule supreme, a benevolent dictatorship that would guide humanity towards its ultimate destiny.

They listened in horror as the speaker described the Order's plans for mass surveillance, for mind control and genetic engineering, for a world where every aspect of human life would be monitored and controlled by the Order's all-seeing eye.

As the presentation drew to a close, the speaker's voice rose to a crescendo.

"The time has come, my brothers and sisters," he said, his eyes blazing with a fanatical light. "The time for the Great Reset, for the birth of a new world order. And we, the Illuminated, will be the ones to lead humanity into the glorious future that awaits."

As the crowd erupted into applause, Jade and David slipped out of the hall. They stumbled on a truth that could change the course of history, a plan so audacious and far-reaching that it defied belief.

34

The rain fell in sheets as Jade and David raced through the streets of London, their breath coming in uneven gasps and their hearts pounding with fear and exhilaration. They'd done it, they'd infiltrated the secret meeting and witnessed firsthand the chilling scope of the Order's plans for global domination.

As they fled through the night, they knew they weren't out of danger. The Order's security would be searching for them, scouring the city with a fine-toothed comb, looking for any sign of the intruders who dared to breach their inner sanctum.

Jade's gown was soaked through, the delicate lace clinging to her body like a second skin. Her hair had come loose from its tight bun, falling in damp tendrils around her face. But she barely noticed the discomfort, she was focused solely on the task at hand.

At her side, David moved with the fluid grace of a trained operative. He shed his tuxedo jacket, the white dress shirt beneath sticking to his muscular frame.

As they rounded a corner, the sound of footsteps behind them could be heard in the distance, the heavy tread of boots on pavement. They exchanged a glance, and quickened their pace, their shoes pounding against the slick cobblestones.

148   T.M JEFFERSON

As they ran, Jade's hand remained clasped around the small, innocuous-looking flash drive she managed to snatch from the podium right before the presentation. It was a tiny thing, no bigger than a thumbnail, but it contained the key to unlocking the Illuminated Order's darkest secrets.

They planned for this moment, studied the layout of the city and mapped out their escape route in meticulous detail. But now, as they fled through the twisting alleys and narrow side streets, they realized no amount of planning could've prepared them for the reality of being hunted by the Order's security force.

They turned down a narrow alleyway, and the sound of a car engine roared behind them, the screeching of tires on wet pavement. They glanced over their shoulders and saw a black sedan barreling down on them, its headlights cutting through the rain like twin laser beams.

With a burst of speed, they sprinted towards the end of the alleyway, their hearts pounding and lungs burning with the effort. Their car was getting closer, the sound of its engine growling louder with each passing second.

As they reached the end of the alley, a narrow, almost invisible gap between two buildings became visible, a tiny sliver of space just wide enough for them to squeeze through.

Without hesitation, they dove for the gap, their bodies twisting and contorting as they forced themselves through the narrow opening, the rough brick scraping against their skin, tearing at their clothes.

As the black sedan reached the mouth of the alley, its headlights sweeping across the empty space where they'd been just moments before, Jade and David emerged on the other side, their chests heaving with exertion and their faces streaked with sweat and grime.

They paused, their eyes meeting in a silent moment of relief and triumph. They'd done it, they escaped the Order's clutches and made it out of the city with the evidence they needed to expose the nefarious schemes.

35

The plane touched down on the tarmac, jolting Jade and David back to reality. As the aircraft taxied to the gate, a sense of relief washed over them. They made it back to the United States, putting an ocean between themselves and the Illuminated Order's clutches. The adrenaline rush of their narrow escape slowly began to fade, replaced by a growing sense of unease about the challenges that lay ahead.

It wasn't until they arrived at Jade's apartment they realized the full extent of the danger they were in. The door had been forced open, the lock splintered and broken. Inside, the place ransacked, drawers and cabinets overturned, papers and belongings scattered across the floor like confetti.

Jade's heart dropped as she looked over the destruction. *Someone was here, searching for something.*

She had a strong feeling of who was behind it.

Beside her, David's jaw clenched. He'd seen this before, witnessed firsthand the ruthless efficiency of the Order's operatives.

They moved through the apartment. Everywhere they looked, they saw signs of the intrusion, the violation of privacy and safety.

When they entered the bedroom the true horror of the situation played out. There, on the bed, lay a single piece of paper, a message scrawled in harsh, angular handwriting.

We have your mother, Jade. If you want to see her alive again, bring us the flash drive. You have 24 hours.

Jade's pulse quickened and her muscles tightened. Her mother, her kind, gentle mother, was in the hands of the Illuminated Order. And it was all because of her, because of the choices she made.

David moved closer, his hand finding hers, his fingers lacing through hers. He pulled her against his shoulder and they stood in silence, not knowing what to say.

Jade clung to him like a lifeline.

They knew the Order would stop at nothing to protect their secrets, to maintain their grip on power. But this ... this was beyond anything they ever imagined.

* * *

THE SUN HAD long since set over the city of Washington D.C. Jade and David huddled together in a motel room on the outskirts of town, their faces drawn and haggard from the events of the past few days.

They'd been on the run ever since they discovered the message, ever since they realized Jade's mother was being held hostage by the same people they'd been trying to expose.

They went underground, moving from one place to another, always looking over their shoulders for any sign of pursuit. The Order's operatives were out there, searching.

But in the midst of fear and desperation, they weren't alone. They had allies out there, people who believed in their cause and were willing to risk everything to help them.

It was late at night when the burner phone rang.

David reached for it. "Hello?"

"David, it's Reynolds." The voice on the other end of the line was familiar.

THE ILLUMINATED ORDER   153

Reynolds was one of their closest allies in the fight against the Illuminated Order, a man of integrity and courage who risked his own career to help them uncover the truth.

"Reynolds, thank God," David said. "We need your help. They've taken Jade's mother, and we don't know what to do."

There was a pause, a moment of heavy silence that seemed to stretch on for an eternity. And then, Reynolds spoke again.

"Listen to me," he said.

David put him on the speakerphone.

"I've been suspended, but that doesn't mean I'm out of the game. I've been doing some digging on my own, and I think I might have a lead on where they're holding Jade's mother."

A surge of adrenaline rushed through Jade's veins. "Where?"

"It's a compound on the outskirts of the city," Reynolds replied. "Heavily guarded, off the grid. But I got a plan to get us inside."

"What kind of plan?" David asked.

Reynolds hesitated, the sound of his breathing heavy and labored over the phone. "The kind of plan that could get us all killed," he said. "But it's the only way to save Jade's mother and take down the Order once and for all."

Jade and David exchanged a glance, their eyes locked in a silent moment of communication.

"We're in," Jade said, her words ringing out like a clarion call in the darkness. "Whatever it takes, we'll do it."

"I knew you would," Reynolds said. "Meet me at the old abandoned warehouse on the edge of town. We got work to do."

The line went dead, leaving Jade and David alone in the silence of the motel room.

36

The abandoned warehouse was a decaying behemoth of rusted metal and shattered windows. Jade and David stood at the entrance, the cool night air biting at their skin as they hesitated, their eyes searching the surroundings for any sign of life.

Jade pulled her jacket tighter around her body, a shiver running down her spine that had little to do with the chill. "I don't like this," she said. "Why would Reynolds want to meet us here, in the middle of nowhere? It doesn't feel right."

"I know it seems strange, but we have to trust him. Reynolds has always been on our side, even when it meant putting his own neck on the line."

Jade shook her head. "But what if this is a trap? What if the Order got to him, turned him against us? We've seen how far their reach extends, how deep their influence goes."

David placed a hand on her shoulder. "Reynolds is one of the good guys. I've known him for years, and he's never once let me down. You remember the Holbrooke case, back when I first started at the agency?"

Jade nodded, her mind flashing back to the story David told her long ago, in a rare moment of vulnerability. "The one where you were undercover, infiltrating that weapons ring?"

"That one," David said, a wistful smile tugging at the corners of his mouth. "I was in over my head, about to be exposed by one of the higher-ups. I thought I was done for, that I'd never make it out alive. But then Reynolds showed up out of nowhere, posing as a corrupt cop on the take. He convinced them I was his informant, that I was feeding him intel on their operation."

"He risked his own life to save yours, even though he barely knew you?"

"That's the kind of man he is, Jade. Loyal to a fault, willing to put everything on the line for the people he believes in. And right now, he believes in us, in the truth we're fighting to expose."

Jade took a deep breath, the knot of tension in her gut loosening. "Okay," she said. "Let's do it. But if anything feels off, if there's even a hint of danger, we get out fast. Agreed?"

"Agreed," David said.

With one last look at the deserted street behind them, Jade and David stepped forward. The atmosphere inside was thick and musty, the scent of old machinery and stale dust hanging in the air. The only light came from a few scattered fluorescent bulbs.

In the center of the room, stood Detective Reynolds, his face lined with exhaustion and his eyes burning with a fierce determination. He looked like a man who'd been through hell and back, a man who'd seen things that no one should ever have to witness.

"Glad you could make it," he said, his voice echoing in the empty space. "I know this isn't exactly the most inviting place, but it's the only safe haven I could find."

Jade checked the room for any sign of danger. "What's the plan?" she asked. "How are we going to find my mother and take down the Order?"

Reynolds motioned for them to follow him, leading them deeper into the warehouse. "I've been doing some digging," he said.

"And I think I've found a way to infiltrate the compound where they're holding your mother."

He led them to a makeshift command center, a tangle of wires and computer screens that looked like something out of a spy movie. "I've been monitoring their communications," his fingers flying across the keyboard. "And I think I've found a weakness in their security protocols."

"What kind of weakness?" David asked.

Reynolds pointed to a schematic of the compound, his finger tracing a series of tunnels and passageways. "There's an old sewer system that runs beneath the compound. If we can access it, we might be able to sneak in undetected."

"And once we're inside?" Jade questioned.

"We find your mother," Reynolds said. "And we take down the Order from the inside."

Over the next few hours, they pored over the details and surveillance footage. They were up against impossible odds, the Illuminated Order was a force to be reckoned with.

As the night wore on, they began to formulate a plan. It was a plan born of desperation and hope, a last-ditch effort to turn the tide of the battle. But as they looked around the room at each other, they knew they were in this together, they would stand united in the face of the darkness.

37

The fifty foot walls of the compound rose from the mist-shrouded forest like a malevolent specter. Perched atop a remote hill in the heart of the Chattahoochee-Oconee National Forest, the facility was a hidden stronghold where unspeakable deeds were rumored to take place.

Wrought-iron gates emblazoned with the Order's symbol open to reveal a palatial mansion of smooth cream stone, crowned with gleaming copper domes. Manicured lawns and pristine gardens surround the compound, dotted with fountains and statues.

Jade, David, and Detective Reynolds crouched at the edge of the treeline, their breath frosting in the chill autumn air as they surveyed the imposing structure before them. The compound was ringed by a double layer of high, reinforced concrete walls, topped with coils of razor wire that shined in the moonlight. Security cameras and motion sensors dotted the perimeter, their unblinking eyes surveying for any sign of intrusion.

"I count at least a dozen armed guards," Reynolds said, his voice low as he peered through a pair of high-powered binoculars. "And those are just the ones we can see. God knows how many more are waiting inside."

160   T.M JEFFERSON

"We're in over our heads, aren't we?" Jade whispered, "How are we supposed to get past all of that, let alone find my mother and get her out alive?"

David patted her back. "We'll find a way, Jade," he said. "We didn't come this far to give up. Your mother's counting on us, and we won't let her down."

Reynolds nodded. "The kid's right," he tucked the binoculars back into his bag. "We've got surprise on our side, and the truth. That's more than the Order's ever had to face before."

He reached into his pocket and pulled out a folded map, spreading it out on the damp ground before them. "Now, listen up. I've been studying this place for weeks, looking for any weakness we can exploit. There's a drainage tunnel on the eastern side of the compound, here." He tapped a finger on the map, indicating a small, easily overlooked feature.

"A drainage tunnel?" Jade said. "Won't that be guarded too?"

Reynolds allowed himself a small, tight smile. "That's the beauty of it. The tunnel is so narrow, the Order probably doesn't even realize it's a potential point of entry. It's not on any of their official blueprints or security plans."

"So we sneak in through the tunnel, make our way to the main building, and find Jade's mother before anyone realizes we're there. It's risky, but it might work." David said.

"It's our best shot. But we'll have to move fast and stay low." Reynolds replied. "Once we're inside, there's no telling what kind of resistance we'll face."

38

As they made their way inside, it was pitch black. The only light came from the beams of their flashlights, cutting through the darkness like knives. They moved slowly, and without warning, all hell broke loose.

The first shot came from above, a burst of gunfire sent them diving for cover. Jade rolled behind a pile of rubble, her heart pounding as she tried to get a bead on their attackers.

"It's a trap! They knew we were coming!"

"Fuck." Reynolds cursed under his breath. "We have to get out of here," he said. "We're sitting ducks."

As the words left his lips, a man emerged from the darkness, a man clad in black tactical gear, holding an assault rifle. He moved with the grace and precision of a trained killer, his eyes cold and merciless behind the visor of his helmet.

"Surrender now," he said, his voice distorted by the electronic filter of his mask. "And maybe we'll let you live."

A surge of anger coursed through Jade's veins, a white-hot fury that burned away the fear and doubt. She rose to her feet, her gun held steady in her hands as she stared down the barrel of the assassin.

"Go to hell," she said, her finger tightening on the trigger.

The assassin moved with blinding speed, his rifle coming up to bear on Jade's chest. But as he fired, David was there, tackling him to the ground.

They rolled across the floor, trading blows and struggling for control of the rifle. Reynolds joined them, his own weapon forgotten as he threw himself into the melee.

Jade watched as the three men fought, their bodies a tangle of limbs and weapons. She had to do something, had to find a way to turn the tide of the battle before it was too late.

A flash of metal in the assassin's hand, the sparkle of a knife blade in the dimmed light. Time slowed down, the world narrowing to a single point of focus as Jade raised her gun and fired.

The bullet struck the assassin in the chest, a spray of blood and bone erupting from the wound. He staggered back, his eyes wide with shock and pain, and then he fell, his body hitting the ground with a dull thud.

David and Reynolds struggled to their feet, their faces streaked with blood and sweat. They looked at Jade, realizing what she'd done.

As they tried to catch their breath, more gunfire erupted through the factory. They kept moving, they had to find Jade's mother and get out of there before reinforcements arrived.

As they were about to give up hope, a soft, muffled cry came from somewhere up ahead.

"Mom?" Jade called out. "Mom, are you there?"

There was a moment of silence. From the shadows, she emerged, a woman with long, dark hair and a face lined with exhaustion and fear.

"Jade?" she said, her eyes wide with disbelief. "Is that really you?"

Jade rushed forward, tears blurring her vision as she dropped to her knees beside her mother. She worked to untie the restraints, her fingers fumbling in her haste. "It's me, Mom. I'm here. I'm going to get you out of here."

Jade's mother grabbed her daughter's hands, squeezing them with a fierce intensity. "I knew you'd come for me," she whispered, her voice cracking with emotion. "I never lost faith."

Jade pulled her mother into a tight hug, burying her face in the crook of her neck as sobs wracked her body. The weight of the past few months– the fear, the desperation, the pursuit of the truth– it all came crashing down in that moment. "I'm so sorry," Jade choked out. "I'm sorry it took me so long."

Her mother held her close, stroking her hair with a soothing touch. "You have nothing to apologize for, my brave girl. You risked everything to save me. I'm so proud of you."

They clung to each other, savoring the bittersweet reunion. But the urgency of their situation soon reasserted itself. Jade pulled back, wiping her eyes with the back of her hand. "We have to go."

With a nod, her mother struggled to her feet. Together, they made their way out, Jade's arm wrapped protectively around her mother's waist.

39

President Adrian Blackwell sat at his desk in the Oval Office, his hands clasped in front of him as he faced the two junior members of the Illuminated Order. Victoria and Jameson, who were standing over him.

"Mr. President, I believe we've made ourselves clear," Victoria said, leaning in close. "The Order's policies must be implemented without delay."

President Blackwell took a deep breath, trying to maintain his composure. "I understand your position, Victoria. But these policies ... they're extreme. The consequences could be devastating."

Jameson's stare was icy. "The consequences of inaction would be far worse, Mr. President. The Order has the nation's best interests at heart."

The President shifted in his seat. The Order's reputation for ruthlessness was known, and the thought of crossing them made him nauseous. But he had a duty to the American people, and he couldn't ignore it.

"I was elected to serve the people, not the Order," The President said. "I need more time to consider the ramifications."

Victoria grinned, "Selected, Mr. President. Never forget that.

166   T.M JEFFERSON

And time is a luxury we don't have. The Order has been patient, but that patience is wearing thin." she said. "We know things about you. Things that could ruin you. It would be a shame if certain secrets were to come to light."

President Blackwell fought to keep his expression neutral. "Are you threatening me?"

Victoria smiled. "We prefer to think of it as a friendly reminder of where your loyalties should lie."

The President rose from his chair, the vein in his neck pulsating. "I won't be bullied into submission. I need to do what's right for the American people."

Jameson stepped closer. "And what about what's right for your family? It would be tragic if something were to happen to them."

The President shifted in his seat. Images of his wife and children flashed through his mind, any harm caused to them was unbearable. He sank back into his chair, his shoulders slumped, and he shook his head.

"What do you need me to do?" he asked.

Victoria and Jameson exchanged a glance. "I'm glad we could reach an understanding, Mr. President," Victoria said, smiling. "The Order will be in touch with further instructions."

As the two turned to leave, the President buried his face in his hands. He'd sworn to protect and serve the nation, but now he found himself a pawn in a game far more dangerous than he ever imagined.

The door closed behind Victoria and Jameson, leaving the President alone in the Oval Office. From this moment forward, his every move would be watched, his every decision scrutinized by the forces that pulled the strings of power. The future of the nation, and the safety of his own family was at stake.

"He who fights with monsters might take care lest he thereby become a monster. And if you gaze for long into an abyss, the abyss gazes also into you."

- FRIEDRICH NIETZSCHE

40

Jade pushed back in her chair, rubbing her tired eyes as she let out a heavy sigh. "There's so much here. Financial records, meeting minutes, encrypted messages ... It's like trying to piece together a million-piece puzzle without the picture on the box."

"The answers we need are in here somewhere, I can feel it." David's eyes widened, and he sat up straight in his seat. "Wait a minute, look at this."

He turned the screen towards Jade, pointing to a series of emails. "These messages are talking about a meeting, a gathering of some kind. And look at the location– the Swiss Alps."

Jade reached into her pocket and pulled out the black business card Victoria slipped her during their encounter at the gala.

"The card," she whispered, her fingers tracing over the embossed lettering. "I think it's an invitation to this meeting."

She flipped the card over and saw the address scrawled on the back in elegant, silver script. "Davos, Switzerland. That's where they're holding the meeting."

"This could be it, Jade. The opportunity we've been waiting for."

170   T.M JEFFERSON

"We have to go. We need to be at that meeting, no matter what it takes." Jade stood up, her mind already racing with the logistics of their trip. "I'll book the flights and make the arrangements. You start packing and gathering whatever equipment we might need."

41

Agent James Ashford strode into the briefing room at MI6 headquarters, his crisp suit and confident demeanor was confirmation to his years of experience in the field. He took a seat at the long table, nodding to his colleagues as they filed in. At the head of the table was Margaret Brentwood, the MI6 section chief, her face lit up by the glow of the large screen behind her.

"Good morning, everyone," Margaret said, tapping a button on the remote in her hand. The screen flashed to life, displaying a map of the Swiss Alps. "Our top priority today is the mission involving Jade Rose and David Montgomery."

James' interest piqued at the mention of the American journalist. "What's the situation, Margaret?" he asked.

"Our sources indicate Jade and David are heading to the Swiss Alps, specifically to Davos Switzerland," Margaret explained. "We believe they're following a lead related to the Illuminated Order." She clicked the remote, and the screen zoomed in on a satellite image of a sprawling mountain compound. "This is the Retenberg Estate, owned by a shell corporation with ties to the Order. We suspect it may be a key location in their operations."

James nodded, his mind already working. He'd been keeping

172 T.M JEFFERSON

tabs on Jade's investigation into the Order, he knew if she was personally pursuing a lead, it must be significant.

Margaret continued, "We believe they may be heading into a dangerous situation."

"And you want me to provide support?" James asked.

"Exactly," Margaret confirmed. "Your experience in the field make you the ideal candidate to assist them. We need you to reach out to Jade and ensure their safety."

James nodded.

"I have no doubt you'll find a way."

"I'll do whatever it takes to ensure the success of this mission and protect our allies."

Margaret gave him a nod of approval. "I know you will. The stakes are high, and the outcome of this operation could have far-reaching consequences. We're counting on you."

As the briefing drew to a close, James stood, ready to spring into action. Time was of the essence, and he needed to make contact with Jade as soon as possible. With a final nod to Margaret, he strode out of the room, his mind already formulating plans and contingencies.

42

The Swiss Alps was a vast expanse of snow-capped peaks and pristine valleys stretching out as far as the eye could see. Jade and David stood at the edge of a clifftop, the fierce winds whipping at their hair and clothes as they observed the breathtaking vista.

"You sure this is the right place?" Jade asked, her voice barely audible over the howling of the wind.

David nodded, his eyes narrowing as he consulted the GPS coordinates on his smartphone. "The coordinates lead right to this spot. The Order's leadership is set to convene here in less than twenty four hours."

The wind picked up, Jade pulled her coat tighter as she stared out over the rugged terrain. "It's so remote," she said. "The perfect place for a secret meeting."

"We have to find a way inside. Stop them before it's too late."

They made their way down the narrow, winding path that led to the valley floor, snow crunching under their boots, their breath clouding in the frigid air. The only sound was the wind, a mournful howl that vibrated off the peaks and through the deep, shadowed ravines.

174   T.M JEFFERSON

As they approached the coordinates, a sprawling compound nestled in the heart of the valley came in to view.

"There it is," David said. "The belly of the beast."

Jade searched the perimeter of the compound for any sign of weakness, any chink in the Order's armor. "We need to find a way inside," she said.

They spent the next few hours scouting the compound, studying its layout and defenses with a meticulous eye. They were up against an intimidating enemy. The Illuminated Order would have spared no expense in securing their most important meeting place.

As the sun set over the mountains, long shadows danced across the valley floor. They found what they were looking for: a small, unguarded service entrance on the far side of the compound, hidden behind a stand of snow-laden pines.

"That's our way in," David said. "We'll wait until nightfall, then make our move."

Jade agreed. They were about to walk into the danger zone without any guarantee of making it out alive.

As the last rays of the sun disappeared behind the mountains, they made their final preparations, checking their weapons and equipment with a practiced eye. They would only have one chance to get this right. The slightest mistake could mean the difference between life and death.

As the night closed in around them and the stars began to shine in the clear, cold sky, they made their move.

Approaching the service entrance, soft mumbling of voices came from inside, the sound of the Order's leadership gathering for their meeting. Jade and David's eyes locked in a silent moment of communication.

This was it, the moment they'd been waiting for. The moment they'd finally come face to face with the enemy they'd been fighting for so long.

With a final nod, they pushed open the heavy double doors and stepped into the room.

What they saw would haunt them for the rest of their lives.

The room was huge, its walls draped in rich textiles and the floor inlaid with intricate patterns of gold and silver. At the far end of the room, a massive stone altar dominated the space, its surface stained with dark, rusty dried blood.

And there, standing before the altar, was a man that could only be the Illuminated Order's grand master.

He was tall and gaunt, his skin pale and translucent beneath the light of the candles that lined the room. His eyes were a piercing blue, cold and calculating as they swept over the assembled crowd.

And what a crowd it was. Jade and David recognized some of the faces instantly– politicians and CEOs, celebrities and royalty, all of them dressed in the same black robes and wearing the same expression of rapt attention.

But it was the person on the altar that drew their gaze, a young woman with long, dark hair and a face twisted in terror and pain. She was naked and bound, her wrists and ankles tied to the four corners of the altar with thick ropes.

The grand master began to speak as Jade and David looked on.

"Brothers and sisters," he said. "We gather here tonight to offer a sacrifice to the great god Baphomet, to renew our vows of loyalty and obedience to the Illuminated Order."

The crowd muttered in assent, their eyes glued to the altar and the struggling form of the young woman. Bile rose up in Jade's throat, a wave of nausea and revulsion threatened to overwhelm her.

But she forced it down, forced herself to watch as the grand master raised a shining silver dagger above his head.

"With this sacrifice," he declared, his voice rising, "we bind ourselves to the will of the Order, to the great work that we have undertaken. We offer this vessel as a symbol of our devotion, a tribute to the power that we wield over the world of men."

And then, with a single, brutal motion, he brought the dagger down, plunging it into the young woman's chest. A sound of pure, unadulterated agony bounced off the walls and through the souls of all who heard it.

As the life drained from her body and the blood poured from her wounds, the grand master continued to speak.

"Behold the power of the Illuminated Order," he said. "Behold the destiny that awaits all who oppose us. We are the future, the true masters of the world, and all who stand in our way shall be crushed beneath our heel."

The crowd erupted in cheers and applause, their voices rising in twisted celebration. Jade and David could only watch in silent horror.

They had to make a move, had to find a way to stop this madness before it consumed the entire world. But in that moment, confronted with the full, terrifying scope of the Order's power and depravity, doubt consumed them, a sinking fear that they might already be too late.

With heavy hearts and trembling hands, they turned to leave, to slip back into the shadows and regroup for the battles to come. But as they did, a voice stopped them dead in their tracks.

"Leaving already?" the grand master's voice cut through the commotion. "And just when things were getting interesting."

Jade and David stopped in their tracks, their hearts pounding as they turned to face the altar. The grand master stood before them, his eyes fixed on theirs. His smile was one of cold satisfaction, a predator who had just cornered his prey.

"Did you really think you could sneak into our private meeting undetected?" he asked. "You've clearly underestimated the Illuminated Order's capabilities. We have eyes and ears everywhere, and nothing happens within these walls without our knowledge."

The grand master took a step forward, his stare never wavering. "Your little infiltration attempt was doomed from the start. We've been aware of your presence since the moment you set foot in this

THE ILLUMINATED ORDER   177

building. But we wanted to see how far you'd go, how much you'd dare to uncover."

He spread his arms wide, gesturing to the room around them. "And now, here you are, witnessing the true power and influence of the Order. But don't mistake this for an invitation. You've stumbled into a world you can barely comprehend, and there will be consequences for your actions."

Jade and David stood their ground. They were outnumbered and outmaneuvered by the Order's members. But they couldn't let the grand master's words shake their resolve. They'd come too far, sacrificed too much, to back down now.

"You may think you have us cornered," Jade said, her voice steady despite the fear rushing through her veins. "But the truth will always find a way to come out. Your secrets, your lies, your manipulations– they won't stay hidden forever. And we won't stop until the world knows the truth about the Illuminated Order."

The grand master let out a harsh laugh, shaking his head in mock pity. "Ah, the naiveté of youth. You still believe in the power of truth, in the ability of the masses to rise up against their masters. But you fail to grasp the true nature of power. It's not about truth or justice or any of those lofty ideals you cling to. It's about control, plain and simple. And the Illuminated Order has been controlling the levers of power for centuries."

He took another step forward, his eyes boring into Jade's. "You have no idea what you've stumbled into, no idea of the forces you're trying to oppose. But you'll learn, soon enough. And when you do, you'll realize just how futile your little crusade really is."

Jade and David could only stare, They were in over their heads. They walked into a trap from which there might be no escape.

The grand master was right about one thing- they stumbled into something far beyond their worst imaginings, a conspiracy that threatened to consume the entire world in darkness and despair.

"You're nothing but insignificant specks in the grand scheme of things. We will not be thwarted by the likes of you."

David reached into his pocket and pulled out a small, spherical object. Before anyone could react, he tossed it at the ground, and a blinding flash of light filled the room, accompanied by a deafening bang.

Chaos erupted as the members of the Order stumbled and shouted in confusion, disoriented by the flash-bang. Jade and David seized the opportunity, pushing through the large crowd and racing towards the exit.

"Stop them!" the grand master's voice cut through the commotion. "Don't let them escape!"

They ran through the winding corridors of the compound, hearts thumping. The footsteps and angry shouts of their pursuers grew louder.

They burst through a set of heavy double doors and found themselves in a courtyard. The cold night air slapping their faces as they ran, searching for a way out.

A black helicopter descended from the sky, its rotor blades whipping the air into a frenzy. The door slid open, revealing the familiar face of their MI6 contact.

"Come on!" he shouted over the noise. "We don't have much time!"

Jade and David raced towards the helicopter, their pursuers hot on their heels. They jumped inside, and the door slid shut behind them just as a hail of bullets pinged off the armored exterior.

The helicopter's rotor blades whirred, kicking up a swirl of snow and debris, Jade collapsed against David, her body shaking of exhaustion and adrenaline. She could feel his heart racing beneath her cheek, his chest rising and falling as he struggled to catch his breath. For a moment, they clung to each other, taking comfort in the warmth and solidity of their bodies.

As they climbed higher, the snowy peaks of the Swiss Alps fell away beneath them, the compound receding into the distance until it was little more than a speck on the vast expanse of white. Jade stared out the window. They infiltrated the heart of the Illuminated Order's power structure, witnessed the ruthlessness of their inner circle, and barely escaped with their lives. The memory of the grand master's cold eyes staring into hers sent a shiver through Jade's body, and she tightened her grip on David's hand.

She leaned her head against his shoulder, drawing strength from his presence. Together, they watched as the snowy peaks gave way to rolling hills and lush valleys, the world below them a patchwork of green and gold.

They looked out over the breathtaking landscape, their hearts filled with a new sense of purpose. They survived this battle, but the war was just beginning.

43

Jade was hunched over the desk in their hotel room, her fingers flying across the keyboard with a frantic urgency. The flash drive she risked everything to obtain was plugged into the laptop, its secrets spilling out before her.

She'd been sifting through the files for hours, her eyes straining against the glare of the screen as she tried to make sense of it all. Financial records, encrypted emails, grainy photographs– each new piece of information only seemed to deepen the mystery, to pull her further down the rabbit hole of conspiracy and corruption.

A photograph, buried deep in a nest of encrypted folders caught her attention. It was a group shot, a gathering of suited men and women with faces that exuded power and prestige. They stood in a lavish ballroom, their smiles cold and calculating beneath the luxurious chandeliers.

But it was the man at the center of the group that drew Jade's eye, a man that was both familiar and utterly foreign to her. It was her father, his face lined with a kind of cruel satisfaction that she'd never seen before. And standing at his side with a hand resting possessively on his shoulder, was Victoria Sterling.

A wave of nausea rose up from the pit of Jade's stomach and her eyes filled with tears. *It just can't be.* Her father had secrets, parts of his life he kept hidden from her. But this ... this was beyond anything she could've imagined.

With trembling fingers, she clicked through to the next file, a spreadsheet filled with numbers and names. Among that complex web of shell corporations and offshore accounts, was a name that made her feel numb all over.

Ether Entertainment. Her father's company, the business he built from the ground up. The company that brought joy and wonder to millions.

There it was, in black and white, irrefutable proof of his involvement with the Illuminated Order. Payments funneled through a dizzying array of front companies, donations made to secret organizations with names that sent quivers through Jade's body.

Her father, the man she looked up to her entire life, the man whose love and guidance shaped her into the person she was today ... was a monster. *I don't believe this is happening.*

A liar, a manipulator, a puppet master pulling the strings of the world from behind the scenes. And she, Jade, had been his unwitting pawn, a tool to be used and discarded in the service of his twisted agenda.

Tears rushed down her face as she stared at the screen, her vision blurring with a kind of raw, visceral pain she had never known before. Everything she ever believed, every truth she ever held dear, was crumbling to dust before her eyes.

She sank into a chair, her legs no longer able to support her weight. Her mind racing, trying to reconcile the image of her loving, supportive father with the cold, ruthless woman that stared back at her.

Tears stung her eyes, a hot, prickling sensation that blurred her vision and made her throat ache with the effort of holding back a sob. *How could he have kept this from me? How could he have lied to me for all these years, pretending to be someone he wasn't?*

The betrayal cut deeper than any physical wound, a singeing pain that radiated from her heart and left her feeling hollow and empty inside. All the times she confided in him, all the moments of laughter and love they shared, she wondered if any of it was real.

Her mind flashed back to her childhood, to the long walks in the park and the bedtime stories he would read to her each night. She always seen him as her hero, her protector, the one person she could count on to be there for her.

But now, as she sat in the ruins of her shattered illusions, she realized she never knew him at all. The man she called her father was a stranger.

Jade's hands trembled as she reached for her phone, her fingers hovering over the keypad. She knew she should call him, confront him with the truth and demand an explanation. But the thought of hearing his voice, of seeing the lies and the deceit written across his face, was more than she could bear.

She closed her eyes, her heart aching with the weight of the decision she knew she had to make. She had to confront him, had to look him in the eye and ask him why he betrayed her, why he chose the Order over his own family.

But as she prepared herself for the confrontation to come, she knew nothing would ever be the same again. The trust that had once been the foundation of their relationship was shattered, the bond between father and daughter forever tainted by the poison of the Illuminated Order.

* * *

JADE'S FATHER, Weston Rose, always dreamed of making it big in the music industry. Born and raised in the South Bronx, he had a natural talent for crafting beats and lyrics that spoke to the struggles and aspirations of his community. But despite his undeniable skills and tireless hustle, he found himself trapped in a cycle of

184   T.M. JEFFERSON

dead-end jobs and broken promises, his dreams of stardom always just out of reach.

It was in the late 1980s, during a low point in his life, when Weston first crossed paths with Victoria Sterling. She approached him after a small gig at a local club, her designer dress and expensive jewelry standing out against the grimy surroundings. She introduced herself as a talent scout with connections to the biggest labels in the business, and she had an offer that was too good to be true.

Victoria promised Weston everything he ever wanted– a record company, worldwide tours, money, fame, and influence. But there was a catch. In exchange for her help, Weston would have to pledge his allegiance to a powerful organization known as the Illuminated Order. He would become a part of their inner circle, privy to their secrets and their plans for the world.

At first, Weston was hesitant. He heard whispers of the Order before, rumors of a secret organization that pulled strings behind the scenes. But Victoria was persuasive, painting a picture of a future filled with wealth and adoration, a life where he could have everything he ever dreamed of.

In a moment of weakness, Weston agreed. He took the oath, swearing his loyalty to the Order and its grand master. And just like that, his fate was sealed.

As he rose through the ranks of the music industry, Weston began to understand the true nature of his bargain. The Order had a plan, a sinister agenda to shape the minds and hearts of the youth through the power of music. They wanted to promote violence, to stir up chaos and unrest, to create a generation of angry, disillusioned young people who could be easily controlled and manipulated.

Weston was a key player in this plan. The music, once a source of hope and inspiration, became a tool of the Order's propaganda machine. His artist crafted lyrics that glorified gang violence, drug use, and misogyny. It was a dark, seductive energy that drew in listeners by the millions.

Behind the scenes, the Order was working to capitalize on the chaos they were creating. They had investments in private prison systems, in security firms and weapons manufacturers. The more violence and unrest there was on the streets, the more money they stood to make.

Weston was sickened by what he'd become, by the knowledge that his music was being used to harm the same people he once sought to uplift. But he was in too deep, trapped by his oath and the fear of what the Order would do to him if he tried to back out.

As the years went by, Weston watched as his daughter Jade grew up, a bright and inquisitive child with a thirst for truth and justice. He knew she would never understand the choices he made, the compromises he accepted in the pursuit of his dreams.

He tried to shield her from the darkness of his world, to give her a life of love and stability despite the turmoil that raged inside of him. But someday, the truth would come out. And when it did, he could only hope Jade would find the strength to forgive him, to understand the impossible choices he faced.

For Weston Rose, the price of fame and fortune had been his soul, his integrity, and his family.

* * *

SITTING at the edge of the bed in the hotel room, Jade wanted to give up. The weight of the last few days, of all the horrors she witnessed and the sacrifices she made, left her emotionally numb.

Beside her, David's face was lined with exhaustion and grief. He lost friends and allies in this fight, seen the true depths of human depravity and cruelty. But he couldn't give up, he had to keep fighting for the sake of all that was good and true in the world.

"Jade," he said. "We can't let them win. We can't let the Illuminated Order's evil go unchallenged."

Jade looked up at him, her eyes red-rimmed and filled with sadness. "I know," she said, her voice hoarse and broken. "But David, the things we've seen, the things we've had to do ... I don't know if I can keep going. I don't know if I have the strength."

David reached out and took her hand. "You're one of the strongest people I know, Jade. You've been through so much, sacrificed so much, but you're still here, still fighting. That takes a kind of strength that most people can only dream of."

A smile came across Jade's lips, her heart swelling with gratitude for David's support. But even as she savored the warmth of his touch and the comfort of his words, grief and despair washed over her, threatening to drag her down into the depths of hopelessness.

"David, there's something I need to tell you. Something I found out about my father."

"What is it?"

Jade took a deep, shuddering breath, her hands clenching into fists at her sides. "My father," she said. "He's involved with the Illuminated Order. He's been using his position in the entertainment industry to spread their propaganda, to influence the minds of the youth and lead them down a path of destruction."

David's eyes widened. He'd always known the Illuminated Order's reach was long and insidious, but to think they infiltrated even the highest levels of the entertainment industry, and were using it to corrupt and mislead an entire generation.

"Jade, I'm so sorry. I can't even imagine how you must be feeling right now."

Jade shook her head, her eyes brimming with fresh tears. "I feel like I don't even know him anymore. Like everything I thought I knew about him was a lie. And the worst part is, I don't know if he's just a pawn in their game, or if he's been a willing participant all along."

David reached out and pulled Jade into his arms, holding her close as she wept against his chest. There were no words that could ease the pain of such a profound betrayal, no platitudes that could make sense of the deceit and manipulation the Illuminated Order had woven.

But they had to find a way to keep fighting no matter how much it hurt. For the sake of all the innocent lives that hung in the balance, and for the sake of the world they swore to protect.

"We'll get through this, Jade," he whispered, his voice fierce with determination. "We'll find a way to stop the Illuminated Order, to expose their lies and bring them to justice. And we'll do it together, no matter what it takes."

Jade clung to him, her tears soaking into the fabric of his shirt.

"You're right," she said. "We can't let them win. We have to keep fighting, no matter what it takes. For the sake of everyone we love, and for the sake of the world we want to create."

44

Detective Marcus Reynolds was slouched over his desk, his eyes bloodshot from the countless hours he spent scrutinizing the evidence they gathered on the Illuminated Order.

As he sifted through the latest batch of intercepted communications, a particular message caught his eye. It was encrypted, but after running it through the decryption software, the contents made his stomach churn.

The message contained detailed information about Jade and David's movements, their plans, and their next steps. But what made Reynolds' blood boil was that this information could only have come from someone within their trusted circle.

With a growing sense of dread, he dug deeper, cross-referencing names and dates, searching for any clue that might lead him to the identity of the traitor. Buried deep within a sea of data, he found it.

An email, sent from a secure server traced back to the Illuminated Order's network. And there, in plain text, was a name he never expected to see.

Dr. Sophia Ramirez.

Reynolds stared at the name on the screen. *I can't believe this.* Dr. Ramirez, the brilliant academic who'd been their guide and ally, the one who provided them with insights into the workings of secret societies. She'd been there from the beginning, earning their trust and leading them through the shadows.

But now, the truth was in front of him. She'd been feeding information to the Illuminated Order all along, using her position of trust to undermine every move. A sudden tightness filled his chest.

He reached for his phone and dialed Jade's number. When she answered, her voice was thick with sleep, he barely managed to choke out the words.

"Jade, it's Dr. Ramirez. She's a mole. She's been working for the Order this whole time."

The silence on the other end of the line was deafening. Jade finally spoke. "Are you sure?"

"I have the proof right here. We need to move fast, before she realizes we're onto her."

"Meet us at the safe-house in an hour." Jade said. "We'll figure out our next move."

Reynolds hung up the phone. He stared down at his palms like they held the answers, his thoughts scrambling, trying to figure out why. Dr. Ramirez, the one person they trusted implicitly, was working against them all along. The depth of her deception knew no bounds.

He gathered his files and headed out into the night. As he drove through the quiet streets, he thought about how long Dr. Ramirez had been deceiving them, how much damage she'd already done.

When he arrived at the safehouse, Jade and David were already there. They pored over the evidence, piecing together the extent of Dr. Ramirez's betrayal.

It was clear she'd been manipulating them from the start, steering their investigation while feeding critical information to the Order. She used her expertise and knowledge to keep them one step behind, allowing the Order to stay ahead of their every move.

THE ILLUMINATED ORDER 191

It was a bitter pill to swallow, but they had no choice but to confront her and uncover the full extent of her treachery.

Confronting Dr. Ramirez would be a dangerous gambit, but they couldn't let her betrayal go unanswered. They had to stop her before she could do more damage, before the Illuminated Order could use her inside knowledge to thwart their efforts once and for all.

In the safehouse, Jade, David, and Reynolds stared at each other in silence. They'd been betrayed by one of their own, but they wouldn't let that stop them.

45

As Jade, David, and Detective Reynolds entered Dr. Ramirez's office, the once-welcoming space now felt like a trap, the walls closing in on them with each passing moment. Dr. Ramirez sat behind her desk, her expression inscrutable, her eyes held an emotion they couldn't quite place.

Jade was the first to break the silence. "How could you?" she said, slamming her hands down on the desk. "We trusted you, and all this time, you've been working for them?"

Dr. Ramirez's lips curved into a smile that didn't reach her eyes. "Trust is a luxury in this game, my dear. You of all people should know that by now."

David stepped forward. "We've seen the evidence, Dr. Ramirez. We know about your communication with the Order. You've been feeding them information about our every move."

"Evidence can be fabricated, Mr. Montgomery. Surely your CIA training taught you that much."

Reynolds shook his head, "Cut the shit, Dr. Ramirez. We've traced the emails back to your private server. There's no denying it anymore. You're working for the Order."

For a moment, Dr. Ramirez said nothing, her eyes drifting to the window and the world beyond. Then, with a sigh, she turned back to face them. "You have no idea what you've stumbled into," she said. "The Illuminated Order is more than just a secret cabal. It's a force that has shaped the course of human history for centuries."

Jade's eyes widened. "What are you talking about?"

Dr. Ramirez rose from her seat, her movements graceful and purposeful as she approached the towering bookshelf that lined the walls of her office. Her fingers traced the spines of the ancient tomes, each one a repository of the Order's secrets.

"The Illuminated Order has been the unseen force guiding the course of human history since the days of the Enlightenment," she said."We've been the invisible hand, the puppeteers pulling the strings of fate, shaping the world to our design."

She turned to face Jade. "You see, the Order understands that true power lies not in the spotlight, but in the shadows. We've worked tirelessly to infiltrate every level of society, to place our agents in positions of influence and authority, where they can guide the course of events to our desired outcomes."

Dr. Ramirez paused, her eyes distant as if lost in the annals of history. "In politics, we've been the kingmakers and the power behind the throne. Our members have whispered in the ears of presidents and prime ministers, have shaped the policies and laws that govern nations. From the halls of Congress to the corridors of Downing Street, our influence knows no boundary."

She ran her fingers along the edge of a specific ancient volume, its pages yellowed with age. "In the world of finance, we've been the hand that moves the markets, that shapes the ebb and flow of wealth and prosperity. Our investments and schemes have toppled governments, and set the stage for the rise and fall of empires. The global economy is our plaything, a tool to be used in the service of our grand design."

Dr. Ramirez's voice took on a note of pride, a hint of the fierce belief that drove the Order's actions. "In science and technology, we've been the force behind the greatest advancements and innovations of the modern age. From the harnessing of electricity to the splitting of the atom, from the mapping of the human genome to the creation of artificial intelligence, our members have been at the forefront of every great leap forward."

She fixed Jade with a piercing stare, her eyes alight with a kind of messianic conviction. "But perhaps our greatest achievement has been in the realm of culture and ideas. Through our control of the media, the arts, and education, we've shaped the fabric of human thought, and have molded the beliefs and values that define the modern world. From the books that line the shelves of every library to the movies that play on every screen, our influence is felt in every corner of human experience."

Dr. Ramirez's voice dropped to a whisper. "The French Revolution, the rise of the Soviet Union, the dawn of the nuclear age ... all of these moments were guided by the Illuminated Order, shaped to serve our purposes and further our goals. The world as you know it is a carefully constructed illusion."

She stepped closer to Jade, her face a mask of cold determination. "And now, as we stand on the brink of a new era, the Order is poised to take the final step, to usher in a world where our vision of enlightenment and progress reigns supreme. The pieces are in place, the stage is set, and soon, the curtain will rise on a future that we alone have the power to shape."

David's eyes narrowed. "How long have you been working for them?"

Dr. Ramirez smiled. "My family has served the Order for generations. It's a duty that's been passed down from parent to child, a sacred trust that cannot be broken."

Detective Reynolds' hand rested on the butt of his gun. "And the grand master? Who is he?"

Dr. Ramirez's eyes sparkled with a dangerous light. "The grand master is the heart and soul of the Order, the one who guides us all. He's a man of immense power and influence, a visionary who sees beyond the petty concerns of nations and governments."

Jade's heart pounded in her chest. "It's him, isn't it? The man we saw at the ceremony in Switzerland. The one who performed the human sacrifice."

Dr. Ramirez nodded, her expression solemn. "Yes, that was the grand master. He's known by many names, but to the Order, he's simply the Architect, the one who shapes the future of the world."

David's hands clenched into fists. "And you're just going to stand by and let him do this? Let the Order manipulate and control everything from the shadows?"

"You still don't understand, do you? The Order is not some sinister force bent on destruction. We're the guardians of humanity, the ones who ensure the world keeps turning, no matter the cost."

Jade's nostrils flared. "No, Dr. Ramirez. What you're doing is wrong. You're taking away people's free will, their right to choose their own destiny."

Dr. Ramirez's smile was sad, almost pitying. "Free will is a myth, Jade. The Order knows this better than anyone. We're all just pawns in a much larger game, and it is our duty to play our parts, no matter how difficult they may be."

Detective Reynolds' grip tightened on his gun. "And what about the human sacrifice? Is that just another part of your grand plan?"

"The sacrifice is a necessary evil, a reminder of the price that must be paid for the greater good. It's a burden the grand master bears, a cross he must carry so others may be spared."

Jade shook her head in a slow, back-and-forth sweep of denial. "I can't believe I ever trusted you."

Dr. Ramirez's eyes softened, a pained expression crossing her face. "I never meant to hurt you, Jade. But you must understand, the Order's work is too important to be jeopardized. We have a duty to protect the world, no matter the cost."

David's voice was cold, his eyes hard as flint. "And what about the cost to the people you're supposed to be protecting? The lives that have been lost, the suffering that's been inflicted?"

"The Order has always known that sacrifices must be made. It's a burden we bear, a price we pay so that humanity may continue to thrive."

Detective Reynolds shook his head. "You're not protecting humanity, Dr. Ramirez. You're enslaving it."

"You may see it that way, Detective. But the truth is, the world needs the Order. Without us, chaos would reign, and all that we've built would be destroyed."

"We're going to stop you," Jade said. "We're going to expose the truth and bring the Order to justice, no matter what it takes."

"You can try, Jade. But the Order is too powerful, too entrenched to be stopped by the likes of you. You're nothing but ants, trying to topple a mountain."

46

Jade, David, and Detective Reynolds stood around the table in the safe house. Dr. Ramirez's information was a goldmine, secrets that unlocked the true scope of the Order's influence. The computer screen was flooded with new data, an array of financial transactions, coded messages, and geopolitical maneuverings painted a chilling picture of the Order's global reach.

Jade pointed to a series of graphs and charts on the screen. "Look at this," she said. "The Order's been manipulating financial markets for decades, orchestrating crashes and booms to line their pockets and consolidate power."

"It's not just the markets," David's finger traced a line of code that scrolled across the screen. "They've been funneling money into wars and conflicts around the world, stoking the flames of chaos to destabilize entire regions."

"It's a classic tactic of the powerful," Reynolds said. "Create a problem, then offer yourself as the solution. The Order's been doing it for centuries, and no one's been the wiser."

Jade couldn't believe what she was seeing. "The Arab Spring, the Ukraine conflict, the rise of populist movements in Europe and the US ... it's all connected."

200 T.M JEFFERSON

David stumbled on an encrypted file. When the decryption software was finished working its magic, his jaw dropped. "Project Zephyr," he said. "Looks like a plan for a coordinated cyber attack on the world's power grids. They're trying to create a global blackout, to plunge entire countries into chaos."

"But why? What could they possibly hope to gain from something like that?" Jade asked.

"Control," Reynolds said. "In the event of a global crisis, the Order positions itself as the savior, the only ones capable of restoring order. They consolidate their power, and the world is left forever changed in their image."

"We have to stop them," David said.

Jade nodded. "We'll need help. Allies who can work with us to counter the Order's moves, to expose their plans before it's too late."

"I might know some people," Reynolds said. "Ex-intelligence, hacktivist groups, people who've been fighting from the darkness for years."

David's eyes met Jade's. They were aware of the risks and dangers that lay ahead.

As they searched deeper into the files, the true magnitude of the Illuminated Order's plan began to take shape. It was a history of deceit and manipulation that stretched back centuries, a conspiracy so vast and intricate that it defied belief.

The Order orchestrated countless wars and revolutions, toppling governments and shaping the course of human events. They infiltrated the highest rankings of power, from the halls of government to the boardrooms of multinational corporations, their influence spreading like a cancer across the globe.

And now, with the advent of new technologies and the rise of global interconnectedness, the Order's power only grew. They controlled the flow of information, manipulating the masses through propaganda and disinformation. They held the keys to the world's economies, using their wealth to bend nations to their will.

As Jade and her team pored over the files, it dawned on them.

The Order's ultimate goal was not just power for its own sake, but something far more diabolical.

They sought to create a new world order, a global totalitarian regime that would enslave humanity under the guise of peace and prosperity. And as the days passed, they grew closer to achieving their twisted vision.

The conference room was bathed in a cool, diffused light, the floor-to-ceiling windows offering a stunning panoramic view of the city skyline. Around the polished glass table sat the junior members of the Illuminated Order, their faces a study in concentration and concern.

At the head of the table, Victoria Sterling's ice-blue eyes searched the faces of her colleagues. "Project Zephyr is entering its critical phase,"she said. "But we're facing a new and unexpected threat– the interference of Jade Rose, David Montgomery, and Detective Marcus Reynolds."

Cassandra Blackwell, the Order's rising star in public relations, frowned, her perfectly manicured fingers drumming a staccato rhythm on the table. "They've been dedicated in their pursuit of the truth," she said. "Jade, in particular, has proven to be an imposing adversary. Her investigative skills and determination are impressive."

Jameson Shaw, the tech prodigy with a razor-sharp intellect, leaned back in his chair. "They're getting too close," he warned. "If they manage to uncover the details of Project Zephyr, it could jeop-

204 T.M JEFFERSON

ardize everything we've worked for. The economic chaos, the social upheaval ... it would all be for nothing."

Victoria's lips pursed in a thin line. "Which is why we need to take action, and fast. We can't allow them to derail our plans, not when we're so close to achieving our goals."

She tapped a button on the console before her, and a holographic display sprang to life in the center of the table. It was a detailed outline of intricate connections and data points, each one representing a key figure or organization in the Order's network of influence.

"We have assets in place," Victoria continued, her finger tracing the glowing lines of the hologram. "Contacts within the media, the police force, even the FBI. We need to leverage every resource at our disposal to discredit and neutralize this threat."

"I can handle the media angle," Cassandra offered. "A few well-placed rumors, some incriminating evidence planted at the right moment ... we can destroy their credibility, paint them as nothing more than conspiracy theorists and attention-seekers."

Jameson's fingers flew across the screen of his tablet. "I can dig into their digital lives, uncover any skeletons in their closets. Everyone has secrets, weaknesses that can be exploited. We just need to find the right pressure points."

"Excellent." Victoria said. "But we need to go further. Detective Reynolds, in particular, poses a significant threat. His position within the department gives him access and resources that could cause us real damage."

She paused, her eyes sweeping over the faces of her colleagues. "I want him neutralized, by any means necessary. If he won't back down, if he won't see reason ... then we'll have to remove him from the equation, permanently."

48

BREAKING NEWS

This is an APB news alert from the Global News Network. We are interrupting regular programming to go live to our correspondent Lila Matsumoto in Washington D.C. Lila, what can you tell us about the developing situation?

"Thanks Jim, I'm coming to you live from outside the J. Edgar Hoover building, headquarters of the Federal Bureau of Investigation. In a shocking development, federal arrest warrants have been issued for three individuals now considered armed and extremely dangerous fugitives."

"The FBI has identified the suspects as Jade Rose, an investigative journalist, and her partner David Montgomery, an ex-CIA operative. They are wanted in connection with a string of crimes including espionage against allied nations, theft of classified intelligence, cyberterrorism, and most disturbingly— conspiracy to commit acts of domestic terrorism here in the United States."

"According to a statement released by the Justice Department, the trio is believed to be at the center of an anti-government militia group that has been operating in secret for years. Authorities claim to have uncovered evidence linking them directly to planned attacks on American soil

designed to 'sow chaos and undermine faith in our democratic institutions.'"

"The announcement comes as a complete shock, as Rose and Montgomery were previously thought to be aiding official investigations into corruption and conspiracy claims regarding a potential 'secret society'. However, Justice officials now assert that this narrative was merely an elaborate cover story masking their true anarchist motives."

"Included in the mountain of evidence cited are intercepted communications, financial transfers to known terror cells, and damning reconnaissance footage that appears to show the suspects casing locations in New York, Washington and other major cities. The FBI is stating unequivocally that this is a national security emergency of the highest order."

"I'm being told a massive multi-agency manhunt is currently underway using every resource at the government's disposal to locate and apprehend these two domestic terrorists before they can strike again. The public is urged to be on high alert and to immediately report any information that could lead to their capture. David Montgomery in particular is considered 'extremely volatile and a direct threat' due to his training with the C.I.A."

"Again, we cannot stress this enough– Jade Rose and David Montgomery are now officially wanted by the FBI, branded as dangerous fugitives waging war against the American people. More updates as this critical situation unfolds."

We'll have continuing live coverage on this accelerating crisis right after a break. Please stay tuned.

* * *

THE GRAINY MOTEL television draped a haunting veil across the dingy room, the flashing images lending an almost surreal quality to the scene unfolding before Jade, David and Detective Reynold's eyes.

On the screen, their faces– Jade's delicate features, and David's chiseled jaw– were plastered beneath garish, sensationalized banners proclaiming them "ARMED AND DANGEROUS" in lurid scarlet type. Right under it, the word "VOLATILE" was stamped like some kind of twisted branding.

"They've stopped just short of putting literal crosshairs on us," David said.

Jade could only nod, mute horror rendering her temporarily robbed of the power of speech. This was a nightmare given corporeal form, a realm of lies and deceit where truth itself became perverted beyond recognition.

As the reporter continued spewing her litany of vile allegations– espionage, planned terror attacks, shadowy militias bent on undermining democracy– something inside of Jade withered and went numb. Was this their legacy now, she and David? Demented bogeymen, anarchist villains woven from whole cloth to be paraded before the terrified masses while the real conspirators pulled their strings?

She caught David's eye, saw the muscle jerking in his clenched jaw, the bright sheen of helpless fury in his gaze like bared steel. He had questions, a thousand of them screaming for voice. But in the silence between them, two people bound together by a pain that clawed at their souls, no words passed his lips.

Because what could either of them possibly say in the face of such monstrous deception? Such a lurid, cunningly calculated lie designed not just to neutralize their efforts, but to vilify and scapegoat them as the same evil they fought? It was an inversion as complete as night becoming day, heroes transformed to villains with no more than a sleight of hand and insidious PR campaign.

The Order's malice, their interminable reach into the power structures meant to protect society from such abhorrent evil, shone through in vivid detail. This was checkmate taken to a brutal, definitive endgame. Jade and David, the warrior pawns destined for sacrifice as black is vanquished by white.

As the report continued on and fresh images of SWAT mobilizations flashed in seizure-inducing montages, visions of jackbooted storm-troopers deployed to hunt them down, Jade's consciousness began to slip away into a welcomed, merciful void of non-existence. This hell realm of gaslighting was simply too much for the human psyche to withstand.

She didn't realize her hands were trembling until David's warm grip encircled her wrist, steadying her, anchoring her back to the nightmare made real. His eyes, when she finally met them, burned with a defiant promise that skewered her shredded despair like a white-hot blade of iron will.

"We're going to burn them," he said. "Burn them all to ashes. For this ... for all of it."

As the television looped its smear campaign again, another sound reached Jade's senses. The distant, growing wail of sirens rushing towards them, the vanguard of a merciless juggernaut mustered against their existence.

David paced back and forth like a caged animal, his hands clenched into fists at his sides and his jaw working with suppressed anger.

The tension between them simmered, the cracks in their relationship widening into a chasm that threatened to swallow them whole. The sacrifices they made, the horrors they witnessed, had taken a toll on both of them, and now it seemed like they were reaching their breaking point.

"We have to strike now," David said. "We can't afford to wait. The Order's getting stronger every day, and if we don't act soon, we might never get another chance."

Jade looked up from the screen. "And do what, exactly? Don't you see what they're doing? We don't have enough information, we don't have enough resources. If we go in half-cocked, we're just going to get ourselves killed."

David slammed his hand down on the table, making Jade jump. "Dammit, Jade, we don't have a choice! The longer we wait, the more people are going to suffer. We have to do something, even if it means risking our own lives."

THE ILLUMINATED ORDER 209

"What about the lives of the people in this room? What about the lives of the activists who've been fighting this fight for years? Are you really willing to sacrifice them, too?"

Detective Reynolds, who was sitting quiet in the corner, spoke up. "Maybe Jade's right. Maybe we need to take a step back, regroup and come up with a better plan."

David whirled on him. "And whose side are you on, Reynolds? The side of the people, or the side of the Order?"

"I'm on the side of justice. The same as I've always been. But I'm not going to risk innocent lives just to satisfy your need for revenge."

Jade stepped between them, her hands held up in a gesture of peace. "Enough, both of you. This isn't helping anyone."

But David wasn't listening. "You know what, Jade? Maybe you're right. Maybe I am too focused on revenge. But can you blame me? After everything the Order's taken from us, after everything they've done to the people we love?"

"I know. I know how much you've lost, how much we've all lost. But we can't let our pain and anger cloud our judgment. We have to be smart about this, or we're just going to end up getting more people hurt."

David's shoulders slumped, the fight draining out of him like air from a punctured balloon. He sank down into a chair, his head in his hands and his voice barely above a whisper. "I'm just so tired, Jade. Tired of fighting, tired of losing the people I care about. I don't know how much more of this I can take."

Jade knelt down beside him, her hand resting on his shoulder. "I know. I'm tired too. But we can't give up. We have to keep fighting, for the sake of everyone who's counting on us."

Reynolds watched from across the room. He'd been in this fight longer than any of them, seen firsthand the toll it could take on even the strongest of souls. And now, as he watched Jade and David struggling to hold on to each other in the face of darkness, he couldn't help but wonder if he made the right choice.

210   T.M JEFFERSON

He thought of his own family, of the wife and children he left behind to pursue this quest for justice. He thought of the sacrifices he made, the pieces of himself he lost along the way. And he wondered, not for the first time, if it had all been worth it.

But even as the doubts and the fears gnawed at him like hungry rats, he couldn't turn back. He'd come too far, seen too much, to ever go back to the life he once knew. He pushed himself to his feet and made his way over to the table where Jade and David sat.

"Listen, both of you," he said. "I know things are tough right now, and I know it feels like we're up against an impossible enemy. But we can't let that stop us from doing what needs to be done."

Jade looked up at him. "But how? How do we keep going, when everything feels so hopeless?"

Reynolds' face softened, his hand reaching out to rest on her shoulder. "We keep going because we have to, Jade. Because there are people out there who are counting on us, who need us to be strong. And because we owe it to ourselves, and to each other, to see this through to the end."

49

President Adrian Blackwell stood by the window in the Oval Office, his back to the room, his posture rigid with contained rage. Senator Jonathan Bishop sat in one of the plush armchairs, his face a mask of apprehension and unease.

The President turned, his eyes blazing with a fury that radiated from every pore of his body. He stalked towards the senator, his footsteps heavy and deliberate on the thick carpet.

"What the fuck is going on, Bishop?" he growled. "I thought you had the Order under control, that you could keep them in line."

Senator Bishop shifted in his seat, his hands gripping the armrests. "Mr. President, I assure you, I'm doing everything in my power to manage the situation. The Order is simply ... eager to see progress on our shared goals."

President Blackwell slammed his fist on the desk, the sudden violence of the action causing Bishop to flinch. "Eager? Is that what you call it? They're breathing down my fucking neck, Bishop. Every day, it's another demand, another threat, another reminder of the leverage they hold over me."

He leaned in closer, his face inches from the senator's, his breath hot and heavy with the scent of whiskey. "I'm the President of the United States, goddamnit. I won't be pushed around by a bunch of shadow-dwelling puppeteers who think they can control the world from behind the scenes."

Senator Bishop swallowed hard. "I understand your frustration, Mr. President. But the Order's influence is vast, their reach extending into every corner of global power. We have to tread carefully, to maintain the delicate balance—"

"Fuck the balance!" President Blackwell roared, his voice jumping off the walls of the Oval Office. "I'm tired of being their lapdog, jumping through hoops to appease their every whim. I was elected to lead this nation, not to serve as a figurehead for some fucking of power-hungry sociopaths."

He grabbed Bishop by the lapels of his suit jacket, yanking him forward until their noses were almost touching. "You listen to me very carefully, Jonathan. You get the Order under control, and you do it now. I want them off my back, out of my business, and out of my fucking sight."

The senator's eyes widened, a bead of sweat trickling down his temple. "I ... I'll do my best, Mr. President. But you have to understand, the Order's plans are already in motion. Project Zephyr, the global economic reset ... these things have been in the works for years. They won't just abandon them because—"

"I don't give a fuck about their plans!" the President snarled, his grip tightening on Bishop's lapels. "If they don't back off, if they don't give me room to breathe, I'll rain holy hell down on them. I'll expose their secrets, dismantle their power structure, and burn their precious Order to the fucking ground."

He shoved Bishop back into the chair, his chest heaving. "And as for you, Senator ... if you can't get them in line, then I'll make your life a fucking nightmare. I'll destroy your career, your reputation, everything you've ever worked for. You'll be lucky to get a job scrubbing toilets when I'm done with you."

Senator Bishop's face drained of color. "Please, Mr. President,

THE ILLUMINATED ORDER   213

let's not be hasty. I'm sure we can find a way to resolve this, to reach a compromise that satisfies all parties involved."

President Blackwell's laughter was a bitter, mirthless sound. "Compromise? There is no compromise with the devil, Bishop. There's only submission or damnation."

He turned back to the window, his eyes fixed on the distant lights of the city. "Get the fuck out of my sight, Senator. And pray you can clean up this mess before it's too late. For all our sakes."

As Bishop stumbled from the room, President Blackwell remained at the window, his shoulders slumped with the weight of the burden he carried.

He had danced with the devil, made a bargain for power and influence he now feared would consume him whole. And as the shadows lengthened and the night deepened, he couldn't shake the feeling that reckoning was fast approaching, the bill for his sins was about to come due.

In the halls of the White House, the most powerful man in the world stood alone, a prisoner of his own ambition, a puppet dancing on the strings of a master he could no longer control.

50

The rain fell in sheets over the city, the sound from the downpour mixed with the sirens and the rumble of traffic on the streets below. Jade stood in the center of her father's office, her hair plastered to her face and her clothes soaked through, the chill of the rain seeping into her bones.

But the cold that gripped her was nothing compared to the icy dread that settled in the pit of her stomach, the sickening realization of the truth she uncovered about the man she once called her hero.

Her father sat behind his desk, calm and composed, his eyes sparkling with a cold, calculating light. He'd always been a master of control, a man who could hide his true feelings behind his charm and charisma. But now, as Jade stared into those eyes, she could see the cracks in that facade, the fear and guilt that danced behind the mask.

"I know everything, Dad," she said. "I know about your involvement with the Illuminated Order, about the things you've done in their name."

Her father's jaw tightened, his fingers curling into fists on the desk before him. "Jade, you don't understand," he said. "The Order is not what you think it is. We're trying to create a better world, a world where everyone can live in peace and prosperity."

Jade shook her head, warm tears stinging her eyes. "A better world? By lying and manipulating, by sowing chaos and discord wherever you go? By planning to plunge the entire planet into darkness and disorder, just so you can seize control in the aftermath?"

"The world is a messy, complicated place, Jade. Sometimes, sacrifices have to be made. The Order understands that, even if you don't."

Jade's heart twisted in her chest, a pain that threatened to tear her apart from the inside out. She always looked up to her father, always seen him as a man of integrity and righteousness in a world that often seemed so dark and corrupt. But now, as she stared into his eyes and saw the cold, ruthless calculation that lurked behind them, she realized she never knew him at all.

"Sacrifices?" she said. "What about the people who'll suffer, the innocent lives that'll be lost? What about the freedoms and rights that'll be trampled underfoot, all in the name of your vision of a perfect world?"

"Jade, listen to me," he said. "You have a choice to make, here and now. You can join us, become a part of something greater than yourself. Or you can continue to fight against us, and face the consequences of your actions."

Jade's breath got caught in her throat. She'd always known her father was a powerful man, he had connections and influence that stretched far beyond the borders of their family. But to hear him speak so casually of consequences, of the price she would pay for standing up for what she believed in...

"I can't do that, Dad," she said. "I can't be a part of something that goes against everything I believe in, everything you taught me to stand for. If you truly loved me, if you truly cared about what was right, you would see that."

For a moment, her father's eyes softened. But then, just as

quickly, the mask slipped back into place, the cold, hard lines of his features settling into a look of grim determination.

"I'm sorry, Jade," he said. "But I have a duty to the Order, a responsibility that goes beyond my personal feelings. If you can't see that, if you choose to stand against us ... then you're no longer my daughter."

The words hit Jade like a punch to the face, a numbing pain that tore through her heart and left her gasping for breath. Her relationship with her father was strained, there were secrets and lies that lurked beneath the surface of their family. But to hear him say those words, to know he was willing to cast her aside so easily...

"Then I guess I never really was," she said. "Because the father I knew, the man I looked up to ... he would never have been a part of something so twisted, so evil. He would've fought against it, just like I'm going to do."

She turned to leave. But as she reached for the door, her father's voice stopped her in her tracks.

"Walk away now, Jade, and you'll be signing your own death warrant," he said. "The Order doesn't take kindly to those who oppose us, and we'll stop at nothing to protect our interests. If you continue down this path, you'll suffer the consequences, and there will be no one left to save you."

51

The opulent boardroom was shrouded in an air of secrecy, the heavy oak doors sealed tight against the prying eyes of the world beyond. The junior members of the Illuminated Order sat around the polished mahogany table.

At the head of the table, Victoria Sterling leaned back in her high-backed leather chair, her ice-blue eyes scanning the room with a calculated intensity. Her blonde hair was pulled back in a severe bun, accentuating the sharp angles of her face and the predatory gleam in her eyes. A holographic display flickered to life, projecting the names of senators and council members on the walls, like pawns on a chessboard. Victoria traced her fingers over the holographic interface, her voice resonating with authority.

"Ladies and gentlemen," she said, her eyes fixed on the name Senator Jonathan Bishop, "the time has come for us to tighten our grip on the levers of power. The pieces are in place, and the stage is set for us to make our move."

Jameson Shaw looked up from his tablet, his fingers moving across the screen with a speed that bordered on superhuman. "I've just intercepted a series of encrypted communications between Senator Bishop's office and the Pentagon," he said. "It seems our dear President is getting cold feet about the new defense budget."

Victoria's lips curved into a razor-thin smile. "Then it's time we reminded him of where his loyalties lie," she said. "Olivia, my dear, I believe this is your area of expertise."

Olivia nodded. "Leave it to me. I have just the right pressure points to push to bring the President back in line." She reached for her phone, her fingers dancing across the screen as she composed a message. "A few whispers in the right ears, a few promises of future favors, and our dear President will be singing a very different tune by the end of the week."

Victoria nodded. "Excellent work, Olivia. And what of our friends in the House and Senate? Are they falling into line as expected?"

Jameson looked up from his tablet once more. "Like a well-oiled machine," he said. "The new legislation we drafted is already making its way through committee, and our allies in the media are primed and ready to sing its praises to the masses."

Victoria leaned forward, her elbows resting on the polished wood of the table. "And the opposition?" she asked.

"Neutralized," Olivia answered. "A few well-placed scandals, a few unfortunate accidents, and the path is clear for us to push through our agenda unopposed."

Victoria leaned back in her chair, a triumphant smile spreading across her face. "Well done, my friends," she said. "The Illuminated Order has never been stronger, and our grip on the reins of power has never been more secure."

She raised her glass of scotch, the liquid shining in the dim light of the boardroom. "To the Order," she said. "And to the bright future that awaits us all."

The others raised their glasses in turn.

As they drank to their own dark triumph, the junior members of the Illuminated Order knew their reign had only just begun, the world itself would soon tremble at their feet.

THE ILLUMINATED ORDER 221

They were the chosen few, the anointed ones, and the power they wielded was beyond the comprehension of mere mortals.

With that kind of power, they would reshape the world in their image, a dark and terrible vision of a future where they alone held sway.

The boardroom thrummed, a dark and pulsing force that seemed to emanate from the walls themselves. As the junior members of the Order set to work, their minds and hearts consumed with the joy of their own dark purpose, they knew nothing and no one could stand in their way.

And heaven help anyone who dared to go against them, who dared to challenge their dark and terrible reign.

For they would be crushed like insects beneath the heel of a merciless and unforgiving god, their screams of agony and despair lost in the howling void of eternity.

52

Senator Jonathan Bishop strode across the manicured lawn, his face a mask of grim determination as he made his way towards the waiting car.

He just finished a tense meeting with the other members of the Order's inner circle, a gathering that left him shaken to his core. The Order's plans were moving forward at a breakneck pace, and the senator found himself questioning the wisdom of their actions, the morality of the path they had chosen.

But there was no turning back, no way to extricate himself from the lies and deceit he helped to spin. He was in too deep, bound by oaths and loyalties that stretched back generations.

As he reached for the car door, movement caught his eye, a shadow seemed to detach itself from the darkness and lunge towards him with blinding speed. The senator's eyes widened, his hand scrabbling for the gun at his waist.

The man slammed into him with the force of a freight train, a gloved hand clamping over his mouth as a blade flashed in the moonlight. The senator felt a pain in his chest, a warm, wet sensation spreading across his shirt as the knife plunged into his flesh again and again.

224 T.M JEFFERSON

He tried to struggle, to fight back against his attacker, but his limbs felt heavy and sluggish, his vision blurring at the edges as the life drained from his body. The last thing he saw before the darkness claimed him was a pair of cold, merciless eyes staring down at him from behind a black mask.

53

Miles away, Jade, David, and Detective Reynolds worked non-stop putting together the final pieces of their plan to bring down the Illuminated Order and stop their attack on the world's energy grid.

As they stared at the live feeds from the Order's key facilities around the globe, the moment of truth finally arrived. The Order's plan was set to be launched in less than 24 hours, and they were the only ones who could stop it.

"Okay, listen up," Reynolds said. "We've got three primary targets—the control hub in Zurich, the backup server farm in Hong Kong, and the power relay station in New York. We need to hit them all simultaneously, disrupt their systems and prevent the activation signal from going out."

"I'll take Zurich," Jade said. "I have contacts there, people who can help me get inside."

David's hand found hers, their fingers intertwining in a silent gesture of support and solidarity. "I'll take Hong Kong," he said. "I know the city, and I've got a few tricks up my sleeve that should get me past their security."

Reynolds took a deep breath. "That leaves New York to me. I've

226   T.M JEFFERSON

got a score to settle with the Order, and I'll be damned if I let them bring the city to its knees."

For a moment, the three of them stood in silence, the gravity of the moment settling over them. The odds were stacked against them. They were going up against an enemy with almost limitless resources and a ruthless determination to see their plan through to the end.

54

The cold rain fell in a mournful cadence as the attendees gathered beneath the gloomy clouds, black umbrellas shielding them from the damp weather. Senator Jonathan Bishop's funeral was a somber affair, his casket draped in the American flag, a symbol of the political legacy he left behind. Mourners whispered condolences, their faces full of grief, while a sea of dark suits and dresses surrounded the grave.

At the back of the crowd, in the darkness, the Junior Members of the Illuminated Order watched with detached expressions. Miss Victoria Sterling, her eyes hidden behind dark sunglasses, stood beside Mr. Jameson Shaw, who examined the proceedings with an emotionless stare. Their presence, while paying respects, held an undertone of cold calculation.

As the casket was lowered into the ground, Victoria whispered to Jameson, "Make sure he's gone. We can't afford any loose ends. His demise opens doors we hadn't anticipated," she said. "The vacuum of power needs to be filled, and we must ensure our interests are safeguarded."

Jameson nodded. "The time has come to solidify our hold on

power. The president must be made aware of our expectations. He's vulnerable. We have an opportunity to tighten our grip further."

Victoria looked down on the casket. "We'll ensure that the President dances to our tune. Senator Bishop's death is but a stepping stone to greater influence."

With grim determination, the Junior Members of the Illuminated Order formulated their plans, their voices devoid of emotion as they discussed the fate of the nation. In their world, sentimentality held no place– only cold-blooded ambition and ruthless determination to achieve their goals at any cost.

55

As Jade stepped onto the streets of Zurich, she was struck by the city's unique blend of old-world charm and modern sophistication. The air was crisp and clean, carrying with it the faint scent of fresh baked bread and rich, aromatic coffee from the nearby cafes.

The narrow, cobblestone streets of the Old Town wound their way through the beautifully preserved medieval buildings.

As she walked, Jade marveled at the city's impeccable cleanliness and order. The streets were spotless, the sidewalks lined with well-manicured trees and tended flower boxes. Even the trams that crisscrossed the city ran with a precision and efficiency that spoke to the Swiss reputation for punctuality and attention to detail.

But what captured Jade's imagination was the breathtaking beauty of Zurich's natural surroundings. The city sat along the shores of the crystal-clear Lake Zurich, its waters sparkling like diamonds in the sunlight. In the distance, the snow-capped peaks of the Swiss Alps loomed majestically, their jagged silhouettes etched against a sky of the purest blue.

Jade was drawn to the Bahnhofstrasse, Zurich's famed shopping boulevard. The street was lined with exclusive boutiques and high-end fashion houses, their window displays showcasing the latest in Swiss luxury and craftsmanship.

Jade eased her way through the crowds, her heart pounding in her chest and her eyes inspecting the faces around her for any sign of pursuit.

A black, luxury sedan skidded to a halt beside her, causing her to stop in her tracks and turn around, its tinted windows hiding the deadly intent of the men inside. Jade's instincts took over, her body moving on pure adrenaline as she dove for cover behind a parked truck, just as a hail of bullets ripped through the air.

She rolled to her feet, her eyes wide with fear. A quick glance at her surroundings revealed an alleyway to her left, a chance at escape she couldn't afford to pass up.

Jade sprinted into the darkness, her boots pounding against the cobblestones as she raced deeper into the twisting maze of back streets and hidden passages.

When she thought there was a chance at losing them, Elias Vale, the Order's notorious assassin stepped out of the darkness. His pale eyes shining with predatory menace as he circled Jade like a wolf sizing up its prey.

Vale exploded into motion. His blade became a silvery blur as he rained down a furious volley of slashes and thrusts. Jade parried and weaved, but the onslaught was relentless. A deep gash opened on her cheek, warm blood trickling down her neck.

She pivoted and retaliated with a side kick, but Vale was fast. He caught her leg and twisted it. The pop of Jade's knee gave way. Agony rushed through her body as she crashed to the ground, fending off Vale's stabbing attacks with weakening blocks.

His blade carved through her defenses, slicing across her ribs with precision. Jade screamed, her vision hazy from the onslaught of pain and blood loss. But she was the hunter now, and surrender wasn't an option.

She whipped her tactical baton from its holster and swung it. The tungsten steel shattered Vale's knife hand in a nauseating

THE ILLUMINATED ORDER   231

crunch of shattering bones. His scream was cut short as Jade followed through, the baton crushing his windpipe in a wet crunch.

Vale staggered, gargling, clawing at his ruined throat as Jade clambered to her feet. Bleeding and in pain, she launched herself at the wounded assassin, raining down blow after bone-pulverizing blow. She wouldn't stop, couldn't stop until he was obliterated.

Vale crashed to the ground– a shattered ruin of the once-formidable killer. Jade stood over his body, chest heaving, knuckles shredded and dripping with blood.

As his eyes dimmed and the life seeped out of him, Vale fixed Jade with one last haunting look. Something like regret flashed across his face before the light was forever extinguished.

Jade felt something deep within her psyche fracture, an innocence forever lost as she stared down at the man she executed. She wanted to feel vindicated, to feel like justice was served.

Instead, all she felt was a creeping hollowness spreading through her soul like a cobweb of cracks splintering outward from her core. She crossed a line from which there was no return, taken a life in the most violent fashion conceivable.

A car screeched to a halt behind her, the sound of doors slamming and angry voices shouting orders. She only had a few seconds, the Order's men would be on her again in moments.

She limped around a corner, searching the street ahead for any sign of an escape route. An old motorcycle leaned against a wall, the keys still dangling from the ignition.

Jade didn't hesitate, moving on pure instinct, she jumped on the bike and gunned the engine to life. The wheels spun on the wet pavement, the machine roaring beneath her as she peeled off down the street, weaving through traffic and pedestrians with reckless abandon.

Behind her, the sound of another engine revving to life, the screeching of tires on asphalt as the Order's car pulled out in pursuit. Bullets whizzed past Jade's head, shattering windows and sending shards of glass flying through the air like deadly rain.

She refused to let the fear take hold, refused to let the weight of the moment crush her spirit.

She gunned the engine, the bike jerking forward like a wild beast, the wind tearing at her hair, and the cold sting of the rain on her face as she pushed the bike to its limits, racing toward the control hub.

As the towering spire of the hub came into view on the horizon, the world exploded in a blaze of light and sound.

A rocket-propelled grenade slammed into the street behind her, the force of the explosion sending her flying off the bike, her body tumbling through the air like a rag doll. Jade hit the ground hard, breath rushing from her lungs in a single, agonizing gasp.

For a moment, the world spun around her, a dizzying kaleidoscope of shapes and colors. As the darkness closed in, and the pain threatened to consume her, she refused to give in, refused to let them win.

She pushed herself to her feet, her body screaming in pain with every inching movement. She could see the control hub ahead, a monolith of steel and glass.

Charging forward, Jade's gun blazed in her hand and her heart pounded with the unquenchable fire of a warrior born. She would make it to the hub, find a way to shut down the systems and stop their plan, no matter the cost.

The corridors of the power relay station was filled with the sound of gunfire and the crunch of broken glass. Detective Reynolds moved like a ghost, his senses heightened to a razor's edge as he fought to stay one step ahead of the Order's elite operatives.

They were everywhere, their black tactical gear blending in with the darkness as they closed in on him from all sides. But Reynolds was ready, his body coiled like a spring and his mind sharp with the clarity of purpose that only came in the heat of battle.

He ducked behind a shattered control panel as a hail of bullets tore through the air above his head. He scanned the room, taking in the positions of his enemies with a single, sweeping glance.

There were five of them, each one armed and trained in the deadliest arts of warfare.

Reynolds was no stranger to combat, his own skills honed by a lifetime of service in the name of justice. He would have to use every trick in his arsenal, every ounce of his strength and ingenuity, if he hoped to make it out of this alive.

He reached for his belt, his fingers closing around the grip of a

234   T.M.JEFFERSON

flash-bang grenade. He counted down the seconds in his head, his muscles tensing with anticipation.

Three ... two ... one ...

He threw himself out from behind cover, the grenade already arcing through the air as he rolled to his feet. The Order's operatives had no time to register the threat before the device detonated, a blinding flash of light and a bang filled the room.

Reynolds was moving before the smoke cleared, his gun barking in his hand as he charged forward. He could hear cries of pain and surprise from his enemies, the sound of bodies hitting the floor as he cut through their ranks like a scythe.

He was running out of time. Every second he spent locked in combat was another second the Order's plan moved closer to fruition. He had to find a way to sever the connection, to cut off the power that flowed through the relay station.

He spotted a bank of transformers at the far end of the room. *If I could overload the system, create a feedback loop, that would fry the circuitry and plunge the city into darkness.*

But before he could act on his plan, a man emerged from behind him, a blade flashing in the light. Reynolds spun, his reflexes taking over as he blocked the blow with the barrel of his gun.

The operative was fast, his movements a blur of speed as he pressed the attack. Reynolds fell back, trying to find an opening, a weakness that he could exploit.

He lunged forward, his gun falling to the floor as he tussled with his opponent hand-to-hand.

They crashed through a bank of computer terminals, sparks flying as they traded blows in a deadly dance of skill and strength. The blood pounded in Reynolds' ears, the adrenaline rushing through his veins like liquid fire.

He had to end this quick, had to find a way to gain the upper hand before it was too late.

He twisted his body, his elbow slamming into the operative's

THE ILLUMINATED ORDER   235

throat with a crunch. The man's eyes widened in pain, his hands scrabbling at his neck as he gasped for breath.

Reynolds didn't hesitate, his fist already connecting to the operative's temple in a blow that crumbled him to the ground like a puppet with its strings cut. He stood over the fallen warrior, his chest heaving with exertion and his mind racing with the knowledge of what he had to do.

He turned back to the transformers, searching the room for anything he could use to create the overload. In the corner, a jagged shard of metal lay amidst the wreckage of the control panels.

Reynolds snatched it up, his fingers tightening around the makeshift weapon as he charged towards the machinery. He could hear the shouts of alarm from the remaining operatives, the sound of their footsteps pounding towards him as they tried to stop him.

With a final, roar, he plunged the shard of metal into the heart of the transformer, the electricity racing through his body like a bolt of lightning.

The pain was indescribable, agony tearing through every nerve. His consciousness slipped away, his vision faded to black at the edges, he'd done it, he severed the connection and bought his friends the precious time they needed.

The last thing he saw before the darkness claimed him was the flicker of the lights overhead, the power dying in a final, shuddering gasp as the city plunged into shadow. He was falling, his body tumbling through the void as the world around him faded to nothingness.

57

David moved through the crowds of Hong Kong's Kowloon district, watching the faces around him for any sign of his pursuers.

He'd been on the run for hours, ever since his meeting with the Jade Dragon was interrupted by a squad of the Order's assassins. They came out of nowhere, their black-clad bodies materializing from the shadows, their weapons already drawn and ready for the kill.

David escaped with his life, his body battered and bleeding from the exchange of gunfire that left three of the assassins dead. It was only a matter of time before they caught up with him, before they closed in for the final blow.

As he ducked into a narrow alleyway, his heart was banging and he could barely catch his breath. Jade Dragon had given him the location of the Order's backup server farm, a heavily guarded facility hidden deep in the city.

If he could make it there, if he could find a way to infiltrate the building and shut down the servers, he might just be able to stop the Order's devastating attack on the world's energy grid. But the odds of making it out of the facility alive were slim to none, the

238   T.M JEFFERSON

Order's security measures were among the most ruthless and efficient in the world.

Footsteps from the far end of the alley caught his attention, the heavy tread of combat boots on concrete. David's heart jumped into his throat, his hand already reaching for the gun at his side as he spun to face the threat.

As he raised his weapon, he was too late. An assassin emerged from the shadows, dressed in tactical gear, his face obscured by a mask and his eyes cold and merciless.

David fired, the gun bucking in his hand as the bullet tore through the assassin's chest. But the man barely seemed to feel the impact, his body jerking as he continued to advance, his own weapon already leveled at David's heart.

David lunged forward, slamming into the assassin with the force of a freight train. They tumbled to the ground in a tangle of limbs and weapons, the concrete scraping against their skin as they struggled for control.

David fought with every ounce of his strength, he could feel the assassin's grip tightening around his throat, the cold steel of a knife pressing against his flesh. He only had seconds left, the Order's killer wouldn't hesitate to end his life in a single, brutal instant.

David closed his eyes, his mind filled with the image of Jade's face, the woman he loved more than life itself. He failed her, failed to stop the Illuminated Order's plan, and now he would pay the price for his failure.

As the darkness closed in, and the assassin's blade began to pierce his skin, David felt a sudden, blinding flash of light explode behind his eyes. The grip on his throat loosened, the weight of the assassin's body slumped against him.

Through the haze of pain and confusion, David saw someone standing over him, a slender, shadowed form with a shock of bright green hair. It was Mei, a member of the Jade Dragon, the young woman who helped him escape the first time.

"Get up," she said. "We don't have much time."

THE ILLUMINATED ORDER   239

David pushed himself to his feet, his body screaming in protest with every movement. Together, he and Mei raced through the side streets of Kowloon as they made their way towards the server farm.

They knew the Order's security would be on high alert, they would stop at nothing to prevent them from shutting down the system. But they had no choice, the fate of the world hung in the balance.

As they approached the fortified walls of the facility, David's mind raced. He had to find a way inside, locate the main server room and plant the explosives that would destroy the Order's backup data, preventing them from launching their attack.

"Cover me," he said. "I'm going in."

Mei nodded. "I got your back," she said, her fingers tightening around the grip of her gun. "Now go, before it's too late."

David took a deep breath. And then, with a final, silent prayer to whatever gods might be listening, he charged forward, his body moving with the grace and speed that belied the exhaustion and pain threatening to overwhelm him.

He made it inside the facility, focused on the task at hand as he navigated the twisting corridors and security checkpoints. The explosives were heavy in his pack, the detonator cold and hard in his hand as he finally reached the server room. He had seconds to act.

As he planted the charges, he felt the first, shuddering vibrations of the impending explosion, Something was wrong. The room was too quiet, the air too still, and the hair on the back of his neck prickled with the sense of an unseen presence.

He turned, his eyes widening in when he saw someone standing in the doorway, a tall, imposing man with a cruel, twisted smile on his face. It was one of the Order's top assassins, Sergei Darkov, a lethal and feared killer in their ranks.

"Did you really think it would be that easy?" Sergei said. "Did you really believe that you could stop us, that you could prevent the dawning of a new age?"

240   T.M JEFFERSON

David's hand tightened around the detonator, his thumb hovering over the trigger. "I don't care about your new age," he said. "I only care about stopping you, and saving the world."

Sergei laughed, a sound that sent chills down David's spine. "The world?" he asked. "The world is already ours, David. And now, it's time for you to pay the price for your interference."

He lunged forward, his blade shining in the light of the server room. David's finger tightened on the detonator, his mind filled with the image of Jade's face.

"Forgive me," he whispered. With a final cry, he triggered the explosives, his world erupting in a blaze of fire and light as the charges detonated, consuming the room and everything in it.

When the smoke cleared, and the dust settled over the ruins of the server farm, there was nothing left but ash, rubble, and the twisted remains of the Illuminated Order's backup system. And there, lying broken amidst the debris, was the body of David Montgomery, the man who gave his life to stop the Order's plan, to save the world from the darkness that threatened to engulf it.

He succeeded in striking a blow against the forces of evil that would be felt for generations to come. But the price was high, the cost too great to bear.

In the end, David had sacrificed everything. He gave his last breath and his final heartbeat in the name of love, in the name of the woman who was his guiding light, his reason for living.

58

The sun had long since set over the city, the streets outside Jade's apartment window were covered in a veil of darkness that mirrored her heart. She sat on the edge of her bed, her body numb and her mind spinning with the news that shattered her world into a million pieces.

David was gone. She knew the risks, understood the dangers they faced in their battle against the Order, but nothing could've prepared her for the reality of his loss, for the gaping wound that his absence left in her soul.

The tears came streaming down her cheeks in an unstoppable torrent of grief and rage. She clutched at her chest, her fingers twisting in the fabric of her shirt as if she could somehow hold herself together, could keep the pain from tearing her apart from the inside out.

Images flashed in her mind, memories of the time she spent with David, the love, laughter and passion they shared. She saw his face, his bright blue eyes and his crooked smile, the way he looked at her like she was the only thing in the world that mattered.

And then, she remembered the way he died. The thought of

him lying there, his body torn apart. It was too much for her to bear. She let out a keening wail of anguish that bellowed through the empty apartment like a ghost.

She failed him, let him down in the worst possible way. She should've been there, should've been by his side in those final, terrifying moments, should've done something, anything, to save him from the fate that claimed him.

For hours, she sat there, lost in her grief, her mind replaying the moments of their time together like a cruel, unending loop. She saw his smile, heard his laughter, felt the warmth of his touch on her skin, and each memory was like a knife to the heart, a fresh wound that bled, ached and refused to heal.

At some point, the tears ran dry, leaving her feeling hollow and drained, a fragment of the woman she'd once been. She stared at the wall, her eyes unfocused and her mind numb, trying to make sense of a world that seemed alien and incomprehensible.

Like a tiny ember flickering to life in the ashes of her grief, something else began to take hold, something fierce and unquenchable. It was anger, a rage that burned through her veins like liquid fire, consuming everything in its path until there was nothing left but a cold, hard core of determination.

She would make them pay, would hunt down every last member of the Illuminated Order and make them suffer for what they'd done. She would avenge David's death, and tear their twisted empire down brick by brick until there was nothing left but dust and ashes.

Like a woman in a dream, Jade rose from the bed, her movements stiff and mechanical as she crossed to the window and stared out at the city beyond. The world had changed, had become a darker, colder place than she ever imagined, but she wouldn't let that stop her, wouldn't let the shadows of despair and hopelessness claim her as they had claimed so many others.

Jade turned from the window, her eyes hard and her jaw set with determination.

The time for grief was over.
The time for vengeance had begun.

59

Jade stood at the center of the safe house, her eyes on the bank of monitors displaying the status of the Order's global network.

Around her, the members of Jade Dragon worked feverishly, their fingers flying across keyboards and their voices low and urgent as they coordinated their efforts to shut down the Order's systems. They'd done it, managed to infiltrate the heart of the beast and strike a blow against the forces that threatened to engulf the world.

A surge of triumph and a sense of victory swelled inside Jade's chest like a rising tide, but something was wrong. The pieces of the puzzle weren't fitting, loose ends were nagging at the back of her mind refusing to be tied up in a neat little bow.

There, on one of the monitors, was a face she recognized, a face that had been plastered across every newspaper and television screen in the world, a face that represented hope and compassion and all that was good in the world.

It was the face of Dr. Evelyn Soros, the billionaire philanthropist and global humanitarian who dedicated her life to fighting poverty and disease, to making the world a better place for all of humanity. She was a beloved figure, a symbol of kindness and generosity that inspired millions around the globe.

But there, on the screen, was a different image of Dr. Soros. She was dressed in the black robes of the Illuminated Order, her face twisted with a cold, malevolent smile as she oversaw the final stages of their plan. And in that moment, Jade knew the truth. She knew the terrible, shocking revelation that had been staring her in the face all along.

Dr. Evelyn Soros was the true mastermind behind the Illuminated Order, the puppet master who'd been pulling the strings from the shadows all along. Her philanthropic image, her facade of benevolence and compassion, had been nothing more than a mask, a lie designed to hide her true, nefarious intentions.

Jade felt as if the ground had been ripped out from under her feet, as if the very foundations of her world had been shattered into tiny pieces. She always looked up to Dr. Soros, always seen her as a shining example of what one person could do to make a difference in the world.

But now, as she stared at the screen, it was all a lie, constructed deception designed to fool the world into complacency while the Illuminated Order worked to bring about their vision of a new world order.

"No," Jade whispered. "It can't be true. It can't be her."

As the words left her lips, she knew it was. The evidence was right there in front of her, undeniable and irrefutable. Dr. Evelyn Soros, the woman who'd been hailed as a savior, a saint, a beacon of hope for all of humanity, was nothing more than a monster, a twisted, evil creature who'd been working to destroy everything Jade and her friends fought so hard to protect.

The room was spinning, the faces of Jade Dragon blurring into a cloud of shock and disbelief. They'd all been played, all been duped by the greatest con in the history of the world, a woman who used her wealth and influence to create a facade of goodness and

THE ILLUMINATED ORDER   247

light, all while working to plunge the planet into darkness and chaos.

"We have to stop her," Jade said. "We have to expose the truth, and show the world who Dr. Soros really is and what she's been planning all along."

60

President Adrian Blackwell strode into the appointed sitting room, his expression stern. This wouldn't be a typical briefing session with his counterparts in the Order's inner circle.

Victoria Sterling and Jameson Shaw were already waiting, twin portraits of menace. As Blackwell took his seat across from them, Shaw flicked open a briefcase, withdrawing a glossy dossier and sliding it across the polished table.

"I trust you've had a chance to review the contents, Mr. President?"He didn't bother waiting for a reply. "The intel paints a rather bleak portrait of our current circumstances. Project Zephyr's timeline has been derailed by the actions of Jade Rose and her cohorts."

"Not to mention the staggering financial and political capital we've hemorrhaged," Victoria cut in. "Our proxy assets, operatives we've cultivated for decades, all compromised in one fell swoop." She stared at Blackwell. "This debacle is unacceptable, Adrian. We're close to overexposure, and I have a pretty strong hunch where the leaks originated."

Blackwell shifted in his chair, a muscle twitching in his jaw. "If you're insinuating I had anything to do with this unraveling–"

"We're not insinuating anything," Jameson interjected. "We

250 T.M JEFFERSON

have countermeasures in place, redundancies to insulate us from these kinds of crises. You were the one who failed to leverage them at the appropriate junctures, Your Excellency."

Victoria reached into her handbag, and Blackwell tensed as she placed a matte black Glock on the table with a dull thud. "Did you think we achieved the Order's standing through half-measures and compromises, Adrian?" Her tone dripped with derision. "That we schemed and plotted for generations only to see our life's work unravel due to lack of intestinal fortitude?"

"Now you listen to me," Blackwell growled. "I'm still the President of the United States. Threaten me again, and every law enforcement agency will be busting through those doors within five minutes."

Jameson barked a humorless laugh as he produced an identical firearm, resting it beside Victoria's. "And tell them what exactly? That a secret sect you voluntarily joined plans to restructure human civilization? You underestimate how overwritten the Order's code is into the machine."

"We've reached the Rubicon, Adrian," Victoria said. "The window is closing, and we need the mettle to do what's required in these dire straits."

She traced the Glock's triggerguard. "You understand that one of us may need to take responsibility, to take the mantle of martyr. To be the sacrifice that rallies the Order's forces and slingshots us into the next vital phase."

Blackwell felt a bead of sweat trickle down his spine as the implications sank in. "You can't be fucking serious. Faking my public downfall, my assassination?" he shook his head slowly. "It'll never work. You'll never get close enough—"

Jameson silenced him by thumbing off the Glock's safety with an audible click. The room constricted in that moment, the air thickening with tension.

"Get close enough?" A cruel smile played across his lips. "Who said anything about getting close, Mr. President?"

THE ILLUMINATED ORDER   251

The weight of their words, their casual brandishing of lethal force all while plotting his undoing as some twisted impetus for the Order's agenda ... it was almost too much for Blackwell to process. How had he allowed himself to become so enmeshed in their chilling worldview?

Swallowing hard against the lump in his throat, he stared into Jameson's dead eyes. "If you're that eager to embrace martyrdom, you malignant bastard, by all means. But I won't resign myself so easily to your psychopathic schemes."

Outside, the first distant wail of approaching sirens drifted in from the street as Jameson's answering smile went feral.

61

Jade stood outside her mother's practice, her heart pounding and her palms slick with sweat. She always looked up to her mother, always seen her as a woman of integrity and compassion.

But as she stood on the threshold of the truth, she couldn't let go the feeling of dread that coiled in the pit of her stomach. She uncovered a secret that threatened to shatter everything she thought she knew about her family, about the woman who raised her and shaped her into the person she was today.

With a deep breath, Jade pushed open the door, stepping into the familiar surroundings of her mother's office.

Her mother sat behind the desk, her head bent over a stack of papers. She looked up as Jade entered.

"Jade," she said. "What brings you here so late?"

Jade swallowed. She rehearsed this moment in her head a thousand times, gone over every possible scenario and outcome. But now, standing face to face with the woman who'd been her rock, her guiding light, she found herself at a loss for words.

"Mom," she said. "There's something I need to talk to you about. Something important."

Her mother set down her pen, giving Jade her full attention.

"What is it, sweetheart? You know you can tell me anything."

Jade took a deep breath. "It's about Dr. Evelyn," she said. "I know the truth about her, about what she's been doing."

For a moment, her mother was silent. She rose from her chair, her movements stiff and mechanical.

"I see," she said. "And what exactly do you think you know, Jade?"

Jade felt a surge of anger rise inside of her, a prickling sensation that made her skin tight. "I know she's been working with the Illuminated Order," she said. "I know she's been using her position, her influence, to manipulate events and control people's lives. And I know she's not the only one."

Her mother's eyes flashed, a hint of something dark and dangerous was lurking. "Be careful what you say, Jade," she warned. "You don't know what you're talking about."

But Jade wasn't backing down, not this time.

"I know more than you think," she said. "I know about the Order's plans, about the role that Dr. Soros has been playing in all of this. And I know you've been involved too, you've been a part of this conspiracy from the beginning."

Her mother's face drained of color, her lips pressing together in a thin, hard line. For a moment, Jade thought she might deny it, might try to convince her she was mistaken, that there was some other explanation for what she uncovered.

But with a heavy sigh, her mother's shoulders slumped, her head bowing in defeat.

"You're right," she said. "I've been involved with the Order, been working with Dr. Soros and the others to shape the course of events."

"How could you?" she said. "How could you be a part of something so evil?"

"Jade, I need you to understand," her mother began, her voice trembling with emotion. "When I first met Dr. Soros, I was just a

THE ILLUMINATED ORDER   255

young woman with a dream. I wanted to make a difference in the world, to use my skills as a dentist to help people in need."

She paused, her eyes distant as she recalled those early days. "Dr. Soros took me under her wing, showed me the ropes of the industry. She was more than just a mentor – she was a friend, a confidante. She believed in me when no one else did, pushed me to be the best version of myself."

Jade reached out, taking her mother's hand in her own. She could see the tension in her mother's shoulders, the way her jaw clenched as she struggled to find the words.

"When she first introduced me to the Order, I was skeptical. But she made it sound so noble, so important. She told me that we were part of something bigger, that we had the power to shape the world for the better."

Her mother's eyes filled with tears, and she looked away, unable to meet Jade's gaze. "I believed her, Jade. I believed in the Order's mission, in the idea that we could use our influence to create positive change. I thought I was part of something special, something that could make a real difference."

She took a deep, shuddering breath, her voice breaking. "But I was wrong. I was so wrong. The Order wasn't what I thought it was. It wasn't about helping people or making the world a better place. It was about power, about control. And Dr. Soros ... she was at the center of it all."

Jade felt a lump forming in her throat, her heart aching for her mother. She couldn't imagine the betrayal she must have felt, the sense of shattered trust and broken dreams.

"I'm so sorry, Jade," her mother whispered, the tears now flowing freely down her cheeks. "I'm sorry for not seeing it sooner, for not being there for you when you needed me most. I was blind, so blind to the truth. And now ... now I don't know how to make it right."

Jade stood up, moving to her mother's side and wrapping her arms around her in a tight embrace. She could feel her mother's

256   T.M JEFFERSON

body shaking with sobs, the weight of her guilt and regret pouring out in a flood of emotion.

"It's okay, Mom," Jade murmured, her own voice thick with tears. "It's not your fault. You were manipulated, just like so many others. But we can make it right, together. We can expose the Order for what it really is, and we can hold Dr. Soros accountable for her actions."

Her mother pulled back, her eyes searching Jade's face. "You've always been so strong, Jade. So brave. I'm so proud of the woman you've become, of the truth you've fought so hard to uncover."

Jade smiled through her tears, her heart swelling with love and admiration for her mother. "I learned from the best, Mom. You taught me to never give up, to always fight for what's right. And that's exactly what we're going to do."

As Jade stared into her mother's eyes, she saw the depth of her pain and regret, she couldn't turn her back on that love, couldn't let the Order's lies and manipulations destroy the one thing that had always been true.

"We can fix this," she said. "We can make it right, bring the Order to justice and expose their crimes for all the world to see."

"You really think so?"

"I know so," she said. "We're stronger than they are, Mom. We have the truth on our side, and we have each other. And that's all we need to win this fight."

For a long moment, her mother was silent, her eyes searching Jade's face as if she was looking for some sign of doubt or hesitation. But Jade's eyes were clear and bright, her jaw set with a fierce determination.

"Okay," her mother said. "I'll help you. I'll do whatever it takes to make this right, to bring the Order to justice."

62

Detective Marcus Reynolds stood before the Chief of Police, his posture rigid and his jaw clenched tight. The chief sat behind his desk shuffling through some papers.

"Detective Reynolds," he said. "Your suspension has been lifted, effective immediately. The department has concluded its investigation into your conduct, and while there are still concerns about your ... unorthodox methods, it's been decided that your skills are too valuable to keep you on the sidelines any longer."

Reynolds nodded, his eyes never leaving the chief's face. "Thank you, sir," he said. "I appreciate the opportunity to return to duty."

"Don't mistake this for a clean slate, Detective. You're still on thin ice, and I'll be watching your every move. One step out of line, one hint of insubordination, and you'll be back on suspension faster than you can blink."

"I understand, sir. I won't let you down."

"And another thing, Reynolds. I know you've been obsessed with the Councilman Thornton murder case, but I'm warning you now– stay away from it. The case is closed, and I won't have you stirring up trouble where there is none."

258 T.M JEFFERSON

"Of course, sir. I understand completely."

The chief studied him for a moment, his eyes searching Reynolds' face for any hint of deception or ulterior motive. But Reynolds spent years perfecting his poker face, he learned to keep his true thoughts and feelings concealed behind a wall of stoic professionalism.

The chief leaned back in his chair, a heavy sigh escaping his lips. "Alright, Detective. You're dismissed. Report to your captain for your new assignment."

Reynolds nodded, his hand snapping up in a crisp salute. "Yes, sir. Thank you, sir."

63

The room was silent as Jade, her mother and Detective Reynolds sat across from Dr. Evelyn Soros.

Dr. Soros sat behind her desk, her face an unreadable mask as she regarded the group before her. "To what do I owe this unexpected visit?" she asked.

"We know everything, Dr. Soros," Reynolds said. "We know about your involvement with the Illuminated Order, and the crimes you've committed in their name."

"I'm afraid I don't know what you're talking about, Detective," she said. "I have no involvement with any criminal organization."

"We have evidence," Jade said. "Financial records, surveillance footage, eyewitness accounts. It all points to you, Dr. Soros. You've been working with the Order for years, manipulating events from behind the scenes."

Detective Reynolds placed a thick folder on Dr. Soros' desk. "This is just the tip of the iceberg," he said. "We have enough evidence to put you away for the rest of your life. And we're not just talking about you– we've made simultaneous arrests across the globe, taking down key members of the Illuminated Order."

Dr. Soros' face drained of color, her hands trembling as she reached for the folder. She flipped through the pages, scanning the evidence laid out before her.

"It's over, Evelyn," Jade's mother said.

Dr. Soros looked up, her eyes locking with Jade's mother in a contest of wills. For a second, the mask slipped– regret and sorrow washed across her face like the ghost of the woman they once admired.

But as quickly as it appeared, it was gone, replaced by a cold, hard resolve. "You have no idea what you've done," she said. "The Order is more powerful than you can possibly imagine. You think you've won, but you've only scratched the surface."

Detective Reynolds shook his head. "That's where you're wrong, Dr. Soros. We've been working on this for months, gathering evidence and building a case against the Order. And now, with the arrests of your associates, we've dealt a crippling blow to their operations."

"Do you know why we do what we do, Detective?" Dr. Soros asked. "Why we dedicate our lives to the Order, even in the face of so much opposition?"

Detective Reynolds remained silent, waiting for her to continue.

"It's because we understand the truth about the world," she said, facing them. "We know that power is the only thing that matters, the only currency that has any real value. And those who possess it have a responsibility to use it for the greater good."

"The greater good. And what exactly does that entail?"

Dr. Soros smiled. "It means creating a world where the strong rule over the weak, where the enlightened few guide the ignorant masses towards a brighter future. It means sacrificing the individual for the sake of the whole, and being willing to do whatever it takes to achieve our goals. There is no other way. The world is a harsh and unforgiving place, and only those with the strength and the will to do what must be done can hope to shape its future. If we falter, if we allow ourselves to be swayed by sentiment or morality, then all our sacrifices will have been for nothing."

THE ILLUMINATED ORDER   261

As if on cue, the door to Dr. Soros' office burst open, and a team of armed federal agents stormed the room. They surrounded Dr. Soros, their weapons trained on her as they read her her rights.

"You have the right to remain silent. Anything you say can and will be used against you in a court of law. You have the right to an attorney. If you cannot afford an attorney, one will be provided for you. Do you understand the rights I have just read to you?"

Jade watched as they led her away, a mix of emotions swirling inside of her. Relief, anger, betrayal, and a deep, overwhelming sadness at the loss of the woman she once admired and respected.

The light in the interrogation room shined down on Dr. Evelyn Soros as she sat still, her wrists shackled to the table in front of her. Her secrets, the burden of her choices, it all seemed to press down on her, threatening to crush her beneath their weight.

As the minutes ticked by, Dr. Soros' mind began to wander, drifting back to the early days of her involvement with the Illuminated Order. The first time she was invited to one of their meetings, the sense of awe and excitement that filled her as she stepped into a world of wealth and power beyond her wildest dreams.

Her fingers traced the outline of the small, gold owl that hung around her neck, a gift from the Order on the day of her initiation. It was a symbol of her dedication, her willingness to sacrifice everything for the sake of the cause.

She thought back to her childhood, to the dingy apartment where she grew up. Her parents were immigrants, struggling to make ends meet in a city that cared little for their dreams. But even then, Evelyn was destined for something more, the world was hers for the taking if only she had the courage to reach out and seize it.

She excelled in school, her brilliant mind and dedicated drive propelling her to the top of her class. But it was in the Order that

264   T.M JEFFERSON

she truly found her calling, a place where her ambition and ruthlessness could be honed into weapons of unimaginable power.

She rose quickly through the ranks, her intellect and deviousness making her a valuable asset to the cause. She made sacrifices along the way, cut ties with anyone who threatened to hold her back or stand in her way. But it was all worth it, she told herself, for the chance to shape the world in her own image.

As she sat in the cold interrogation room, Dr. Soros wondered if it was all a mistake. The Order's plans had been exposed, their crafted web of lies and deceit unraveling before the eyes of the world. And she, one of their masterminds, had been brought low, reduced to a common criminal in the eyes of the law.

The gold owl around her neck shined in the light, a reminder of the vows she took and the sacrifices she made. As the door to the interrogation room swung open, Dr. Soros smiled, a cold, ruthless expression that sent a chill through the bodies of all who saw it.

The game was far from over, and she still had one final card left to play.

65

Beaking News: Global Arrests Made in Connection to Secret Organization

In a stunning development that has sent shockwaves through the international community, law enforcement agencies across the globe have carried out a series of coordinated arrests targeting key members of a secret organization known as the Illuminated Order.

The arrests, which took place simultaneously in multiple countries, are the result of a months-long investigation into the Order's alleged criminal activities, including financial manipulation, political corruption, and conspiracy to subvert democratic institutions.

Among those taken into custody was Dr. Evelyn Soros, a renowned philanthropist and medical researcher who has been accused of using her position and influence to further the Order's agenda. Dr. Soros, who has long been a prominent figure in the global health community, has denied any wrongdoing and is expected to contest the charges against her.

Other high-profile arrestees include several prominent business leaders, politicians, and even members of the aristocracy, all of whom are alleged to have played key roles in the Order's operations.

According to a statement released by Interpol, the international law enforcement agency that coordinated the global operation, the Illuminated Order has been operating in the dark for decades, using its wealth and influence to shape world events and manipulate the course of history.

"This is a major victory in the fight against corruption and the abuse of power," said Interpol Secretary General Jürgen Stock. "The Illuminated Order has long been a source of concern for law enforcement agencies around the world, and today's arrests are a testament to the tireless work and dedication of the men and women who have been investigating this case."

The arrests have sent shockwaves through the global political and financial systems, with many wondering just how deep the Order's influence may have reached. Markets have reacted with volatility, and there are concerns about the potential economic fallout from the disruption of the Order's network of financial interests.

Governments around the world have also been quick to react, with many praising the coordinated law enforcement action and pledging their support for the ongoing investigation.

"The Illuminated Order represents a clear and present danger to the stability and integrity of our democratic institutions," said U.S. President Adrian Blackwell. "We stand in solidarity with our international partners in this fight against corruption and the abuse of power, and we will not rest until every member of this criminal organization is brought to justice."

As the dust settles on this unprecedented global operation, attention is now turning to the long and complex legal process that lies ahead. With so many high-profile individuals implicated in the case, and with the potential for further arrests and revelations in the coming days and weeks, it is clear that the fallout from the Illuminated Order investigation will be felt for years to come.

For now, however, the focus is on the brave men and women of law enforcement who have worked tirelessly to bring this organization to light. Their dedication and sacrifice have given hope to millions around the world who have long suspected that the levers of power were being manipulated by unseen forces.

THE ILLUMINATED ORDER   267

And while the road ahead may be long and difficult, there is a sense of optimism and determination in the air— a belief that, with truth and justice on their side, the forces of good will ultimately prevail.

This is Lila Matsumoto reporting for Global News Network. We will continue to bring you updates on this developing story as more information becomes available.

The United Nations Security Council chamber was in an uproar, the normally staid and composed diplomats and world leaders shouting over each other in a racket of anger, disbelief, and recrimination. On the large screen at the front of the room, the evidence of the Illuminated Order's misdeeds played out in damning detail, the scope and scale of their conspiracy laid bare for all to see.

"This is an outrage!" the American ambassador shouted, his face red with fury. "The Illuminated Order has been manipulating world events for decades, and we had no idea. How could this have happened?"

"It's clear that the Order has infiltrated governments and institutions at the highest levels," the British Prime Minister said. "We must take immediate action to root out their influence and bring those responsible to justice."

But not everyone in the room was so eager to condemn the Order. The Russian and Chinese ambassadors sat silent, their expressions inscrutable as they watched the chaos unfold around them.

"We must not be too hasty," the Chinese ambassador said. "The Illuminated Order has done much good in the world, and we cannot discount their contributions to global stability and progress."

The room erupted in angry shouts and accusations, the American and European leaders rounding on the Chinese ambassador with fury in their eyes.

"Good?" the German Chancellor spat. "You call manipulation, murder, and conspiracy good? The Order must be stopped, and anyone who stands in the way of justice will be held accountable."

In the days and weeks that followed, the world reacted to the revelations about the Illuminated Order with a mixture of shock, anger, and disbelief. Some countries, like the United States and many European nations, were quick to condemn the Order and pledge their support for bringing its members to justice. They launched investigations and issued arrest warrants, determined to root out the Order's influence from their governments and institutions.

But others, like Russia and China, were more circumspect. They acknowledged the Order's misdeeds but also pointed to the many ways in which the organization helped to maintain global stability and promote economic growth. Some even suggested the expose was nothing more than a Western propaganda campaign, designed to undermine their rivals and assert their own dominance on the world stage.

As the geopolitical fallout from the Order's exposure continued to unfold, Jade and her team would have to be more vigilant than ever. The Order was wounded, but not defeated, and they would stop at nothing to protect their interests and maintain their grip on power.

As she watched the world leaders argue and debate, Jade allowed herself a moment of satisfaction, a small smile tugging at the corners of her mouth. She struck a blow for truth and justice, shined a light into the darkness and exposed the Order's crimes for all to see.

67

In the heart of the Middle East, Amir Al Fayed sat in his opulent palace, his eyes glued to the television as the news of the Illuminated Order's conspiracy played out before him. For decades, he'd been one of the Order's most reliable allies, his regime propped up by their money and influence.

But as the truth about the Order's activities were exposed, a sinking sensation formulated in the pit of his stomach. It was only a matter of time before his own people turned against him, before the anger and resentment that was simmering beneath the surface for so long boiled over into open rebellion.

In the days that followed, his worst fears were realized. Protests erupted in the streets, angry mobs storming government buildings and clashing with security forces. The once-loyal military began to fracture, with some units joining the protesters and others fighting to maintain control.

As the destruction spread and the death toll mounted, Amir Al Fayed fled, his loyal bodyguards spiriting him out of the country in the dead of night. It was only a matter of time before the revolution consumed him, before the house of cards that the Order built came crashing down around him.

272   T.M JEFFERSON

* * *

JADE STOOD on the steps of the Capitol, watching as the sun set over the city. The weight of the past few months seemed to settle on her shoulders, a mixture of exhaustion and relief.

She thought back to all the moments of doubt, of fear, of wondering if she had the strength to see this through. But in the end, it was the strength of her convictions, the belief in the power of truth, that carried her forward.

The road ahead wouldn't be easy. The Illuminated Order may have been exposed, but the work of healing, of rebuilding trust and faith in the institutions they corrupted, was only just beginning.

As she stood there, bathed in the golden light of the fading day, Jade felt a sense of hope, of possibility. She'd seen the worst of what humanity was capable of, but she'd also seen the best– the courage, the resilience, the commitment to justice and truth.

And with that knowledge, that deep and abiding faith in the human spirit, no matter what challenges lay ahead, Jade would keep fighting. For the truth, for justice, and for the belief that, in the end, the light would always triumph over the darkness.

68

The courtroom was packed as the bailiff called the room to order. At the defendant's table, Dr. Evelyn Soros sat still, staring straight ahead. Beside her, a team of high-powered attorneys shuffled papers and conferred in hushed tones.

As the judge took her seat, the lead prosecutor, a sharp-eyed woman named Nadia Khalifa, rose to her feet. She approached the jury box, her eyes sweeping over the twelve men and women who held Dr. Soros' fate in their hands.

"Ladies and gentlemen of the jury," she began, her voice ringing out clear and strong in the silent courtroom. "We are here today to seek justice, to hold accountable those who have abused their power and influence to manipulate the course of history."

She paused, letting her words take effect before continuing. "The defendant, Dr. Evelyn Soros, stands accused of numerous crimes, all committed in service to a secret organization known as the Illuminated Order. For decades, this group has operated in the shadows, pulling the strings of governments and corporations alike, all in the name of their agenda."

As Khalifa spoke, images began to appear on the screens positioned around the courtroom. Grainy surveillance photos, bank statements, and email exchanges, all painting a damning picture of Dr. Soros' involvement with the Order.

"Through her position as a respected philanthropist and medical researcher, Dr. Soros has used her influence to further the Order's goals, funneling money and resources to their various front organizations and shell companies. She has manipulated public opinion, silenced critics, and even resorted to violence and intimidation to protect the Order's interests."

The prosecutor's voice grew more impassioned as she continued, her eyes blazing with a righteous fury. "But perhaps most disturbingly, we have evidence that Dr. Soros and the Illuminated Order have been involved in a global conspiracy to subvert democratic institutions and undermine the very foundations of our society. They have rigged elections, orchestrated financial crises, and even gone so far as to plan the overthrow of legitimate governments, all in the name of their own vision for the future."

As Khalifa laid out the case against Dr. Soros, the jury listened, their expressions ranging from shock to disgust. In the gallery, Jade and her mother sat side by side.

For Jade, the betrayal of her former mentor cut deep, a wound that would take years to heal. But as she struggled with the emotional fallout of Dr. Soros' actions, she had no choice but to see this through, to ensure that justice was served and the truth was brought to light.

As the prosecutor wrapped up her opening statement, the courtroom seemed to hold its breath, the weight of the moment was heavy on all those present. And yet, even in the face of such overwhelming evidence, Dr. Soros remained impassive, her eyes fixed on some distant point beyond the walls of the courtroom.

It was a chilling reminder of the depths of her delusion, the belief in her own righteousness that led her down this dark path. And as the trial began, it would take every ounce of Jade's strength and determination to see this fight through to the end, to ensure the Illuminated Order's reign of terror was brought to a final, decisive close.

69

As the trial progressed, the prosecution called forth a series of witnesses, each one painting a damning picture of Dr. Soros and the Order's crimes. But it was the testimony of those closest to the defendant that captivated the courtroom, their words ringing out with a raw, unbridled emotion that could not be ignored.

First to take the stand was Detective Marcus Reynolds, his face lined with the weight of sleepless nights spent chasing down leads and piecing together the puzzle of the Order's deceit. As he spoke, his voice was low and steady, each word chosen to convey the depth of his conviction.

"In all my years on the force, I've never seen anything like this," he said, his eyes fixed on the jury. "The scale of the Illuminated Order's crimes is staggering, the depths of their corruption is beyond anything I could've imagined. And at the center of it all, pulling the strings, was Dr. Evelyn Soros."

He went on to detail the evidence he uncovered, the paper trail of money and influence that led straight to the defendant's door. But it was the toll the investigation had taken on him personally that drove home the impact of Dr. Soros' betrayal.

"I've lost friends and colleagues to this case," he said. "Good people, people who dedicated their lives to serving and protecting, only to be cut down by the Order's assassins. And for what? For the sake of some dream of power and control?"

As Reynolds stepped down from the stand, the courtroom was silent, the weight of his words hanging in the air. But it was the testimony of Jade and her mother that brought the human cost of Dr. Soros' crimes into sharp focus.

Jade took the stand, her eyes red-rimmed and her hands trembling as she recounted the moment she learned of her mentor's true nature. "I trusted her," she said. "I looked up to her, wanted to be just like her. And all the while, she was using me, manipulating me to further the Order's agenda."

She spoke of the countless hours she spent with Dr. Soros, the long conversations about medicine and politics, about the power of knowledge to change the world. And she spoke of the bitter realization that it had all been a lie, designed to conceal the rot beneath the surface.

"She was like a second mother to me," Jade said. "And now, knowing what she's done, the lives she's destroyed ... it's like a part of me has died along with that trust."

Jade's mother took the stand. She was a woman of quiet strength, her face showed lines of a life spent in service to others. But as she spoke of Dr. Soros' betrayal, her voice trembled with a raw, unfettered anger.

"I took an oath to do no harm," she said. "To use my skills and knowledge to heal, to make the world a better place. And to find out that someone I trusted, someone I admired, took those same ideals to serve their own selfish ends ... it's a violation of everything I stand for."

She went on to detail the ways in which Dr. Soros used her influence to manipulate the medical community, to suppress research that threatened the Order's interests and promote treatments that lined their pockets. And she spoke of the lives that were

THE ILLUMINATED ORDER   279

lost as a result, the patients who suffered and died because of the Order's greed and hubris.

As she stepped down from the stand, the courtroom was silent. It was clear to all those present the true cost of the Illuminated Order's crimes could never be measured in dollars or cents, but in the shattered lives and broken dreams of all those they touched.

For Jade and her mother, the wounds inflicted by Dr. Soros' betrayal would take a lifetime to heal. But as they looked to the jury, to the twelve men and women who held the power to bring the Order to justice, they had no choice but to keep fighting.

70

As the prosecution rested its case, the defense team for Dr. Evelyn Soros wasted no time in launching their counterattack. Led by the renowned trial attorney, Kai Donovan, they began to systematically pick apart the testimony of each witness, seeking to cast doubt on their credibility and motives.

Kai was a master of his craft, his sharp intellect and even sharper tongue honed by decades in the courtroom. As he rose to begin his cross-examination of Detective Reynolds, his eyes shined with the intensity of a predator, like a shark circling its prey.

"Detective Reynolds," he began. "You've painted quite the picture of my client as some sort of criminal mastermind, pulling the strings of a vast conspiracy. But isn't it true that your investigation into the Illuminated Order was deeply personal, motivated by your own vendetta against the defendant?"

Reynolds bristled at the accusation, his jaw clenching. "My investigation was motivated by a desire for justice," he said. "To bring to light the crimes committed by Dr. Soros and her associates, and to hold them accountable for their actions."

Donovan smiled. "Ah yes, justice," he said. "The same justice that led you to pursue this case with a single-minded obsession, to

282   T.M JEFFERSON

the exclusion of all else? The same justice that blinded you to any evidence that might contradict your pre-conceived notions of my client's guilt?"

Reynolds struggled to respond, and Donovan pressed his advantage, his voice rising with each question. "Isn't it true, Detective, that you have a history of misconduct, of cutting corners and bending the rules in pursuit of your own agenda? And isn't it possible that your actions in this case were driven not by a desire for truth, but by a need to satisfy your own ego and ambition?"

The detective's face flushed with anger, his fists clenching at his sides as he fought to maintain his composure. But as he opened his mouth to respond, it was clear that Donovan's words hit their mark, sowing seeds of doubt in the minds of the jury.

And so it went, with each witness called to the stand.

Jade found herself subjected to a brutal line of questioning about her own motives, her past relationship with Dr. Soros picked apart and twisted to paint her as a spurned protégé, driven by jealousy and resentment.

Her mother, too. Her medical expertise called into question and her personal life dragged through the mud. Donovan seized on every inconsistency, every moment of hesitation, seeking to undermine their credibility and cast doubt on the mountain of evidence against his client.

Through it all, Dr. Soros sat impassive, her face, a mask as she watched the proceedings with a detached, almost clinical interest. It was as if she were observing the trial from a distance, a spectator to her own fate.

As the day wore on, the tension in the courtroom grew. The jury, once so certain in their convictions, now seemed to waver, their expressions showing doubt.

For Jade and her allies, it was a bitter pill to swallow, a reminder of the uphill battle they faced in bringing the Order to justice. They'd always known Dr. Soros and her team would fight tooth and nail to avoid accountability, but to see it play out in real-time, to feel the ground shifting beneath their feet with each carefully crafted lie and half-truth ...

It was a sobering reminder of the power and influence wielded by their adversary, a testament to the depths of corruption and deceit that ran through the heart of their society.

As the trial wore on, Jade found herself caught in a maelstrom of conflicting emotions, her heart torn between the pursuit of justice and the painful betrayal of her former mentor. With each passing day, the weight of Dr. Soros' actions seemed to press on her, a suffocating burden that threatened to crush her beneath its weight.

In the quiet moments between testimonies and cross-examinations, Jade's mind would drift, replaying the countless hours she spent with Dr. Soros, the long conversations and shared laughter that once filled her with such warmth and inspiration. She could still vividly recall the way her heart swelled with pride every time Dr. Soros praised her work or shared her latest findings with her.

In those moments, Jade was part of something greater, her own aspirations and goals intertwined with the groundbreaking work they were doing together. She would hang on Dr. Soros' every word, her eyes wide with wonder as she absorbed the older woman's wisdom and experience.

Under Dr. Soros' guidance, Jade felt a sense of purpose and direction that previously eluded her. The path ahead seemed clear and full of promise, each day bringing new challenges and opportunities to learn and grow.

She began to see herself through Dr. Soros' eyes, as a rising star in the field with limitless potential. The older woman's confidence in her abilities was intoxicating, and Jade pushed herself harder than ever before, determined to live up to the faith that had been placed in her.

Those early days were a turning point in her life, a time when she discovered not just her passion for the work, but also the strength and resilience that would carry her through the trials to come. Dr. Soros had given her a gift beyond measure, and now, amidst the pain and betrayal, Jade clung to those memories as a reminder of the person she'd once been, and the person she still hoped to become.

But as she sat in the courtroom, watching the woman she once admired unveil her true nature, those memories turned bitter and sour, tainted by the knowledge of all that was lost.

Jade's mother, seated beside her, could sense her daughter's turmoil, the way her hands trembled and her eyes grew distant and unfocused. In the brief recesses between court sessions, she would take Jade aside, her voice low and soothing as she tried to offer comfort and support.

"I know how much she meant to you," she said, her hand resting gently on Jade's shoulder. "And I know how much it hurts to see her like this, to realize that the person you thought you knew was nothing more than a lie."

Jade nodded, her throat tight with emotion as she struggled to find the words. "I just ... I don't know how to reconcile it all," she said. "The Dr. Soros I knew, the one who inspired me and believed in me ... how could she be the same person who did all those terrible things? How could I have been so blind, so naive?"

Her mother's eyes softened. "You weren't blind, Jade," she said. "You saw the good in her, the potential for greatness. That's not a weakness, it's a strength. It's what makes you who you are, what drives you to fight for what's right."

Jade's eyes filled with tears, the knot in her chest tightening.

"But what if I was wrong?" she asked. "What if I put my faith in the wrong person, trusted the wrong cause? What if everything I've done, everything I've fought for, has been for nothing?"

Her mother pulled her close, wrapping her in a fierce, protective embrace. "Listen to me," she said. "You are not defined by the actions of others, by the choices they make or the paths they choose to follow. You are defined by your own heart, your own conscience, your own sense of what is right and what is wrong."

She pulled back, her hands framing Jade's face as she looked deep into her daughter's eyes. "And I know that your heart is true, that your cause is just. You've faced challenges and setbacks that would've broken a lesser person, but you've never wavered, never lost sight of what truly matters."

A warm glow blossomed in Jade's chest, hope and strength cut through the darkness of her doubt. Her mother was right, the betrayal of Dr. Soros didn't diminish the importance of their fight, the righteousness of their cause.

But the pain lingered, throbbing in the depths of her heart. It would take time to heal, to come to terms with the loss of the mentor she once held so dear. But she couldn't let that pain consume her, couldn't let it cloud her judgment or dull her resolve.

As she returned to the courtroom, her head held high and her eyes clear and focused, Jade made a vow to herself, a promise that she would see this fight through to the end, no matter the cost.

As Dr. Evelyn Soros took the stand, silence fell over the courtroom. All eyes were on the woman at the center of the storm, the woman who'd once been hailed as a visionary and a philanthropist, but who now stood accused of the most heinous of crimes.

For Jade, the moment was almost surreal, a strange and jarring disconnect between the mentor she'd once known and the cold, inscrutable stranger who now sat before her.

As Dr. Soros began to speak, her voice was calm and measured, her demeanor one of quiet confidence and self-assurance. "I know that many of you have come here today seeking answers," she said, her eyes sweeping over the crowd. "Seeking to understand the truth behind the accusations that have been leveled against me, and against the organization to which I have dedicated my life."

She paused, letting her words hang in the air for a moment before continuing. "But the truth, as is so often the case, is far more complex than any simple narrative could ever capture. It's a web of interwoven strands, a tapestry of light and shadow that defies easy categorization or understanding."

Jade's stomach churned. She sensed Dr. Soros was building towards something, some revelation that would upend everything she thought she knew. Beside her, Detective Reynolds leaned forward in concentration as he tried to anticipate the woman's next move.

"The Illuminated Order is not what you think it is," Dr. Soros said. "It's not some sinister cabal, some shadowy conspiracy bent on world domination. It's a force for good, a beacon of hope and progress in a world all too often consumed by darkness and chaos."

She looked at Jade, her eyes burning into the younger woman's with an intensity that was almost hypnotic. "Jade, my dear, you of all people should understand this. You've seen firsthand the work we do, the lives we've touched and the futures we've shaped. You know our cause is just, that our mission is one of the utmost importance."

Jade's heart skipped a beat, a swell of confusion and uncertainty rose inside of her. She thought she knew Dr. Soros, thought she understood the depths of her mentor's betrayal. But now, faced with the woman's impassioned words and the strange, unsettling conviction in her eyes, she found herself doubting everything she once believed.

"But ..." Jade began. "But what about the evidence? The money trails, the covert operations, the lives lost and destroyed in pursuit of your goals? How can you justify that, how can you possibly claim to be a force for good?"

Dr. Soros smiled. "Oh, my dear girl," she said. "You still have so much to learn, so much to understand about the way the world works. The sacrifices we've made, the difficult choices we've been forced to undertake ... they're all in service of a higher purpose, a greater good that transcends the petty concerns of any one individual."

She leaned forward, her eyes gleaming with a fervor that was almost fanatical. "The Illuminated Order is not some simple organization. It's an idea, a vision of a world remade in the image of progress and enlightenment. And sometimes, in pursuit of that vision, hard decisions must be made, and prices must be paid."

Jade felt a surge of anger settle over her. "And who gets to make those decisions?" she asked. "Who gets to play God, to decide who lives and who dies in service of your grand vision?"

Dr. Soros' smile only widened, a look of almost maternal pride crossing her face. "Why, we do, of course," she said. "The chosen few, the enlightened ones who have been gifted with the knowledge and the will to shape the course of human history. And you, Jade, could be one of us, if only you could find the courage to embrace your true potential."

Jade recoiled as if she had been slapped. To think her mentor, the woman she once loved and admired above all others, could be so callous, so utterly devoid of empathy or compassion ...

It was almost too much to bear, a betrayal that cut deeper than any knife ever could.

As the courtroom erupted into chaos, as the lawyers and the spectators began to shout and argue and demand answers, Jade found herself strangely calm, a quiet, unshakable resolve settling over her like a mantle.

She knew now, with a clarity that was almost blinding, that Dr. Soros was lost, that the woman she once knew was nothing more than a front, a disguise concealing a heart of pure, unadulterated evil.

The courtroom was a commotion, the disclosure of Dr. Soros' true nature sent tremors through the crowd. Jade sat in silence, her mind swirling with the ramifications of her former mentor's words, the depth of her deceit was a wound that cut straight to the bone.

Stillness fell over the atmosphere, a clear shift in the air that drew all eyes to the back of the courtroom. There, standing tall and proud in the doorway, was a woman Jade never expected to see again, a ghost from her past she thought was lost forever.

It was Dr. Sophia Ramirez, the brilliant researcher and former ally who disappeared without a trace months before, vanishing into the shadows of the Order's expansive and deadly network.

As she strode down the aisle, Jade felt a burst of emotions wash over her– shock, confusion, and hope that perhaps, against all odds, they'd found an unexpected ally in their darkest hour.

Dr. Ramirez took the stand. She took a deep breath, her hands trembling as she gripped the edges of the witness box.

The prosecutor approached, her voice calm and measured as she began her questioning. "Dr. Ramirez, can you please tell the court about your involvement with the organization known as the Illuminated Order?"

Dr. Ramirez took a deep breath. "My family has been involved with the Order for generations," she said. "It was a legacy passed down from parent to child, a sacred duty that we were honor-bound to fulfill."

She paused, her eyes distant as she lost herself in the memories. "I was initiated into the Order at a young age, groomed to take my place among the ranks of the elite. It was a world of secrets and shadows, of power and influence wielded behind closed doors."

The prosecutor nodded. "And what was the nature of this power and influence, Dr. Ramirez? What exactly did the Order seek to achieve?"

"Control," she said. "The Order sought to shape the course of human history, to bend the will of nations to their own agenda. They infiltrated governments and corporations, pulling the strings from behind the scenes like puppeteers."

"And what role did you play in this conspiracy, Dr. Ramirez? Were you a willing participant, or were you coerced into coopretation?"

"I believed in the Order's mission," she said. "I know many of you have questions. Questions about where I've been these past months, and why I've chosen this moment to come forward and speak the truth."

She paused, her eyes sweeping over the crowd before coming to rest on Dr. Soros, who sat stone-faced and impassive in the defendant's chair.

"The truth is," Dr. Ramirez continued, "that I've been living a lie, a deception that has eaten away at my soul and haunted my every waking moment. I've been a member of the Illuminated Order, and a willing participant in their twisted schemes."

A gasp rippled through the courtroom, shock and disbelief seemed to shake the building. Jade leaned forward in her seat, her heart throbbing in her chest as she tried to process the enormity of what she was hearing.

"But I cannot remain silent any longer," Dr. Ramirez said. "I cannot stand by and watch as the Order continues to sow havoc and destruction, to manipulate and control the lives of innocent people in pursuit of their own selfish ends."

She fixed Dr. Soros with a penetrating stare, her eyes blazing with anger. "Evelyn, you've been my mentor, my friend, and my confidante for years. But now, I see you for what you truly are– a monster, a corrupt creature who'll stop at nothing to achieve your goals."

Dr. Soros' face remained impassive, but Jade could see the rage and betrayal dancing behind her eyes, the coiled tension in her body that spoke of a fury barely held in check.

"I have evidence," Dr. Ramirez continued. "Documents, recordings, and firsthand accounts that'll expose the true nature of the Illuminated Order, and the depths of perversity to which they've sunk in their quest for power."

She reached into her pocket, and withdrew a small flash drive. "On this device is everything you need to know, everything you need to bring the Order to its knees and hold them accountable for their crimes."

Excitement and anticipation ripped through the courtroom. A surge of hope and vindication washed over Jade, she couldn't shake the sense of unease that churned in the pit of her stomach.

She knew, with a certainty that chilled her to the bone, that the Illuminated Order wouldn't take this betrayal lightly, they would stop at nothing to silence Dr. Ramirez and anyone else who dared to stand against them.

The moment Dr. Sophia Ramirez stepped down from the witness stand, the courtroom erupted into a frenzy, a chaotic swirl of shouted questions and flashing cameras threatened to drown out all rational thought. Reporters from every major news outlet in the country surged forward, their microphones and recorders thrusting towards the startled faces of the key players in the trial.

"Dr. Ramirez!" one reporter shouted, his voice straining to be heard above the rest. "Can you comment on the allegations you've made against Dr. Soros and the Illuminated Order? What made you come forward after all this time?"

Dr. Ramirez hesitated, her eyes moving nervously from one eager face to the next. She knew her testimony would be explosive, that it would draw the attention of the world's media. But nothing could've prepared her for the sheer intensity of the scrutiny, the weight of a thousand eyes and lenses all fixed on her with unrelenting focus.

"I ... I did what I had to do," she stammered. "The truth had to be told, no matter the cost. I couldn't live with myself any longer, knowing what I knew and remaining silent."

Another reporter, a woman with sharp eyes and a sharper

tongue, pushed her way to the front of the pack. "And what about your own safety, Dr. Ramirez? Aren't you concerned about retaliation from the Order, now that you've betrayed their trust and exposed their secrets?"

Dr. Ramirez's face paled. "Of course I'm concerned," she said. "I know the risks, the danger I've put myself and my loved ones in by coming forward. But some things are more important than personal safety, more important than any one life. The truth is one of those things."

As the reporters continued to swarm around Dr. Ramirez, their questions grew more insistent and invasive. Jade seen firsthand the toll this trial had taken on her former friend and ally, the sleepless nights and haunted eyes that spoke of a burden almost too heavy to bear.

Watching as the media vultures circled, picking at the bones of Dr. Ramirez's trauma and sacrifice, Jade's rage bubbled inside of her, a fury that threatened to consume her from the inside out.

She pushed her way through the crowd, her elbows jabbing into ribs and her feet trampling on expensive leather shoes. "Enough!" she shouted, her voice cutting through the babble like a knife through butter. "Can't you see what you're doing to her? She's risked everything to be here, to tell the truth and bring the Order to justice. And all you can think about is getting your sound bites and your headlines."

The reporters fell silent, their faces flushing with a mix of shame and indignation. For a moment, the only sound in the courtroom was the soft whir of the cameras and the ragged breathing of Dr. Ramirez, who clung to Jade's arm like a drowning woman to a life raft.

But the reprieve was short-lived. Like a pack of hungry wolves, the reporters soon regrouped, their questions growing more pointed and aggressive as they sensed the opportunity for a juicy scoop slipping away.

"Miss Rose!" one of them called out. "As the former protégé of

THE ILLUMINATED ORDER   299

Dr. Soros, how do you feel about the revelations that have come to light during this trial? Do you feel betrayed by your mentor, or do you still believe in the work of the Illuminated Order?"

Jade's jaw clenched, her eyes narrowing to slits as she turned to face the reporter. "How do I feel?" she said. "I feel like I've been living a lie, like everything I ever believed in was nothing more than a facade, a mask concealing a rotten, corrupted core."

She took a step forward, her eyes sweeping over the assembled reporters with a force that seemed to physically push them back. "But I also feel more determined than ever to see this through, to make sure the truth comes out and justice is served. The Illuminated Order may have fooled me once, but they won't fool me again. And they won't fool the world, either. Not if I have anything to say about it."

There was a moment of silence, a shift in the air as the reporters absorbed the raw, unadulterated passion in Jade's words. And then, like a dam bursting, the questions began to fly once more.

"Do you believe the evidence she provided will be enough to bring down the Illuminated Order?"

"What do you say to those who claim this trial is nothing more than a witch hunt, a politically motivated attack on one of the world's most respected humanitarians?"

Jade gritted her teeth, her jaw clenched tight as she pushed her way through the throng of reporters, her eyes fixed straight ahead. Any misstep, any unguarded moment or carelessly chosen word, could be twisted and manipulated by those who sought to discredit their cause, to paint them as nothing more than conspiracy theorists and troublemakers.

She came too far, sacrificed too much, to let the opinions of others sway her from her course. So, she stepped up to the podium, the sea of microphones and cameras converging on her like a pack of hungry wolves. Jade took a deep breath, her voice ringing out clear and strong across the courthouse steps.

"Today, we have taken a momentous step forward in the fight

for truth and justice," she said, her eyes blazing with conviction. "With the testimony of Dr. Sophia Ramirez, we've exposed the true nature of the Illuminated Order, and the depths of corruption and deceit that have allowed them to operate in the shadows for far too long."

She let her words sink in for a moment before continuing. "But this is only the beginning. The road ahead will be long and hard, and there will be those who seek to discredit and undermine our efforts at every turn. But we will not be silenced, we will not be cowed by fear or intimidation."

Jade looked over the crowd, taking in the sea of faces that stretched out before her, the reporters and the onlookers, the supporters and the skeptics alike. "We're fighting for the very soul of our nation," she said, her voice rising with each word. "For the right to live in a world where the truth is not a commodity to be bought and sold, where justice is not a game to be played by the wealthy and the powerful."

She raised her fist in the air, a gesture of defiance and determination that sent a surge of energy through the crowd. "And we will not rest until that world is a reality, until the shadows of the Illuminated Order are banished from the earth, and the light of truth shines forth for all to see."

The crowd erupted in a roar of approval, and the energy and purpose washed over her, a sense of clarity and focus cut through the noise and the chaos. Jade knew with a certainty they would prevail, the truth would win out in the end, no matter the cost.

The media frenzy would continue, the pundits and the talking heads would spin their webs of speculation and innuendo. But Jade and her allies remained focused on the horizon, their hearts filled with the conviction that they were on the right side of history.

75

Jade sat at the edge of her seat as the closing arguments began, each side presenting their case with a fervor and passion that belied the exhaustion and strain of the long trial.

The prosecutor painted a convicting picture of Dr. Soros and the Illuminated Order, her words dripping with righteous indignation as she recounted the litany of crimes and abuses that had been laid bare over the course of the proceedings.

"Ladies and gentlemen of the jury," she said, her eyes sweeping over the faces of the twelve men and women who held the fate of the accused in their hands. "Over the past several months, you've heard testimony from a wide range of witnesses, each one shedding light on the dark and twisted ways of the Illuminated Order and its leadership."

She paused, letting the weight of her words sink in. "You have heard from victims and whistleblowers, from experts and insiders, all painting a picture of an organization that has operated in the dark for far too long, manipulating world events and sowing chaos and destruction in the name of their own agenda."

The prosecutor's voice rose, her finger jabbing towards the defendant's table where Dr. Soros sat. "And at the center of it all, pulling the strings like a puppeteer, sits the woman before you today. Dr. Evelyn Soros, a woman who has used her position of power and influence to commit unspeakable acts, all while presenting a façade of benevolence and philanthropy to the world."

As the prosecutor laid out the case against Dr. Soros in detail, Jade felt hope and vindication stirring in her heart. After all the trials and tribulations, all the sacrifices and losses they endured, it seemed justice might finally be within reach, that the truth might at last prevail over the forces of evil and deceit.

As the closing arguments reached their crescendo, the feeling that something wasn't right gnawed at Jade's stomach. And as the defense rose to deliver their own closing statement, that feeling only grew stronger, a sense of dread that seemed to permeate the very air of the courtroom.

The defense attorney, a slick and polished man with a shark's smile, wasted no time in launching into his own version of events, painting Dr. Soros as a victim of a conspiracy, a woman who'd been unfairly targeted and maligned by those who sought to bring down the Illuminated Order and its noble mission.

"My client has been the subject of a witch hunt," he said, his voice dripping with scorn and derision. "A politically motivated attack orchestrated by those who fear the truth, who seek to silence anyone who dares to challenge the status quo and fight for a better world."

He gestured towards Jade and her allies. "These so-called 'whistleblowers' and 'witnesses' are nothing more than pawns in a larger game, manipulated and coerced into providing false testimony in order to further their own agendas and bring down a woman who has dedicated her life to serving others."

As the defense attorney continued his tirade, a sinking sensation tickled Jade's gut, a growing realization that the tide might be turning against them. The jury, once so focused and attentive, now seemed to distant, their expressions clouded with doubt and uncertainty.

THE ILLUMINATED ORDER 303

After what seemed like an eternity of waiting and deliberation, the verdict was read, the words ringing out like a thunderclap in the stillness of the courtroom.

"Not guilty!"

Jade felt as if the floor had dropped out from beneath her, shock and disbelief covering her like a tidal wave. She'd been so sure, so convinced the evidence they presented would be enough, that the truth would win out in the end.

But as she watched Dr. Soros rise from her seat, a triumphant smirk playing across her lips, Jade realized they had been outmaneuvered, that the Illuminated Order's reach and influence extended far beyond what any of them had ever imagined.

The implications of the verdict were staggering, the ripple effects would be felt across the world as the news spread like wildfire. The Illuminated Order won, emerged victorious from the crucible of the trial, and now there would be no stopping them, no force on earth could stand against their agenda.

A crushing sense of despair washed over Jade, a feeling of hopelessness and futility threatened to overwhelm her entirely. But even in the depths of her despair, she couldn't give up, the fight was far from over.

76

The early morning light filtered through the curtains of Dr. Sophia Ramirez's bedroom. The air was thick with an unsettling stillness, a heavy silence broken only by the persistent buzzing of flies.

Detective Marcus Reynolds stepped cautiously into the room, his heart heavy with dread. He received the call just moments ago, a frantic voice on the other end of the line stammering out news that Dr. Ramirez had been found dead in her home.

As he took in the scene before him, Reynolds felt a wave of nausea wash over him, his stomach churning at the sight of the body lying on the floor. Dr. Ramirez lay on her back, her eyes wide and staring, her mouth frozen in a silent scream. Her once vibrant face was now a mask of terror, the life drained from her features like the color from a faded photograph.

The room itself was in disarray, furniture overturned and broken, shards of glass littering the floor. It was clear a struggle had taken place, a violent confrontation had left the brilliant doctor broken and lifeless on the ground.

Reynolds moved closer, his eyes scanning the scene for any clues, any hint of the monster who had committed such a heinous act. He noted the defensive wounds on Dr. Ramirez's hands and arms, the blood had pooled beneath her body, the signs of a desperate fight for survival.

As he stood over Dr. Ramirez's body, his eyes were drawn to a shimmer of gold amidst the chaos and destruction of the crime scene. There, against her throat, was a small, intricately crafted owl pendant, its eyes seeming to stare back at him with an eerie, knowing gaze.

With a trembling hand, Reynolds reached out, his fingers closing around the delicate chain. He could feel the weight of the pendant in his palm, could sense the power and significance it held.

For a moment, he hesitated. But then, with a sudden, decisive motion, he yanked the chain from Dr. Ramirez's neck, the clasp breaking with a tiny, almost imperceptible snap.

He held the pendant up to the light, his eyes narrowing as he studied the intricate details of the owl's design. He knew this was more than just a simple piece of jewelry, it was a symbol of something far greater and more sinister.

And as he slipped the pendant into his pocket, his jaw clenched with grim determination, Reynolds had just taken the first step down a dangerous and uncertain path. But he had no choice, the secrets of the Illuminated Order were too great to be left unchallenged.

As he continued to search for answers, Reynolds knew in his heart this was no random act of violence, no senseless tragedy born of chance or circumstance. This was a deliberate and calculated move, a message sent by the Illuminated Order to anyone who dared to stand against them.

Dr. Ramirez was a threat, a dangerous loose end that needed to be tied up. She risked everything to bring the truth to light, to expose the dark doings of the Order and its leadership. And now, in the most brutal and horrifying way possible, she paid the ultimate price for her bravery.

As the crime scene investigators began to arrive, their cameras

THE ILLUMINATED ORDER 307

flashing and their voices hushed with shock and disbelief, Reynolds stepped back. He thought of Jade and the others, the brave few who stood beside Dr. Ramirez in her fight for justice, and he felt a renewed sense of determination.

They couldn't let this stand, couldn't let the Illuminated Order get away with such a blatant and despicable act of violence. They had to find a way to bring them to justice, to make them pay for the lives they destroyed and the horrors they wrought.

Reynolds looked down at Dr. Ramirez's body, his heart heavy with grief and resolve. He knelt beside her, his hand reaching out to gently close her eyes, a final act of respect for a woman who had given everything in the name of truth and justice.

"I'm sorry, Dr. Ramirez," he whispered, his voice choked with emotion. "I'm so sorry we couldn't protect you. But I promise you this– we won't let your sacrifice be in vain. We'll find the ones who did this, and we'll make them pay. You have my word."

He rose to his feet, his eyes hard with determination as he turned to face the shattered remains of the bedroom window. The Illuminated Order thought they could silence the truth, thought they could crush the spirit of those who stood against them.

But they were wrong.

As long as there were people like Dr. Ramirez, like Jade and the others, the fight would go on. The truth would be heard, and justice would be served, no matter the cost.

Reynolds took one last look at the scene. Then he stepped out into the morning light, ready to face whatever challenges lay ahead.

For the memory of Dr. Sophia Ramirez, and for all those who had fallen in the fight against the forces of darkness and evil ...

He would not rest until the job was done.

77

"Good evening, and welcome to Global News Network. Our top story tonight: markets around the world are in freefall as the extent of the Illuminated Order's control over key industries and institutions is revealed.

According to leaked documents and insider testimony, the Order has been manipulating everything from energy prices to the supply of rare earth minerals, using their wealth and influence to shape the global economy to their own ends.

The fallout from these revelations has been swift and severe. Stock prices have plummeted, with some companies losing billions of dollars in value overnight. Governments around the world are scrambling to contain the damage, but many experts fear the worst is yet to come.

In a statement released earlier today, the International Monetary Fund warned that the Order's actions could trigger a global recession, with millions of jobs and livelihoods at risk. The statement called for immediate action to regulate and oversee key industries, and to hold those responsible for the Order's crimes accountable.

But even as the world struggles to come to terms with the scale of the Order's influence, some are asking how such a vast conspiracy could have gone undetected for so long. And with many of the Order's leaders still at

310 T.M JEFFERSON

large, there are fears that the organization could strike back, plunging the world into even greater chaos and uncertainty.

We'll have more on this developing story as it unfolds. For Global News Network, I'm Lila Matsumoto. Good night."

78

The Oval Office was quiet, the only sound the muted ticking of the clock on the mantel. Outside, the rose garden lay bathed in the golden glow of late afternoon, but Adrian Blackwell paid it no mind. His focus was inward, steeling his nerves for the address to come.

He could still scarcely believe how the events unraveled, the lies and deceptions laid bare for all the world to see. The shadows he willingly cloaked himself in, thinking he was immune to their corrosive effects, now threatened to swallow him whole.

A knock at the door jolted him from his thoughts. "It's time, Mr. President."

Blackwell rose, straightening his tie with a steadying exhale.

Time to put on the performance of a lifetime.

As he strode through the corridors towards the press briefing room, his thoughts strayed to those shadowy partners who maneuvered him to this ledge– Jameson Shaw, Victoria Sterling, and their cohorts in the Illuminated Order's uppermost echelons. No doubt they would be watching with bated breath, judging whether he still possessed the fortitude to play his role in their unfolding saga.

Entering the briefing room, he was awash in the blinding bril-

312 T.M JEFFERSON

liance of klieg lights and a forest of microphones. He blinked against the assault, composing himself with a diplomatic's mask before taking his place at the podium. No trace of the tumult churning within could be betrayed to the wolves lying in wait.

"My fellow Americans ..." he began, letting the words roll forth with patented sincerity. "In the wake of the shocking revelations concerning the so-called Illuminated Order conspiracy, I come before you tonight to address the grave implications thrust upon our nation."

Each sculpted phrase flowed like honeyed poison from his lips, denouncing the Order and their schemes as unequivocally as he once committed himself to their grand agenda behind closed doors.

"The evidence brought forth at the trial of Dr. Evelyn Soros has understandably raised serious concerns about whom we can trust to uphold the sacred institutions that preserve our liberties. Allegations of secret societies infiltrating the highest levels of power and authority cut to the very core of what we hold dear as Americans."

As he stared into the camera's unblinking eye, he knew the Order's lieutenants were judging every nuance of his performance with surgical precision.

"However, I stand here today to reassure you– we will not surrender our way of life, nor the future of this great republic, to the cowardly forces of disinformation that seek to divide and demoralize us from within. The rule of law remains inviolable. Justice remains sacrosanct. And those premises will never be open for negotiation or compromise ... Not on my watch. Not while I draw breath to execute the duties entrusted to me by the American people."

He continued. "Make no mistake– this administration condemns the purveyors of these lurid conspiracy theories in the strongest possible terms. Fantastical claims of shadow governments and Machiavellian puppet masters are the ramblings of paranoid cynics, not credible threats to our national security or sovereignty."

THE ILLUMINATED ORDER   313

He leaned into the podium, his expression hardening with emphasis.

"While I cannot comment on the sensitive details of any ongoing investigations, I can promise this– any individuals, organizations or hostile forces seeking to subjugate our freedoms or destabilize our democratic institutions from within ... will be rooted out, neutralized, and brought to the scorching light of justice."

He paused and looked into the cameras.

"To my fellow citizens viewing this address– rest assured your government remains steadfast and protective in the face of all threats, both foreign and domestic. We will endure, and we will overcome these forces of chaos and discord. United, vigilant, and committed to the self-evident truths of liberty upon which this nation was forged. For as long as Old Glory still waves eternal over this land of the free and home of the brave, America's resilience in upholding our cherished ideals shall never be extinguished. That is my vow to you. That is the undying promise I shall keep, without fail, until my final breath. Thank you. God bless you all, and may God forever bless these United States of America."

As the lights dimmed and the press corps buzzed with reaction, he turned to make his exit– never perceiving the tiny green laser sighting dot that danced briefly across his brow. If he had, perhaps he would've glimpsed the horrible truth, the sheer depths of the vipers' nest he sworn himself to protecting.

Perhaps. But for now, the performance of 'President' must go on, no matter how degraded that sacred office had become in reality. With each passing day, Blackwell was aware, the end drew nearer. And when that final reckoning arrived, there would be no pageant left to shield him.

Only the wages of his own wretched transgressions left to pay.

EPILOGUE

Washington, D.C., 2025

The grand hall of the National Archives echoed with the footsteps of the assembled guests, their faces illuminated by the soft glow of the chandeliers overhead. They gathered to witness a moment of profound significance, a turning point in the history of the nation and the world.

At the center of the room stood Jade Rose, her eyes shining with a fierce determination that became her hallmark. Beside her, Detective Marcus Reynolds and Dr. Sophia Ramirez's family stood in quiet solidarity, their presence a testament to the sacrifices that were made in the name of truth and justice.

As Jade stepped forward to address the crowd, her voice rang out clear and strong. "Today, we honor the memory of those who've fallen in the fight against the Illuminated Order," she said, her eyes sweeping over the sea of faces before her. "We remember their courage, their sacrifice, and their commitment to the principles of freedom and democracy."

She spoke of the long and perilous journey that brought them to this moment, of the battles fought and the secrets uncovered.

316   T.M JEFFERSON

She paid tribute to the bravery of Dr. Ramirez, whose death had galvanized a nation and sparked a global movement for change.

As the ceremony continued, the scene shifted, years melting away like the pages of a history book. In the aftermath of the Illuminated Order's exposure, the world had undergone a profound transformation. Governments were reformed, corrupt institutions dismantled, and the power of the secret cabal finally broken.

But the fight was far from over. In the shadows, new enemies emerged, seeking to fill the void left by the Order's demise. The Children of the Light, a radical offshoot of the Order, rose from the ashes, their ranks swelling with the disaffected and the disillusioned.

Cassandra Blackwell, a former protégé of Dr. Soros, had taken up the mantle of leadership, her charisma and ruthless ambition was a potent weapon in the struggle for power. She moved in the highest circles of society, her influence spreading like a virus through the halls of government and the boardrooms of industry.

But as the shadows lengthened and the threats multiplied, Jade and her allies remained steadfast in their resolve. They learned the lessons of the past, and forged unbreakable bonds of trust and loyalty in the crucible of adversity.

As the ceremony drew to a close, Jade's voice rang out once more, a clarion call to action and a promise of hope. "The road ahead will not be easy," she said, her eyes blazing with conviction. "But we will not falter, we will not yield. For we have seen the face of true evil, and we know the price of complacency."

She raised her fist in the air, a gesture of defiance and determination that sent a wave of energy through the crowd. "Together, we will build a world where the truth is not a commodity to be traded, where justice is not a game to be played. We will stand against the darkness, and we will prevail. I never asked to be a hero, never sought out the mantle of a champion. But when faced with the choice between silent complicity and the hard, dangerous road of resistance, I knew there was only one path I could take. The truth is a flame that cannot be extinguished, and the human spirit is a force that cannot be conquered. And as long as there are those who are willing to stand up and be counted, to rage against the dying of the light, then there will always be hope for a better tomorrow."

As the applause rose to a crescendo and the guests began to disperse, Jade and her companions lingered in the grand hall. They became the guardians of a new era, the custodians of a future that hung in the balance.

The legacy of the Illuminated Order was not one of fear or oppression, but of resilience and hope. And as long as there were those willing to stand against the darkness, to fight for the light of truth and justice, that legacy would endure, a beacon of inspiration for generations to come.

The world changed, but the struggle continued. And Jade Rose and her allies would be there, on the front lines of history, ready to meet the future head-on, no matter the cost.

And they would not rest until that promise was fulfilled, until the last shadow of tyranny and deceit had been banished from the earth, and the dawn of a new age could begin.

"The truth will set you free, but first it will piss you off."

- GLORIA STEINEM

BOOK CLUB DISCUSSION GUIDE

Dear Reader,

Thank you for joining Jade Rose on her thrilling journey to uncover the secrets of the Illuminated Order. I hope her story has entertained, challenged, and inspired you, just as writing it has done for me.

The questions that follow are designed to enhance your reading experience and encourage deeper reflection on the themes, characters, and events of the novel. They can be used for personal contemplation or as a springboard for lively discussions with friends, family, or book club companions.

As you think about these questions, I invite you to explore your own interpretations and reactions to the story. The beauty of fiction is that it comes alive in the imagination of each individual reader, sparking unique insights and perspectives. Trust your instincts, and don't be afraid to challenge assumptions or propose alternative viewpoints.

Most importantly, I encourage you to share your thoughts and reactions with others. Stories have the power to connect us, to bridge divides and foster empathy. By discussing "The Illuminated Order" with fellow readers, you'll enrich your own understanding of the novel and forge deeper connections with those around you.

Thank you again for your support and enthusiasm. I hope Jade's story continues to resonate with you long after you've turned the final page.

Happy reading and happy discussing!

* * *

1: How does Jade Rose evolve as a character throughout the novel? In what ways does her journey mirror the classic hero's journey archetype, and how does she subvert or challenge it?

2: The Illuminated Order is portrayed as a shadowy organization pulling the strings of world events. How realistic or plausible do you find this concept, and what real-world parallels or inspirations can you draw from history or current events?

3: The novel grapples with themes of power, corruption, and the erosion of democracy. How effectively does the story explore these ideas, and what insights or perspectives does it offer on these pressing issues?

4: Jade's relationship with her mentor, Dr. Evelyn Soros, is a core emotional thread of the story. How does their dynamic evolve over the course of the novel, and what does it reveal about the complexities of trust, loyalty, and betrayal?

5: The action sequences in "The Illuminated Order" are visceral and intense. Which scene or set-piece stands out to you as the most impactful or memorable, and why?

6: The novel features a large cast of secondary characters, each with their own motivations and secrets. Which supporting character did you find most intriguing or compelling, and why?

7: The ending of "The Illuminated Order" is both satisfying and open-ended, hinting at a larger conspiracy still at work. What are your predictions or hopes for a potential sequel or series?

8: The author weaves in elements of real-world conspiracy theories and secret societies into the narrative. How did this affect your reading experience, and did it make the story feel more grounded or more fantastical?

9: Jade is a journalist who risks everything to uncover the truth. In what ways does her character and her mission reflect the role and importance of the free press in a democratic society?

10: "The Illuminated Order" is a thriller that also grapples with weighty themes and ideas. How effectively does the novel balance its entertainment value with its social and political commentary?

11: The novel features a complex web of conspiracies and counter-conspiracies. Were you able to follow the various threads and revelations, or did you find yourself getting lost at times? How does the author manage the flow of information throughout the story?

12: The settings of "The Illuminated Order," from Washington D.C. to the remote Swiss Alps, are vividly rendered. How did the author's descriptions of place enhance or affect your reading experience?

13: The Illuminated Order itself is a fascinating and enigmatic entity. What was your impression of the organization, its goals, and its methods? Did your perception of them change over the course of the novel?

14: The novel features several twists and turns, from shocking betrayals to unexpected alliances. Which plot twist caught you most off guard, and how did it affect your understanding of the story?

15: "The Illuminated Order" taps into the current cultural zeitgeist of distrust in institutions and anxiety about the concentration of power. How do you think this novel reflects or comments on our current social and political moment?

ALSO BY T.M JEFFERSON

The Union

King

My America

The Don of New York

These Streets Ain't For Everybody

Printed in the USA
CPSIA information can be obtained
at www.ICGtesting.com
LVHW032119230524
781104LV00014B/256